Steller's Orchid

Steller's Orchid

a novel

Thomas McGuire

Book design by Mark E. Cull

ISBN 978-1-59709-860-1 (tradepaper)

The National Endowment for the Arts, the Los Angeles County Arts
Commission, the Ahmanson Foundation, the Dwight Stuart Youth
Fund, the Max Factor Family Foundation, the Pasadena Tournament
of Roses Foundation, the Pasadena Arts & Culture Commission
and the City of Pasadena Cultural Affairs Division, the City of Los
Angeles Department of Cultural Affairs, the Audrey & Sydney Irmas
Charitable Foundation, the Kinder Morgan Foundation, the Meta
& George Rosenberg Foundation, the Allergan Foundation, and the
Riordan Foundation partially support Red Hen Press.

First Edition
Published by Boreal Books
an imprint of Red Hen Press
www.borealbooks.org
www.redhen.org

PART I

Seattle, 1977

Ignoranti, quem portum petat,
nullus suus ventus est.

If one does not know to which port one is sailing
no wind is favorable.

—Seneca

"You need to use the full range from dark to bright in every drawing. The hand only needs pencil pressure but the eye has to understand and that takes longer."

The portfolio was part of Alyson's art school application. I turned another page as she watched with uncharacteristic diffidence. She wore tattered jeans and a thrift-shop flannel shirt. Her hair, once cut short and dyed lavender, was growing back to blonde. She looked nothing at all like her namesake grandmother, my sister Alyson.

I stopped at a sketch of a girl sitting on a driftwood log on an otherwise empty beach, her face turned away. A commonplace subject, the kind of artwork you would find at any street fair, but Alyson had used a focal point that would never have occurred to me. She had tucked the image in one corner, making the empty space the real story.

"This is really good," I said to her. "You've gone way past me."

"I like your work, Uncle John. You've got a great sense of line."

"I'm a good draftsman but never an artist." Alyson gave me a wry look as though I was fishing for a compliment but I was not. For a long time I had attempted nothing beyond illustrations for my botany work. I felt a pang of envy for Alyson's talent. And for her youth.

"One thing you still need to learn is that light can cast its own shadow."

"How's that work?" Alyson wrinkled her nose.

"Just watch a campfire, or a guttering candle."

"You're being a little obscure."

"Some things you can't learn in a classroom. I found out about light and dark a long way from school. In Alaska when I was your age."

"You mention Alaska a lot but then change the subject whenever I ask anything."

"The Arctic plays tricks with light and dark. So does memory." Her drawing of the girl on the beach had struck too close to home.

"Uncle John, I want to know what happened."

"It's a long story."

"We've got all night."

"Okay, but for once you have to listen. Just listen."

CHAPTER 1

I had to lie and threaten blackmail to get the job, which may have been why the gods frowned on it from the beginning. I was supposed to clerk in my father's law office that summer, work that I loathed. When the botany department posted an offering for a plant survey in southwestern Alaska I thought I might have found my ticket out. And so, in New Haven, Connecticut, on the last day of March, 1924, I walked up Hillhouse Avenue toward the home of Professor and Mrs. Walter Arbuthnot.

The maid who answered the door led me to a book-lined study. The professor was seated in a wheelchair, looking through a window at an elm tree still gaunt with winter. He turned his chair and considered me as though judging a horse.

"John Lars Nelson," he said after a long moment. "You are from Seattle?"

"Yes, sir."

"And your family has connections with the Alaskan fisheries?"

"Well, sir." I cleared my throat and skated onto thin ice. "My grandfather built a cannery in Bristol Bay as an extension of our Puget Sound packing business. I grew up working on the boats. When Grandfather died two years ago the family sold the business but my father's law firm still handles their accounts."

"Bristol Bay, you say?"

"Yes, sir. At Pilot Point on the Ugashik River." I was being a bit devious. In my application letter I had mentioned that my family once owned a cannery in Alaska and that I had worked on a company fish tender. Both statements were true, but the implied connection was not. My work in the company fleet had been in Puget Sound. I had never visited Alaska, never been north of Seattle. My only connection with Pilot Point had been watching the big windjammers depart in the spring with the Norwegian and Italian fishermen and the Chinese cannery workers, then return in the fall with the season's pack. I had hoped to work in Ugashik during my college summers but once the canneries were sold the law office became my fate.

The professor continued to study me. "Do you know the work of Georg Wilhelm Steller?" he asked.

"Steller? No, sir." The name was not at all familiar.

"A very gifted man. He was ship's doctor and naturalist on Bering's Alaska expedition in 1741. The voyage itself was a bit of a fiasco. Bering lost contact with his second ship and made only two landfalls, first at Cape St. Elias, and then further west in the Shumagin Islands, the area that interests us now." Arbuthnot gestured at a map pinned to the wall. It showed a group of about a dozen small islands scattered like windblown seeds near the beginning of the Aleutian chain.

"Bering stopped to fill the ship's water barrels. A seaman named Nikita Shumagin died of scurvy and was buried ashore. Bering named the island for him but over time the name shifted to the entire group. The island where they landed is now called Nagai, a name I had never heard till six months ago."

"Nagai." I tried the name on my tongue, dark and bitter as an acorn.

"Steller was able to botanize onshore, but his collection was lost in the wreck of the *St. Peter.*"

"They were shipwrecked?"

"On a small island off the Siberian Coast. Bering died that winter but come spring the survivors built a small boat from the wreckage and made it back to Petropavlovsk. Steller was among them but died not long after in mysterious circumstances. But the shipwreck is not important. What matters is Nagai."

Arbuthnot rolled his wheelchair over to a work table with obvious effort. On campus he more commonly used crutches. The squeak of their rubber tips and the rasp of his breath heralded his passage down the corridors of the biology building. He was a bit of an outlier there, not an academic botanist but a plant hunter who had somehow become director of the Marsh Botanical Garden, the college's botanical facility. Arbuthnot was British but had grown up in India and worked around South Asia. No one knew how he had secured his appointment.

I was an outsider as well, and not just because I was from the West Coast. I had entered college as an art major. I quickly found that I had no real talent but was good at natural history drawing. I did a series of life-cycle drawings for the museum and gradually drifted into a botany major. But even that was low-status. At Yale all of us science majors were shunted to the Sheffield School to keep us away from the soon-to-be lawyers and stockbrokers, in case science was contagious. Even my class designation, 1925S, carried the scarlet letter.

Still breathing heavily, Arbuthnot unfolded a map of Nagai on top of the table and beckoned me closer. I bent to study the map. The island was shaped something like an oak leaf—elongated but deeply lobed, a series of headlands and deep, narrow bays. On the south end of the island there was a promontory connected to the main island by a threadlike spit named Saddlers Mistake. On the north end was a similar, though broader, spit named Pirate's Shake. Between the two stretched a convoluted coastline.

"A complex topography," Arbuthnot said as if following my thoughts. "Searching it will be difficult but that is what we want you to do. The brief for the expedition authorizes a survey of the Alaska Peninsula and neighboring islands but that's something of a subterfuge. The real focus will be Nagai."

"Because Bering landed there?"

"Because of what Steller found." Arbuthnot sat back and steepled his fingers. "Steller came my way by chance. My wife collects botanical art. Her special interest is orchids, particularly Chinese brush-and-ink drawings. Last year a dealer in Shanghai wrote her about a very fine Ch'ing Dynasty drawing that had come on the market.

From the estate of a White Russian named Zagoskin. Audrey purchased it but it arrived in a bulky European frame. When she had it reframed a packet of letters was discovered behind the mat. Letters that Steller wrote to his wife, Brigitta Helena, in 1741."

"Zagoskin," I said, lost in the swirl of strange names and places. "How did he end up with the letters? Was he related to the wife?"

"Who can say? Not much is known of Brigitta Helena. She had planned to accompany Steller to Kamchatka but for some reason turned back at Moscow. He never saw her again." Arbuthnot paused for a moment. "I think we can infer she was a bit of a handful. Steller was quite young when he first came to St. Petersburg. He studied under a Dr. Daniel Messerschmidt and when the man died Steller promptly married his widow. Fell under her spell somehow. You can't help but wonder . . ."

A soft knock at the door interrupted him. A woman entered the study, dressed in coat and hat as though she had just come in from the street. "Walter, I hope I'm not too late," she said. "Town was absolutely beastly." As she crossed the room I had a confused impression of auburn hair framing a face pale and fine as porcelain.

"Audrey," Arbuthnot said, "this is John Lars Nelson. John, my wife Audrey."

She took off her gloves and extended one hand, palm downward. I took it somewhat awkwardly. She held my hand a bit longer than customary while studying me with jade-green eyes.

"So this is your chosen chevalier. But he is so young, Walter, to send out amongst the heathens."

"Older than you were on your first trip to China."

"China," Mrs. Arbuthnot said. She reached up and unpinned her hat. "Let's not get started on that subject or we'll be late for tea. Annie has set the table in the conservatory. John, perhaps you could help Walter? I'm afraid this is one of his bad days."

Arbuthnot objected briefly but I took the handles of his chair and wheeled him out of the study and down a long corridor. I felt an unwilling intimacy, smelling his hair oil and feeling the heft of his body in the chair. His wife walked ahead of us. She looked a lot younger than Arbuthnot, whippet-slim and very graceful.

The house was rather grand for a professor's salary. The conservatory faced south. Mrs. Arbuthnot opened the glass doors and a puff of moist heat escaped like the breath of a dragon. There was a faint hiss of steam from the coiled radiators and the tiled floor lay in squares like scales. Beyond the windows the brick-walled garden lay drab and brown but the tables within held dark green plants with vivid blooms. I wheeled the professor to a glass-topped table where their maid was setting a tea service.

"Come, John, you must have a brief tour." Mrs. Arbuthnot beckoned me to the plant tables. "We have space here for only a few of our favorite orchids. Mostly tropical. The heat is good for Walter's bones, and for the cattleyas, but the mountain orchids don't fare so well."

She stopped to touch a bloom. "*Labiata*," she said so softly she could have been speaking to herself. The plant was lavender with a full lip, its color so brilliant and petals so extravagant that it cast a spell. Was it a cattleya? I had no idea. I picked up a lump of the fibrous material that filled the boxes and rolled it in my fingers.

"The roots of the Osmunda fern, from the Jersey pine barrens." Mrs. Arbuthnot took my hand and pressed till I felt the moisture. "The best of all potting mediums, even for the epiphytic orchids."

"Audrey, would you fetch the Steller letters?" Arbuthnot interrupted. "I was just about to show John when you arrived."

A ripple of tension crossed the room. Audrey dropped my hand with a flicker of a smile, then turned and walked away. I watched her go; it would have been hard not to. 'Epiphytic,' I thought. Orchids that drank the wind.

I sat opposite the professor as he poured tea. He had massive shoulders and the blunt, worn hands of a working man. The porcelain teapot looked frail in his grasp. The tea he poured was pale green and aromatic.

"Dragon Well tea," he said. "From the mountains in Chekiang province. Hard to find in New Haven. No one understands tea here.

Or any other plant for that matter." He took a sip and looked at me. "You probably know that Evan Hamilton agreed to do the survey but then had to back out. The job is a bit much for an undergraduate to tackle but it's late now for recruiting and Evan suggested your name. Your professors speak well of you and your Alaskan connection is a strong selling point."

"Thank you, sir. I'm pretty eager to try fieldwork." I tried to look stalwart and capable. Evan was a graduate student and close friend. When he had given up the chance to do the survey I had twisted his arm and even threatened blackmail with his fiancée over our past escapades to make him drop my hat in the ring.

Mrs. Arbuthnot reappeared carrying a sheaf of typescript and a packet of letters. I stood to hold her chair and caught another brief smile. The professor untied the red ribbon that bound the packet and selected a single letter. The envelope was stained and brittle but the letter appeared to be in good condition.

"Do you know German?" Arbuthnot asked.

"German, not Russian?"

"The expedition was Russian but Steller was German. Bering himself was Danish. The language is not important; we have a translation for you. But I wanted you to see the original document. It's more compelling. This is the second longest of the letters, written while they lay at anchor off Nagai."

He handed the letter to me. It was on two pages with closely spaced lines. The writing was angular and spiky, the letters formed oddly in slashes of black ink. Looking at it I tried to picture a small sailing vessel anchored near a bleak and rocky island, while onboard a young man wrote to a wife he would never again see.

Arbuthnot began to read from the typescript: "I have this day returned from a walk ashore. The island is perhaps forty versts in length and mountainous, with rough gray and yellow rock covered with the green of low vegetation. I saw many birds including sea parrots, auks, and Greenland pigeons. I also saw marmots and foxes, but no larger mammals and no sign of human habitation. The island is treeless and the plants are much like those I found at Cape St. Elias but with one quite extravagant exception, my love. In a low valley I found a brilliant crimson orchid. A color like your garnet necklace, or perhaps more like rubies. The petals are full and voluptuous with a labellum slightly more than a vershok in width . . . ."

Arbuthnot paused and lookessd at me above his glasses. "That would be about five centimeters. A not inconsiderable bloom. So, what do you make of this at first reading?"

"I don't know what to say. Somehow I never thought of the North as home to orchids."

"Orchidaceae are in fact the most widespread of all plant families, but all northern orchids have modest blooms. Steller himself described several, which brings up a troublesome point. Nowhere in the journal or his plant lists does Steller mention such a remarkable orchid, only in the letters."

"Are you sure the letters are real? Is the handwriting even the same?"

"There is a photostat of Steller's journal in the Library of Congress, made by a man named Frank Golder in Moscow seven years ago. I traveled to Washington to see it only to find that what Golder had photographed was itself a copy, written in three different hands. So there was no way to compare. But what possible reason could there be for forgery? We paid nothing for the letters, only the painting, so what is there to gain? Even if the letters were forged a century ago it makes no sense. Who was being defrauded and why? No, I'm convinced the letters are authentic. Steller simply chose to keep his find a secret. Understandable, if you know anything about orchid collecting. They are not like other plants."

"No, sir." I was not an orchid fancier but I did know something of their strange world, its passions and intrigues. And I knew that the scent of orchids was akin to the scent of money.

As we talked, Audrey walked to one of the orchid benches. The light from the one western window fell in a long slash across the bench, setting its few blooms ablaze. She stood in the shadows but reached into the light to touch a flower, effectively upstaging her husband.

Arbuthnot shuffled the papers as though they were a hand he had been dealt. "Finding Steller's orchid would be a tremendous coup for us. There's a vacuum in the orchid world just now. Kew is in disarray since Robert Rolfe died—he founded the *Orchid Review*, you know. Oakes Ames at Harvard has ambitions to fill Rolfe's shoes but with Steller's orchid we can surpass them all."

"Good God, Walter," Audrey interrupted. "Don't you dare turn this into another petty academic squabble." She walked swiftly to the table and picked up the typescript. "Listen, John," she said and began to read: "'The flower glowed like a flame with a fragrance more intoxicating than new wine. I am enclosing a bloom for you. Know that I carried it next to my heart and kissed each petal. It is late now and I just awoke from a tortured dream. I was sitting beside you in a meadow, covering your hands with kisses. When I reached for you half-drugged with sleep I awakened with a flood of tears. I am but a wanderer, a rover on earth. Are you more than that?'"

Audrey looked at me with widened eyes and cupped her hand in an oddly beckoning gesture. I looked down at the letter I was still holding. There was a faint discoloration as though a flower had been pressed there years ago. Whether the flower had been deep red and voluptuous I could not say.

CHAPTER 2

A deckhand with a red neckerchief secured the battens on the SS *Victoria*'s forward hatch. I leaned against the ship's rail and watched him work. On this beautiful June day, Mount Rainier floated cloud-like and distant above the Seattle skyline and the pennants on the *Victoria*'s masts tossed and snapped in a brisk westerly. The waterfront was a kaleidoscope of movement and color. We were an hour past the scheduled departure for Nome but goods and people still crowded Pier 2.

My father had dropped me at the pier head with scarcely a backward glance. I was all alone and nervous of the challenge ahead. Misleading Arbuthnot about my experience suddenly seemed a very foolish gambit. Plus, I had weathered quite a storm of disapproval when I arrived home. I had not told my parents about the expedition beforehand, for fear they would veto it. My father was furious but I told him it was too late to back out and reminded him of his own boyhood summers in Ugashik. Eventually I talked him around to a grudging acceptance.

Traveling to Nome on the *Victoria* was my next gamble. The only scheduled service to the Shumagins was the mail boat, the *Starr*, which departed from Seward on the Kenai Peninsula on the tenth of each month. But I had lingered too long in New Haven and then my train west was delayed by a landslide in the Rockies. I reached Seattle just too late to catch the boat that would connect with the *Starr*'s June sailing. Rather than wait till July I decided to take a chance on the *Victoria*. The *Starr* was a slow boat that dawdled along the Alaska Peninsula, making seven stops before reaching the Shumagins. The *Victoria* was an ex-Cunard liner that would take me nonstop to Nome in only ten days.

Nome was a good distance beyond the Shumagins but it was the hub city of the Bering Sea. I counted on finding a fisherman or trader who could help me backtrack to the Shumagins. My grandfather preferred to take ship on the *Victoria* and then charter to Pilot Point whenever he visited our cannery, so I knew it was possible to get that far at least. I might need to hopscotch with more than one ride but with luck I could reach the islands well before the *Starr's* July visit. There was some risk involved but my collecting season was short and anything was preferable to cooling my heels in Seattle for another month.

On Pier 2, a woman stepped from a cab and began to walk up the *Victoria's* gangplank. She wore a blue dress and carried a parasol. Long, reddish hair flowed from beneath her bonnet and I thought for a shocked instant she was Audrey Arbuthnot. I pushed my way through the crowd but then saw the woman was tall and coarse-featured, her face heavily painted. She gave me a bold stare and passed by just as the ship's whistle blew to warn visitors ashore.

A tug nosed the *Victoria* across the waters of Elliott Bay. I watched till the city's skyline began to dwindle, then turned and headed for my cabin. I had booked a room on the upper deck for $115. The ship was large but the room was small, with two Pullman-style bunks and a washstand. The carpet bag with my clothing and drawing equipment sat on the bunk.

Plant hunters do not travel light. I had a plant press, reams of collecting paper, plant identification texts, and a host of smaller equipment such as spirit lamps, tweezers, and magnifying glasses. I also had a Wardian case for carrying the orchid home. In the seventeenth century the British botanist Nathaniel Ward designed a glass-topped box that could keep plants alive on long sea voyages. The one I carried was beautifully made, a gift from Mrs. Arbuthnot.

All this collecting paraphernalia was stowed in the *Victoria*'s hold, in an old steamer trunk the Arbuthnots had lent me. The trunk had faded decals from Bombay, Shanghai, Cartagena, and other exotic locales. It made me feel like a seasoned traveler.

In my cabin I also had a battered tin vasculum—a box with a leather shoulder strap for carrying specimens in the field. Professor Arbuthnot had used this one in China; now it held my copies of Steller's letters and journal. I took out the journal and sat on my bunk and began to read about the confusion and delays in the departure of the *St. Peter* and *St. Paul* from Avacha Bay in Siberia. Butterflies formed in my stomach at the thought of my own voyage and the problems ahead.

The dinner gong sounded and I relocked the vasculum and headed for the dining room, which was down a flight of stairs on the saloon deck. After a moment's search I found the table the purser had assigned me.

"Flowers?" The man seated to my right tugged his mutton-chop whiskers dubiously. He had introduced himself as Francis X. Fitzgerald and asked why I was bound for Nome. Fitzgerald wore a bright checked suit and had a free and easy manner. He said that he was returning to Nome after a trip outside "for his health." The other two men at the table were dour and uncommunicative. Old prospectors, I assumed.

"It's a survey of flowering plants," I said. "But it's actually in the Shumagin Islands. What's the best way to get there from Nome?"

"I dunno. Won't be easy. Not much traffic goes that way." Fitzgerald took a clasp knife from his pocket and used it to cut his meat. "Still, anything's possible. There's lots of small schooners in Nome. Some of the skippers are pretty desperate, now the Siberia trade's gone tits up. They'd sail right off the edge of the world, you offer them enough money."

The *Victoria* had begun to roll in a less gentle fashion and I could hear the clink of cutlery sliding across plates. Suddenly my forkful of mashed potatoes and gravy did not look appetizing.

"I have a letter of introduction to Olaf Swenson; you wouldn't happen to know him?" My father had done some legal work for Swenson and had written a letter for me. This tenuous connection was my sole entry to the maritime world of the Bering Sea.

"Olaf? Hell, yes, everybody knows Olaf. Him and the *King & Winge*."

"The *King & Winge*?"

"His schooner, an old codfish boat."

"That Olaf be one fine man," said one of the other men in a thick accent. "Not like some of dem, rob you blind." He looked at Fitzgerald, who laughed aloud.

"Old Olaf and me, we don't always see eye to eye. But he won't help you none. He'll be taking the *King & Winge* north to the pack ice, trading furs and hunting walrus. He may be gone already. But I got a few friends who could be useful."

"Thanks anyway but I think I can manage." I was anxious for help but Fitzgerald's interest was a bit too prying.

There was apple pie for dessert but I needed air and I went on deck to walk the stern promenade. The *Victoria* rolled even more as she stuck her bow into the big swell that curled through the Strait of Juan de Fuca. I could feel the vibration of the engine through the deck and prickles of perspiration formed along my spine despite the cold wind. My old nemesis—seasickness. During my deckhand days on the fish packer any rough weather found me puking over the lee rail, much to the amusement of the old Norwegian skipper and his mate. I had hoped that the motion of a big ship like the *Victoria* would be easier.

I was staring at the distant, unmoving shoreline to quell my stomach when Francis X. Fitzgerald appeared and took my arm and said, "I was just gonna slip into the lounge and smoke a cigar but I need somebody to yarn with."

He steered me through a door into what had been the ship's saloon. At the long mahogany bar we both ordered ginger ale. The bubbly ginger drink felt cool on my troubled stomach but Fitzgerald produced a flask from his pocket and added a shot of whiskey to our drinks. Other men were doctoring their setups from hip flasks, showing varying amounts of discretion depending on their degree of contempt for Prohibition.

The woman with the red hair was sitting at a nearby table. Fitzgerald cast a roving eye her way. "*Poule deluxe,*" he said with a wink then said to me, "C'mon, kid, you can tell old Francis. What are ya really after? Nobody's gonna pay your way out there to pick posies."

"People go all over the world doing plant survey but nothing's been done in the Shumagins. That's a big opportunity for a botanist." I thought that I had to be careful what I said or I might start a gold rush to the Shumagins based on rumor alone.

"There can't be any real money in it."

"Mostly knowledge, but that's worth something."

"Not in the North, it isn't." Fitzgerald gestured to the steward to bring more ginger ale, which he again freshened with whiskey. "Fur or metal, that's your ticket. I got a good tin prospect up near Wainwright. I just need a grubstake to get it on its feet. Gotta do somethin'. I used to be in the Siberian trade but that's shot to hell what with the Bolsheviks."

Fitzgerald looked around the room as he pulled a cigar from his vest pocket and lit it. "See that guy over there with the long, beaked nose?" He pointed with his cigar at a thin man wearing a silver derby with a tiny rim. "Arne Larson. When Siberian ivory dried up him and me figured to go walrus huntin' ourselves. We outfitted a schooner and hired five or six Eskimos from Diomede Island. Told 'em they could have the hides and meat and we'd keep the ivory. Arne's still doin' it but I got out. I'd introduce ya only we had a fallin' out when we split the sheets. Nah, tin's the thing for me, now. I got tired of battling the ice day and night. And the rot and stink of the hides. Ya never got away from the smell."

Fitzgerald had a way of constantly waving his cigar as he talked. My eyes could not let go of the glowing end as it moved in circles. My vision was a little blurred and the loud checks of Fitzgerald's coat seemed to grow and shrink. The ship was rolling more and more and the steward was busily securing things behind the bar. I felt a drop of sweat slide down my cheek and I picked up the cool glass of ginger ale and held it against my forehead.

"You okay, kid?" Fitzgerald asked. I slid partway off the bar stool and measured the distance to the door.

"Yeah," Fitzgerald continued, "once we killed five, six walrus we'd tow 'em to an ice floe and butcher 'em. Only first the Eskimos'd boil a billy of tea and have a feast. They'd cut open a walrus's stomach, pull out a slimy handful of oysters and eat 'em raw."

I bolted for the door, followed by Fitzgerald's laughter. On deck I grabbed a stanchion and took long, shuddering gasps of air. I felt the bile rise in my throat but then mercifully recede, leaving a taste like old pennies. I inhaled again shakily and looked around. Inshore I could see a fishing boat bound for shelter with its running lights lit. Clinging to the rail I headed for my cabin on trembling legs, accompanied by the prolonged hiss of waves cutting along the side of the vessel. Once inside I pulled off my shoes and flung myself on my bunk, completely alone and wretched as an orphan.

I awoke from a dream of foreboding monsters and crashing ice floes. The ship's motion was considerably worse. The bitter copper taste was thick in my mouth and I sat up and began methodically to put on my shoes. Everything loose in the cabin moved in a drunken dance. My coat swung on its hook by the door and my fountain pen rolled across the floor then back, random as a waterbug.

The vasculum fell from the table with a clatter. I bent over to pick it up but my stomach began to somersault and I grabbed my coat and bolted through the door. The roll of the ship threw me against the rail. I leaned over the side and vomited and watched what was left of my dinner fall to the sea. I stayed clinging to the rail till a second fit of retching emptied my stomach. I felt better, then, but lightheaded and weak as a newborn.

I buttoned my coat and walked toward the foredeck, gulping the fresh air. The sun was setting and the light splintered off the waves in unruly facets. The wind was a full gale from the north and the ship was taking the heavy seas on the starboard bow. The cargo mast scribed a giddy arc against the sky. As the boat rolled the dying rays of the sun caught the big anchor winch, highlighting the rust-marred paint and silvering the spray that whipped across it.

The top of a wave broke over the starboard rail and sluiced across the foredeck and I turned back. In the stern someone stood by the rail, the only other person outside. In the fading light I thought it was a woman in a gray dress.

As I approached my cabin my stomach began to move again like a pump gaining suction. A series of hammer-like convulsions shook me and I leaned far over the rail and retched and retched again but there was nothing in my stomach other than a little liquid that I watched spindle down to the waves.

The boat took a sudden steep roll to port and I clutched desperately at the rail as I began to tilt overboard. A strong hand grabbed my collar and yanked me back. I sat down heavily on the wet deck and looked up to thank my benefactor. I expected a burly prospector but it was the woman in the gray dress. To my further surprise she was a girl about my own age.

"You shouldn't be out here," she said with a look of concern as she hauled me to my feet. "Where's your cabin?"

She had an Indian's high cheekbones and I could see thick, dark hair coiled beneath her bonnet but her eyes were gray-blue, a mirror of the evening light.

"Thanks, I'm quite all right, really. Just needed a little air." Then another fit of retching seized me and I leaned over the rail and heaved till I expected blood to come gushing out my mouth. The girl held me by the shoulders till the fit passed.

"Where's your room?" she asked again.

"Twenty-eight,"—I gestured weakly—"but I'm a lot better now. I'll be fine."

Ignoring my words, she put an arm under my shoulders and walked me to the cabin. She was nearly as tall as I. Once in the cabin I flopped onto my bed like a spent fish and closed my eyes.

The girl knelt to pull off my shoes and then gave a little chuckle. I opened my eyes and she said, "Whyever are your shoes on the wrong feet?"

"Long story," I muttered, remembering the obsessive care with which I had laced the shoes. She grinned and I could see that one of her front teeth was slightly chipped.

She took a clean washcloth and dampened it at the little basin and put it on my forehead. She wetted another, gave it to me and said, "You might try sucking on this, it'll make your mouth taste better."

She stooped to pick up the vasculum that still lay on the floor. She eyed it curiously and tried the padlock. "Hey, wait a minute," I said and tried to sit up but my stomach rolled again. I closed my eyes and sucked on the washcloth. The door clicked, I looked and the girl was gone. The wind shrieked in the rigging.

CHAPTER 3

One week out from Seattle the *Victoria* sighted land. By mid-afternoon we were coasting along the south shore of Unimak Island, the first link in the Aleutian chain. The Shumagin Islands were a day's sail to the east but we were headed west and then north, into the Bering Sea.

Towering above us a cone-shaped mountain trailed a plume of cloud like a windblown scarf. "Mount Shishaldin," Francis X. Fitzgerald said as he sauntered up. "Nasty big bugger. Wouldn't want to be around when she blows her top."

"Look," I said and pointed at two seals floating on their backs, each clasping a front and rear flipper so they were curved like two strung bows.

"Fur seals," Fitzgerald said. "Used to be a lot of money huntin' 'em but not no more. The government grabbed all the rookeries. Seems like a man no sooner 'n figures out how to make a buck than somebody puts the kibosh on it." He spat over the side. "Hell, five years ago we was rollin' in dough tradin' in Siberia. Two hunnerd and fifty dollars for one black fox pelt. Plus sable, white fox, ivory. Up to twenty-five bucks a pound for mastodon ivory."

"Mastodon ivory?"

"They dig it out of the muck."

"What would you trade for it?"

"Any damn thing. Sugar, whiskey, guns. Hell, I made a killin' sellin' goddamn hand crank Victrolas over there. Bought a bunch for twenty dollars each in Nome. Traded one for the prettiest eleven-foot polar bear hide ya ever saw. Traded another for twenty-five white fox skins. And six records for six tusks."

"What kind of music did they like?" I asked, curious.

"Didn't matter. I gave 'em brass bands, some damn opera called Don Jovanny. I even had John McCormack singin' 'The Nut-Brown Maid,' but I tell ya there ain't nothin' in the County Down like the nut-brown maids they got up here." Fitzgerald gave me a sly dig in the ribs. "One of them wraps her legs around you and you'll hit high notes McCormack never dreamed of."

He laughed and strolled away. Fitzgerald was my closest acquaintance onboard the ship but after talking with him I always wanted to check to see if my wallet was still in my pocket. I took a quick turn around the nearly deserted deck. The cold wind kept most of the passengers in their cabins. I was looking for the young girl who had befriended me during the storm. I had not seen her since that night and I was beginning to wonder if she was part of a dream sequence. I had even tried to sketch her but could only remember her eyes.

I stood alone in the bow, hands in pockets and shoulders hunched. Despite the cold I was anxious for my first glimpse of the Bering Sea, the country where you traded Mozart for mastodon tusks. At the south end of Unimak Pass we ran through a cloud of sooty shearwaters. There were hundreds, thousands of them, curving in long arcs above the water, flecks of dark against the slate-gray sky. A kaleidoscope of birds.

This country was so wild and empty that it filled me with both excitement and dread. My spirits rose and fell with the bow of the boat. One instant I felt as though I were headed for the stars, the orchid in easy reach. The next I plunged toward the cold depths, feeling hopelessly over my head.

The dinner bell sounded but I ignored it and stayed on deck till I was shaking with cold. The sun was low in the north, the port side now deep in shadow. When I turned and walked aft I saw a figure standing near my cabin. Seeing me he straightened and walked quickly away. When I reached my room I found the door unlocked.

A quick glance showed the vasculum was missing and I turned and sprinted after the man, all the way around the stern promenade and then down the stairs to the saloon deck. I stopped at the foot of the stairs to look around. Further aft was the companionway to the steerage deck. I glimpsed a bit of gray disappearing like a rat down a hole and I gave chase.

A miasma of bunkered coal and bilge water wafted up the shadowed stairwell. A door clanged shut somewhere below and then I could hear only the incessant thrum of the engine. Halfway down the steel-grated stairs I kicked something that rattled down ahead of me. When I reached the bottom I found the vasculum, its hasp twisted and broken. The light at the foot of the stairs flickered dimly with the pulse of the engine but thirty feet ahead I saw someone bent over scattered leaves of paper. I ran forward and grabbed the person by the arm.

"What the hell are you doing . . . ." I said as I hauled him upright. Only it wasn't a man, it was the girl I had been seeking. A brief flicker crossed her face. Fear, anger, guilt? I could not tell, but she tucked the papers under her arm and looked at me with steadfast eyes.

"What brings you down here?" she asked.

"I might ask you the same."

"My room is right here," she said and, as if on cue, the door opened. A child with a tousled head regarded us gravely. From somewhere beyond her a querulous voice said, "Natasha, what's all that row? Who is that?"

"In a minute, ma'am," the girl said. With a conspiratorial gesture she shooed the little girl inside and closed the door, then looked at me again.

"I want my papers," I said.

"How do I know they're yours?"

"Just give them back." I was irritable from cold and hunger and from the feeling I was off my own ground. The girl continued to look at me then opened her hand and let the papers fall to the floor. She turned on her heel and entered the cabin, very gently closing the door behind her. Somehow the quiet closing of the door was so dismissive that it annoyed me more than anything yet. I knelt and began to gather the papers, blowing the coal dust off them. Another door opened and a man looked out. He was in stocking feet and shirtless, his suspenders dangling. No doubt the commotion had awakened him.

"Did you see anybody go by a few minutes ago?" I asked, but he shook his head sleepily and closed his door again. He must have thought I was crazy. I stuffed the papers into the vasculum and headed back topsides. Colder now, the sun was about to dip below the northern horizon. I ducked into the almost-empty saloon and grabbed a couple of sandwiches from the tray left out for the first-class passengers. Francis X. Fitzgerald sat at the bar with another man. He gestured for me to join them but I waved and left. The last thing I wanted was more Fitzgerald stories.

Once in my room I wolfed down one of the sandwiches and tried to put the papers in order. Nothing seemed to be missing. With a little food in my belly and the warmth of the cabin I started to feel better, though a bit foolish. Here I had been looking for the girl to thank her and when I found her I all but accused her of theft. Natasha, the woman had called her. What was she doing on the steerage deck? I thought those berths were for men only.

I debated telling the purser about the break-in. If I mentioned finding the girl with the papers it could prove awkward for her and I thought it unlikely she was the culprit. But who could the intruder have been, and why would he or she want my papers? I suppose for a sneak thief the padlock on the vasculum would be incentive enough. At any rate my cache of money was still safe, half in the money belt I wore and half in the lining of my trunk in the hold.

I ate the second sandwich and straightened a rumpled page of typescript that was now marked with a misshapen heel print, presumably from the fleeing burglar. The letter was one Steller had written to his wife the evening Bering made his first landfall near Cape St. Elias. I remembered that the journal entry for that day included an analytical description of the four-chambered heart of a seal. In contrast the letter read: "My passion for nature has become a tor-ment. Where once I saw only flowers now I see your image in every blossom, the curve of your lips in every petal. Oh, my love, I long for the wings of the crane to carry me to your side where I may taste again the foaming cup of bliss . . ."

What strange torment, the words as flamboyant as any orchid. The overheated imagery reminded me of the German Romantics I had been forced to read in a long-ago literature class. Goethe, maybe, but the memory swam in depths just beyond my grasp.

I looked again at the letter. "Alone on this desolate coast I look to the evening star which conceals itself in the rolling waves of the ocean and I wonder which is more obsessive—desire or the memory of desire?"

What did that last phrase mean? This whole journey was an exer-cise in echoes and shadows. I lay down on my bunk. Light still came through the porthole, pale as the petals of a night-blooming flower.

The ship's whistle gave a long blast that was then repeated at two-minute intervals. I kept my eyes screwed shut but sleep was gone. I struggled up and looked out the porthole to find that the ship was ghosting along in a thick morning fog. I dressed and went outside. There was no wind at all. The rail was slick with water and drops fell from the rigging.

The deck was deserted but someone stood alone in the bow. I saw that it was the girl. I walked up and stood at the rail near her. "Hello," I said diffidently but she did not look my way. I cleared my throat. "We've met twice now but I still don't know your name. I'm John Lars Nelson."

After a heartbeat she said, "Natasha Christiansen."

"Another Norwegian," I said.

"Partly." The ship's whistle sounded overhead. The boat seemed imprisoned in a bowl of fog but the girl continued to stare westward.

"What's out there?" I asked.

"The third mate told me we'd be passing the Pribilofs about now. If it wasn't foggy we might be able to see them."

"The Pribilofs? Aren't they the fur seal islands?"

"Yes. I was born on St. Paul. My father worked for the American Fur Company."

"And your mother?"

"She was Aleut. From the village."

"You're going back to see them?"

"They are both dead." She turned away from the rail and began to walk toward the starboard side. I hesitated a moment then followed her.

"Look, I'm sorry about being rude last night," I said when I caught up with her. "It's no excuse but I was cold and hungry and my papers were missing."

"And you thought I took them?"

"No, no. Not exactly, I mean . . . well, actually . . ." I wound my scarf more tightly around my neck. It was a blue-and-white Yale scarf that my roommate Palmer had given me, enjoining me to nail it to the mast like a flag when my ship sank. Which was exactly how I felt now.

I tried another tack. "That lady in the cabin, are you working for her?"

"Mrs. Kelly? I only just met her in Seattle. She offered to pay part of my fare if I helped watch her four little girls. We're not even supposed to be in steerage. It took a lot of tears and pleading from Mrs. Kelly to get that cabin. It's meant to be part of the infirmary."

"How's it working?"

"Not very well. Mrs. Kelly has been so seasick she still hasn't gotten out of bed. The little girls were supposed to sleep two to a bunk but the older two squabble so much I had to give one of them mine. I've been sleeping on the floor."

That explained the rumpled dress and the dark circles under her eyes. But at least she was speaking to me now. We reached the stern companionway and Natasha turned and said, "I should go check on the little girls. If they start bothering their mother she'll get angry."

"Please, not yet. Walk around the deck with me. Just one more round."

"I really shouldn't . . ."

"But you owe it to me. You saved my life that first night so now you're responsible for me. Nelson's first law of entangled destinies."

"I didn't really save your life. I just tucked you in bed."

"Then you owe me a bedtime story. That's the second law."

Which brought the first real smile I'd seen from her. She turned and accompanied me back along the port side, glancing west toward the Pribilofs.

"I saw two fur seals by Unimak Island yesterday," I said. "They were floating on their backs, clutching their flippers."

"People call that their 'teacup' posture." She circled her arms and mimed it very prettily.

I laughed and flipped the ends of my scarf over my shoulder.

"That's a very jaunty scarf," Natasha said.

"Oh, this, it's just a school scarf. From Yale . . . ." I stopped short, embarrassed by how much I sounded like a prep-school moron. Next I'd be prattling about debutante balls. The idiot child of privilege.

"Yale," she said. "I've heard of it. It's a Congregationalist school, isn't it?"

"Sort of. Used to be, anyway. Now they mostly worship football."

"I just finished a teacher training course at Nebraska Wesleyan," she said shyly. "Two years."

"Nebraska? What on earth took you from the Pribilofs to Nebraska?"

"The school in Unga was run by Methodists. Both of the teachers went to Nebraska Wesleyan and they encouraged me to go there."

There were a few more people on deck now. A man stopped to light a cigarette, his eyes following Natasha till the match burned his fingers. One of Natasha's words circled at the back of my mind till it rose like a trout. "Unga? That's in the Shumagins, isn't it?"

"Yes, it is."

"But that's where I'm going. I've got a job there this summer."

"Then you're going in the wrong direction. But what on earth brings you from Yale College all the way to Unga?" She grinned as she mimicked me.

"It's botanical work. I'm supposed to make a survey of flowering plants."

"Flowers, how curious." She laughed.

"What do you mean, 'curious'?" I asked, slightly irked.

"Oh, I don't know. I've never heard of such a thing. But the flowers are wonderful. They come in waves. From spring to fall there's always something blooming—lupine and columbine and shooting stars and many, many more. I missed them in Nebraska."

"You can show me. I need a guide, or at least somebody to get me there."

"But I'm not going there. I've been offered a job teaching in one of the Department of Education Native Schools. But why didn't you go to Seward and catch the mail boat?"

"Bad timing, like everything I do." We turned and walked back aft and I told her a little of my travels and the plan for the summer. The *Victoria* broke free of the fog bank, like flying out of a cloud. The sea changed from gray to a brilliant blue. Small ice floes dotted the surface of the water.

"Will I see you in Nome?" I asked.

"I may not be there long. I don't know just where I'll be teaching. One of the village schools, I hope, maybe Wales or White Mountain. But it's up to Dr. Westmoreland in Nome."

I gave her a sidelong glance. With the high cheekbones and lustrous hair she was an exotic flower herself, despite the dowdy dress. I was so distracted that I stumbled against one of the lifeboat davits and nearly fell. Natasha grabbed my arm to steady me and again I was startled by the strength of her grip.

"John Lars, you really have to learn to watch where you're going."

"It's a problem I have." I tried to hide my ruffled vanity. She had pronounced my two names with an odd rhythm, as though they were one.

We reached the stern companionway. "I have to go now," Natasha said and gave me her hand and a brilliant smile. She disappeared down the stairs holding the hem of her dress in her right hand. I could see that the heels of her shoes were worn down.

Alyson

"Natasha, she's the girl you mention sometimes?"

"Have I?"

"Once when we were drunk you called her the ideal woman. Whatever the fuck that means." Alyson reached into the top pocket of her shirt and pulled out a hand-rolled cigarette.

"What's that?"

"A doobie. Want a hit? Good for your glaucoma."

"No thanks."

Alyson lit it, shook out the match, and said, "Uncle John, I want the whole story."

"I'm trying."

"No you're not. You're dancing around something, I can tell. Something you don't want to talk about."

"Well, yeah, maybe . . ." I reached for the joint, took a long draw and held it. Alyson looked at me, surprised that it was obviously not my first time.

"We'd have to backtrack a bit." I let the smoke out in a long stream.

"To New Haven?"

"Did I ever tell you about the old Yale library? The building was Portland brownstone. There was no central heating, so in the winter some of the faculty wore their commoners' gowns against the chill. Watch them shuffle by in the dim light and you'd swear you were in a monastery. It was my refuge for four years."

"Now you're really changing the subject."

"No, I'm not. The library was where my troubles began."

CHAPTER 4

The cascade of creamy white blossoms with slender spurs looked like a shower of stars. *Angraecum articulatum*. If the painting was this breathtaking what would the actual flower be like?

I was seated at a long oak table in the library's main reading room, looking at Henry George Moon's watercolors of orchids in the *Reichenbachia*, a four-volume orchid florilegia published in the 1890s. I had come to the library to do background research on the Alaskan project. The job appeared to be mine for the taking but my first encounter with the Arbuthnots had left me wary. When I left their home that day the professor had enjoined me to secrecy. A bit too cloak-and-dagger for me. Hidden letters and mysterious orchids had little to do with the botany I knew.

Unfortunately, the library offered next to nothing about Georg Wilhelm Steller. All I found was a summary of his work in the fourth edition of Willamm Coxe's *Account of the Russian Discoveries between Asia and America*, published in England in 1805, and an even briefer mention in Pennant's *Arctic Zoology*, from 1785. Apparently much of Steller's scholarly work had disappeared. What survived was archived in the Russian Imperial Academy, which did me little good.

Orchids were an easier target. The library had many holdings but for me the best find was the *Reichenbachia*. I was staring transfixed at Moon's *Angraecum* when a light touch on my shoulder startled me. I looked up to see Audrey Arbuthnot, wearing a raincoat and carrying an umbrella. I pushed my chair back to stand up but she increased the pressure of her hand to hold me in place and then sat down next to me, leaving her hand on my arm. She was a toucher; I already knew that.

"So you've discovered Henry Moon," she said in a low voice.

"This is unbelievable."

"Let me take you deeper into the garden." She turned the pages to an orchid whose throat was a frilled magenta pathway marked by sulfur-yellow patches. Looking at it made me feel as though I was about to spiral down into an inescapable whirlpool.

"Oh, my God," I said and a man at a nearby table looked up and coughed pointedly. Audrey leaned closer and touched a finger to her lips. From the folio pages came a scent of dust and parchment but her breath was like apple blossoms. She moved her hand to my forearm. I flinched away, salmon at the first brush of the net. I looked at the clock on the far wall.

"Do you have to be somewhere, John?" she asked in an almost-whisper.

"I have a microbiology class in Sheffield in fifteen minutes."

"I'll keep you company that far." She stood and waited for me to gather my books.

Outside a light rain was falling; its cool touch helped clear my head. "I had a talk with my adviser about the survey," I said as we walked along Chapel Street.

"And what did he say?"

"He saw some merit in it," I said guardedly.

"Some merit?" She laughed. "Just who might your adviser be?"

"Professor Taylor."

"Lord Liverwort, isn't that what the students call him?"

"Some do."

"Better watch your step or he'll have you mired in a laboratory cataloging mosses for the rest of your life."

"He's been a good friend to me," I said a bit stiffly.

"He was a little too friendly with me at one faculty party after his third glass of sherry," Audrey said with a tone of mock indignation, then laughed merrily. She had an unusually high, sweet voice and a laugh like a wind chime. I could not help laughing as well but then felt a bit disloyal, as though I had changed sides at the beginning of a game.

In truth, Professor Taylor had not been at all enthusiastic about the expedition. He considered both the Arbuthnots and their plant-hunting background a bit too raffish to be quite acceptable. "The glamour that is evil," he had muttered darkly while staring out the window at New England's rather severe version of spring. I had been careful not to mention Steller's orchid, not just because of the Arbuthnots' demand for secrecy. I knew that Professor Talyor thought orchids overly flamboyant. He was a good soul but he had made his reputation with a monograph on the reproductive cycle of the Bryophyta. I was beginning to have something far more adventuresome in mind.

"Walter gets livid when the other professors look down their noses at him," Audrey said. "He's a better plantsman than any of those old maids. Put them in the mountains and they'd be screaming for their mothers. That's why this orchid is so important to Walter. They couldn't ignore him then. Or so he thinks."

We crossed Elm Street, scattering pigeons from the rain-dark pavement. As we reached the other side the rain suddenly intensified. Audrey opened her umbrella and handed it to me. It just managed to shelter us both if I walked close beside her and bent over slightly. She slipped her arm in mine.

"I was just looking at some issues of the *Orchid Review*," I said. "I was pretty amazed at the excitement about new plants. And the amount of money."

"The money doesn't count, only the passion. When I was in China I burned to find some fabulous orchid, something that would bear my name forever."

"I thought you already had a flower named for you."

She arched her eyebrows. "My, you have been doing your homework."

"Somebody mentioned it and I kind of looked it up."

"My husband's little gift. But asphodel, I mean, really!"

"The flower of the Elysian Fields, or so they say."

"Ah, yes. The flower of forgetting. And forgetting and forgetting." She laughed again. "We were so impossibly young."

"Just when were you in China?"

"Oh, before the war."

Rain colored the cut-granite blocks of the building, and tilted black umbrellas fled the street. I looked down at Audrey; her step was light and her figure girlish but she had to be in her mid-thirties or beyond, closer to my mother's age than my own. The quickening of desire confused me and I moved a step away, causing rain to drip down my collar from the edge of the umbrella. She pulled on my arm to draw me back.

"I'm counting on you to find Steller's orchid for me."

"I haven't even decided if I'm going yet."

"Oh, yes, you have." She tightened her grip till I felt the bite of her nails. A raindrop coursed down my spine. We had almost reached the Sheffield School. I could see the observatory perched on the clock tower like an absurd top hat. I was already late for my class but I kept walking.

The rain slackened and almost stopped as we reached the corner of Hillhouse Avenue. Audrey took back the umbrella, shook the rain from it and folded it.

"This is as far as I can take you today, John. I have to meet a friend. But I'm glad I found you. I know this is a little premature but I wanted to give you a present." She reached into her handbag, brought out a J. Press box and opened it to show a brilliant blue silk necktie.

I took an involuntary step backward. "No, no, I couldn't possibly . . ."

"A gift, John, not a bribe." She knit her brows in a pretty frown. "You could say 'thank you.'"

"Sorry, I didn't mean . . . ." I stammered.

"Just hold still." She turned up my collar and loosened my old brown tie. I looked around but mercifully the streets were empty.

"Why do all botanists dress like impoverished undertakers?" She shook her head as she looped the new tie around my neck. I blushed and took another step backward but she pulled the tie as though it were a halter.

"Don't be so skittish. I've done this before." Her fingers were light and deft as she tied the knot. "There," she said, stepping back. "Much better. I was going to get you a crimson one, like Steller's orchid, but it really wouldn't be your color."

Mist glistened in her auburn hair and changed the color of her eyes. Her face was as pale as the rain-washed light. She widened her eyes and I felt like Aladdin at the gates of the enchanted garden, but then her gaze broke away and she shivered.

"Cold?" I wanted to throw my coat over her shoulders. Or at her feet.

"No," she said in an odd tone. "No, for a moment you reminded me of someone. Someone long ago and far away." She shrugged her shoulders gracefully. "And someone completely forgotten."

"Completely?"

"More than completely. The effect of asphodel." She laid two fingers on the inside of my wrist. "Not a bribe, John Nelson, but perhaps an enticement."

She began to walk away, up Hillhouse. A frayed brown oak leaf rode the current in the street gutters. Caught in a vortex, it plunged into a storm drain, headed for the sea. I fingered the tie that was cool and rich and silk to the touch. Audrey turned and blew me a farewell kiss. I remembered that Aladdin's garden was not only enchanted but forbidden.

A figure in a silk dressing gown embroidered with dragons held a long iron fork over a bed of glowing coals. It was my roommate Palmer. He had built a fire in the grate and was toasting a piece of bread.

"What did you find out about your man Steller?" he asked as he turned the toast.

"Not much at all. The library was pretty barren." I collapsed on our threadbare sofa and looked at the chessboard on the table in front of me, a game left unfinished from the night before. I was playing white and was up by a pawn. The black queen was in a vulnerable position but was it a gambit? Palmer liked risky moves.

"I still can't figure out what's going on," I said. "The job is quite a plum, so why me? Why not some graduate student? Or even a junior faculty member? My Alaskan connection wasn't that much of a selling point, even after I exaggerated it."

"Arbuthnot needs somebody he can push aside. A faculty member would want his own name on any discovery." Palmer's toast caught fire and he waved it around the room like a beacon but then dropped it on the coals where it flared and died. "Sad to say, my friend, you are no more than a pawn in the greater game of academic preferment."

"You're probably right, but I think I'll go anyway. Find out what's at the back of the north wind."

"Trolls, demons, hags."

"Maybe, but you should see Audrey Arbuthnot, Palmer. Not your average faculty wife."

"I do know *la belle* Arbuthnot. By reputation at least. She's what you might call notorious in certain circles." Palmer was a fount of gossip, usually accurate. He sat down in the armchair opposite the chess table and lit a cigarette. His eye lingered on my bright blue necktie.

"I did a little asking about your new friends." Palmer blew a smoke ring and poked a finger through it. "Arbuthnot is an odd duck, a bit of a chancer, really. He has no academic degrees and no prior teaching positions, just some murky connection to the Kew Gardens in London. There were quite a few raised eyebrows when he got his job."

"Palmer, I know all that. But truth is, Arbuthnot's got tons more field experience than anybody in the department. He's been places and done things they've never dreamed of." I had already adopted Audrey's viewpoint.

"Perhaps. But the delightful Audrey, now there's a story." Palmer looked at my necktie again. "She comes from old money. Very old and very large. Boston money. She was raised a proper bluestocking but kicked over the traces, married some scholarship boy, and decamped to China. Two years later she reappears with a new husband, the first having been beheaded by bandits."

"Beheaded?"

"So the story goes. She then took off for South America, coming back this time with a crippled husband and a pet monkey. Bit of bad luck, taking up with Audrey. The monkey at least had the good grace to die and now she entertains herself with a series of human pets."

"Palmer, that's ugly. She's quite nice."

"Easy, Nels. I just don't want you losing your head out there."

Palmer reached for the black queen but then withdrew his hand without touching her. I could take the queen in two moves, but was it a trap?

"The upper Yangtze is incredible country. Steep mountains and deep-cut canyons. Even the names are dramatic—Tiger Leaping Gorge, Jade Dragon Snow Mountain. Virtually impassable but it's a botanical treasure trove. It's where I met Audrey."

Professor Arbuthnot and I were working on equipment lists but he had stopped to spin another yarn about China.

"I had a contract with Veitch, the big London nursery. A man named Kentledge claimed to have found a new orchid in the gorges of the Ch'i Chiang River. He hadn't shown anyone a specimen but was trying to sell a map. Then he was found in an opium den with his throat cut and his luggage gone. I'd met Kentledge and took him for a grifter but Veitch wanted me to check out his story. Audrey was freelancing in the area. She caught wind of the orchid and was dead set on finding it. She needed a guide and I knew the country and the flora so she proposed . . . ." Arbuthnot hesitated for a moment, his eyes glazed with some personal distance. "Well, you had to know Audrey back then. Persuasive and relentless. Just a slip of girl, all big eyes and soft touch, but tough as steel underneath. And hard to say no to."

"Did you find the orchid?" I found it odd that Arbuthnot had so far made no mention of Audrey's first husband. Perhaps, for once, Palmer's gossip was incorrect.

"We looked long and hard but winter caught us. I didn't believe in the orchid in the first place and I knew that snow would close the Do-Kar-La Pass. Audrey still hasn't forgiven me for turning back, but I didn't fancy being stranded in some mountain village. Winter is cruel up there. Plus, there was a bandit gang in the area led by a renegade monk called the White Wolf."

"The White Wolf?" I asked. "And opium dens and cutthroats? Sounds like a Fu Manchu novel."

"I can assure you the White Wolf was most definitely real. His band attacked us at a river ford on the way back and scattered our porters. Audrey and I barely escaped."

"Is that what plant hunting's really like?"

"Not every day." Arbuthnot laughed. "Mostly it's just a long slog. You probably won't have to deal with bandits in Alaska though any area as remote as the Shumagins will be mostly lawless. And you shouldn't have to bribe any officials. In China we needed government passes to travel anywhere and that always led to cash payments and lies about our true destination. One thing you'll find, even in Alaska, is that no one will believe you're after plants. Turn your back for one minute and they'll rifle your bags, trying to figure out what you're really up to."

"I'm not sure that's quite what I signed on for," I said, though in truth it was.

"The hunt is addictive, John. You might get hooked; I certainly did. On the danger, the gamble, the strange places and stranger people. New Haven feels like a cage in comparison."

I thought that Arbuthnot's wheelchair made an even tighter cage than Connecticut. I wanted to know what confined him to the chair but of course could not ask and he never volunteered an explanation.

By now we had met many times to plan the expedition. I enjoyed the professor's company when his talk veered to his past adventures and he became amiable and expansive and full of practical advice. At such times he was almost a friend but more often his manner was brusque and heavy-handed and his ego easily bruised. I was surprised by the gaps in his botanical knowledge. He was an encyclopedia about orchids and other flowers with commercial possibilities but was disdainful of the more humdrum plant families and dismissive of my questions about them. Palmer had been right in that surmise, at least. I was just a glorified errand boy who could be discarded afterwards. I chafed at that notion. Credit and the honor of naming any discovery should go to the actual finder.

A deeper problem lurked beneath this surface tension. I was falling increasingly under Audrey's spell. I tried to time my visits so that she would be present but that could be hard to predict. We did meet alone a few times, more by her contrivance than mine. She knew the carrel where I liked to study in the library and stopped by more than once. I soon realized she was not only beautiful but piercingly intelligent. I found that she was the one who had translated the Steller letters. She was fluent in both German and French, spoke a little Mandarin, and her Latin was better than mine. Also her botany. And she was a better storyteller even than her husband. She would talk of Asia and South America in a tone so soft and beguiling that I would have to lean close to catch every word and soon my head would be spinning.

One week after the professor told me that China story I returned to their home. Rain darkened the new leaves on the elm trees as I knocked on the door. On my first visit I had thought the bronze door knocker was an iris but now I saw it was an orchid, the labellum polished by the touch of many hands.

"I'm afraid Walter had to go to the city," Audrey said when she answered the door. The city was, of course, New York, which meant the professor would not be back till quite late, if at all. I also knew that Wednesday was the maid's day off. Audrey led me to the conservatory and beckoned me to sit beside her. Together we looked out at the rainswept garden. One of the conservatory windows was partway open and a fine mist darkened the tile floor beneath it. Audrey leaned back against the wicker sofa and lightly stroked the blue beads she wore around her neck.

"So you intend to follow in Steller's footsteps?" she asked.

"Depends on which footsteps."

"Perhaps the ones toward Brigitta Helena, the merry widow." She crossed her legs and kicked one foot slowly, idly. "Do you think she deserved such passionate letters?"

"I don't really know." Through the sound of the rain I heard the faint drone of a bee. I watched it circle and land on a bright magenta orchid and crawl inside the cup.

"Walter hates to see that," Audrey said. "He absolutely loathes accidental fertilization in the greenhouse. But I find the bees amusing—they become so covered with pollen that they tip over and thrash in circles, completely besotted." She laughed and bit her lower lip.

A hanging lamp swung slightly near the French doors, its shadow moving fitfully on the tiled floor. Audrey loosened the ribbon that bound her hair and shook her head and the hair cascaded to her shoulders. I was acutely aware of the shape of her legs beneath her light dress. We both sat poised on the edge of something. I had known that the professor would not be home and I suspected that Audrey was aware of that and knew why I had come.

"Walter was so dashing when we first met," she said suddenly. "A breath of fresh air after my rather cloistered upbringing. He grew up very hard. His father was manager of a tea plantation in the hill country of India but he died of drink and Walter was cut loose when he was only fourteen. Somehow he drifted into plant hunting but he learned his botany in the jungles and mountains, not in the classroom. In the old days he would have rushed to Alaska the instant we found the letters. It's sad to see him so reduced."

"What happened to him?"

"We were in Colombia. He fell sixty feet from a tree and broke his back. It was my fault. I had dared him to climb after an orchid, taunted him, actually."

"Did he get the orchid?"

"It had already been named." She shrugged. "So now Walter's half a man and our buccaneering days are over."

"Why don't you come with me?" I blurted out. "I could use your help and it would be one last adventure."

"One last adventure," Audrey said with a rueful smile. She twined a lock of her hair around her fingers. "I've never shown you the drawing that started all this, have I? It's in my room upstairs." Audrey gave my hand a gentle tug to pull me to my feet then led me to the staircase. Briefly I thought that Arbuthnot could never manage the climb but then I pushed his image from my mind and followed Audrey up the stairs, the sway of her hips perfect as a metronome.

Down the hall and into the room that held her bed. On the wall were half a dozen Chinese brush-and-ink drawings. I instantly knew which one had hidden the Steller letters, so compelling was its depiction of orchid, bamboo, and rock. And I knew that I could never match the artist, not in a thousand lifetimes.

"I can't believe I own this," Audrey said. "It's by Cheng Hsieh, one of the best ever. He was early Ch'ing dynasty. The dealer said this one probably dates to 1740."

"Almost the same year as Steller," I said and then was embarrassed by the pedantry. Bering's voyage was not at all on my mind. My throat was dry and my hands trembled, but not at the beauty of the painting.

"I have something to give you." Audrey put her hand on my spine and turned me toward a bedside table that held a wooden box with a glass lid.

"This is the Wardian case I promised you. It was a gift to me in China but I want you to take it. For luck, to make sure you bring the orchid home."

"But it's so beautiful." The case was a work of art, not a simple specimen box. The wood was dark and highly polished. The corners were immaculately done in a kind of dovetail joint.

"Chinese mahogany." Audrey took my hand and drew it gently along the surface of the case. Her hand was cool and soft and the wood had a patina like satin. Without saying anything she entwined her fingers with mine. I looked at her but she kept her head lowered so that the soft billow of hair shielded her face. I could see the faint

rise and fall of her breast. Somewhere in the house a clock ticked—
the slow release of a coiled spring. Still holding my hand Audrey
turned toward the bed.

Alyson

"What a conniving bitch," Alyson said.

"It was my idea more than hers."

"No, it wasn't, she just made you think so. She wanted to get her hooks in you from the get-go. So you'd do what she wanted."

"But the thing is I wanted to be seduced. Most young men do. I was looking for that kind of adventure and I sure found it."

"I'll bet she didn't have any women friends."

"Maybe not." Women never like femme fatales. I knew that Alyson had also left a trail of broken hearts but I doubted she had ever been manipulative or scheming. Simply indifferent, but that could be just as painful.

"Being with Audrey was a revelation for me. Remember, the world was different back then. I was shy around women and inexperienced sexually, like most people my age."

"Whereas nowadays we all fuck like rabbits."

"I would have too, given the chance. But it was different in more ways than just sex. Audrey was a better botanist than any of us but if she had wanted to run the Marsh Garden, or teach, or lead an expedition, she'd have been laughed at."

"That hasn't changed much, Uncle John."

"Maybe not enough, but it was way worse back then. Even Audrey's money wasn't her own. She had a large trust fund but the purse strings were held by the trustees until she married, at which point her husband took control."

"That definitely sucks."

"For centuries it was just common law. The arrangement was a little outdated by Audrey's time but I expect her family knew she was reckless and designed the trust to keep a tight rein on her."

"How'd she like that?"

"About as much as you would have. So, she fought back with the only weapon left, her beauty. A devil's bargain, maybe, but I can't think ill of her. That spring she made all the colors brighter, all the sounds sweeter."

"I still don't like her. Why didn't her husband just boot her out? He must have known what was she was up to."

"Audrey wasn't all that discreet, that's for sure. Maybe she was trying to goad Arbuthnot into leaving her. The only legal reason for divorce back then was adultery, which meant he could divorce her but she had no grounds to divorce him. Only he was too smart to take the bait and he hung on to keep his hands on her money. But at heart I think it was more about blood than coin. Some deep game I still don't understand."

"I still don't like her. And what about her first husband, the one she beheaded?"

"Bandits did it, not Audrey, but even that was hearsay. It's funny, though. All the times we talked about China, Audrey never once mentioned a first husband, nor did the professor. That bothered me; it was kind of ruthless. Maybe she married just to have access to her inheritance, and chose someone she thought was a pushover."

"Sounds like you did learn something about him."

I shrugged and handed the joint back to Alyson. She took a hit, then let out a long curl of smoke, studying me all the while.

"So, what happened next?"

PART II

Nome

"Oh, thou poor man! What misfortune can have brought thee into my country? Seest thou what miserable lives we have? I have never seen any stranger here in summer. Whence dost thou come, and whither dost thou intend to go?"

—Carl Linnaeus, quoting an old woman he met while botanizing in Lapland as a young man

The constant drone of the engine changed pitch and the ship shuddered as the screw reversed. As I left my cabin I heard a distant shout and then a loud rattle as the anchor chain plummeted through the hawsehole. The day was cold and gray and a raw wind swept the deck.

A cluster of buildings perched on the nearby shore. Nome may have been the principal town on the Bering Sea but on this bitter cold day it looked forgotten and left behind. Nonetheless a launch carrying a brass band had come out to serenade the *Victoria's* first arrival of the season. The sound of tubas and trumpets mingled with the eldritch cry of the seabirds.

Natasha was standing by the starboard rail alongside a short, stout woman shaped something like a duck. Gathered around them were four smaller versions of the lady. The little girls had their hair pinned in two short tufts that stuck straight up and made them look more like quail than ducks, as though their mother had accidentally hatched the wrong brood. I was working my way across the crowded deck to speak with them when Francis X. Fitzgerald grabbed my arm and drew me to the rail. The *Victoria* lay in an open roadstead. Nearby a revenue cutter and a gaggle of small schooners swung at anchor.

"You're in luck, kid, the ice must still be solid in the Bering Strait or these boats wouldn't be here. That's the *King & Winge* over there, your buddy Swenson's boat, so you'll get to talk to the old man after all. Just don't tell 'em ya know me."

"Those boats look awfully small."

"The mosquito fleet. There'll be more in the Snake River, on the west end of town. Maybe one's your ride, kid." He slapped me on the shoulder and strolled off.

Natasha was no longer abovedecks. I grabbed my carpetbag and boarded the motor launch that was lightering the passengers ashore. There was no wharf in Nome—if one were built the ice would destroy it come winter—and the launch was simply run up on the shingly beach. I jumped ashore but the land felt unsteady after ten days aboard the ship and I nearly sat down in surprise.

The beach looked as though a tidal wave of human activity had swept across the lonely sand and then receded. There were cans and bottles, shovels with broken handles, odd bits of rusting machinery. The town was no more prepossessing. Buildings leaned alarmingly, their sides scoured free of paint by the wind-driven sand. Grime clouded the blank windows and coated the sea grass that grew in tufts along the planked boardwalk. The road itself was a confusion of muddy ruts.

I stopped before a large false-fronted building that stood slightly askew. This was the Golden Gate, reputedly Nome's best hotel. It looked a little tawdry and overdressed, brooding over its glamorous youth now twenty years gone by. I booked a room for $2.50, dropped off my carpetbag, and returned to the lobby. From the lounge I could hear the click of billiard balls and I looked in at the usual collection of idlers. A man in shirtsleeves stared at me expressionlessly as he chalked his cue.

The hotel clerk sat on a high stool, his hair slick with brilliantine. "I need to arrange passage to the Shumagin Islands," I said to him. "You wouldn't have any idea how to go about that?"

"The Shumagin Islands?" He frowned and lightly touched his hair. "Never heard of them."

"South of the Peninsula? Sort of on the way to Seward?"

"Sorry. Doesn't ring a bell."

"Well, do you know where Olaf Swenson lives?"

"Front Street, two blocks down." He waved an arm. "Ask anybody on the street."

No one answered my knock at Swenson's home. I stood uncertainly for a moment then decided to walk the road to Anvil Mountain. I needed to stretch my legs and feel the land. On the outskirts of town aging miners sat in the doorways of tiny shacks and ragged children played in the muddy streets. I passed an old woman wearing an ankle-length caribou parka decorated with what appeared to be squirrels' tails. Her face was dark and wrinkled and she had four blue lines tattooed on her chin. She looked at me with eyes that did not seem to focus.

On the lower slopes of the mountain I found delphinium, gentian, primula, pyrola and white dryas. The tension that had accompanied me from New Haven fell away. When I had first studied the Linnaean binomial system it was like encountering a language I already knew. The beautiful symmetry of the branching patterns was instantly clear. Now, alone in the hills of Nome with only the wind for company, I felt a sense of kinship with Linnaeus when he went collecting in Lapland as a young man, or perhaps with Steller when he first traveled to Kamchatka.

I came upon a single plant of alpine phlox with lavender blossoms. I picked one of the tiny, precise flowers and examined it with my magnifying glass. But then memory intruded and I saw instead a *Vanda coerulea* in the Arbuthnot's conservatory—complex curves unfolding to frilled ends, a throat deep and beckoning. And I saw the curve of Audrey's ivory-white throat as she bent to sniff the bloom.

I drew a deep breath and tossed the phlox blossom in the air and watched the wind play with it till it came to rest.

The next morning I found Olaf Swenson at home going over account books. He was a tall, seemingly austere man with a neatly trimmed mustache. He motioned me to sit down while he read my letter of introduction.

"John Lars Nelson, yes. How is your father?"

"Quite well, sir, thank you."

"He represented me in a legal action a few years back. Quite ably, I might add. I also knew your grandfather." He tapped the letter. "So you need to get to the Shumagins, John."

"Yes, sir."

"I'm afraid I won't be as much help as I'd like. I'll be going north, probably within the week."

"Do you know of anyone headed south?"

"Not just offhand. All the money's being made up north right now, at the edge of the pack ice. There used to be a man, Isaac Soboloff, who ran a regular trade route south of Unimak but he died last year. I haven't heard of anyone planning to pick up his business but let's go see what we can find out."

Swenson took his coat and hat from a clothes tree and we left his home and turned west toward the Snake River. Swenson walked like my grandfather—very erect with the hands clasped behind the back.

"How much money do you think I'll have to spend to get to the Shumagins?" I asked him.

"Difficult to say. If someone's going that way they may take you for very little. But if you have to charter a boat you might end up paying two hundred a week or so."

My stomach plummeted. I might exhaust my budget without ever reaching Nagai.

Before we had walked very far we came upon Arne Larson, still wearing the silver derby with the tiny rim. "Arne," Swenson said, "I'd like you to meet John Nelson."

"I saw him on the *Victoria*." Arne stopped to light a cigarette, cupping his hand around the flame as though he were on the back deck of a schooner. "There was a lot of talk about your flower hunting." He tipped me a wink as he shook out his match.

"John needs to get to the Shumagins, Arne. Do you know anybody headed south?"

"Nobody, now Isaac's gone." Larson blew out a jet of smoke. "Except maybe Jay Davis."

"Jason Davis?"

"I seen him and Li Po getting set to launch the *Amy Galoshes*. I heard they bought all Isaac's charts off his widow. Anyway they wouldn't dare take that old tub into the ice."

"Jason Davis," Swenson said again slowly. "Didn't they spend a winter or two in King Cove?"

"Yup. Can't imagine why. Those two always got some crazy scheme going."

"Do you think they might be leaving soon?" I asked.

"Quick as possible, I'd guess. Before the bank or some irate husband gets ahold of Davis." Larson winked again and then walked on, his laugh trailing behind him.

"The *Amy Galoshes*?" I said to Swenson. The boats in Nome certainly had strange names.

"To me she's still the *Starik*. She was Siberian-built but Davis renamed her. I never thought of Davis for your trip. Last summer he and Li Po were salting red salmon in Bristol Bay and selling them here. From Ugashik—that was your grandfather's cannery, wasn't it?"

"Yes, sir, Pilot Point."

"Well, Jason Davis might be your best chance."

A row of abandoned buildings fronted the road that ran along the left bank of the Snake. On the riverside several mud-colored hulks rotted quietly alongside less-moribund schooners that had been hauled high and dry and chocked in place with timbers. Some distance off two men stood beneath a schooner's stern. Closer by a larger schooner floated in the river; judging from the clutter of tools and timbers it had only just been launched. Two men and a woman stood on the afterdeck studying a chart. One of the men was Francis X. Fitzgerald. He gave me a brief nod. Swenson stopped for a moment and clasped and unclasped his hands behind his back.

"Good day to you, Captain Gottschalk," he said. "I see you've managed to get the *Seal* in the water."

"Looks that way, don't it, Captain Swenson," the man holding the chart said with a mocking emphasis on "Captain." The man was short and muscular. He was in shirtsleeves and hatless and his gray hair was cut as short as iron filings. Vertical grooves around his mouth deepened as he bared his teeth in a wolfish grin. He looked as though he had been hammered out of hot iron and thrust into an ice floe to harden.

"Are you going walrus hunting this year, Captain Gottschalk?" Swenson asked very formally.

"Gotta do somethin'," the man said and spat into the river.

"Let's hope for better ice conditions this year." Swenson tipped his hat to the woman as we left.

When we reached the other schooner a tall man in dungarees and a collarless shirt swung a mallet with a long, thin head as he worked a caulking iron along a seam in the stern. A spool of white cotton dangled before him. A Chinese man wearing baggy blue pants, a quilted jacket, and a cap without a bill carried a bucket of tar with which he was paying the seams that had already been caulked. The ring of the mallet stopped as we drew near.

Swenson nodded first to the Chinese man and then said, "Morning, Captain Davis. I'd like you to meet John Nelson. John is looking for a ride to Bristol Bay and beyond. I thought maybe you could help him."

Davis offered me his hand, which was long and slender though heavily calloused. "This is Li Po," he said, indicating the other man. I extended my hand to him as well but he held up his own pitch-covered hand in a kind of salute.

"And why is John Nelson going to Bristol Bay?" Davis asked.

"Actually, it's the Shumagins I'm trying to reach," I said. "I'm going to do a plant survey there."

Davis leaned against the rudder of his boat. "*Emilia Galotti*" was painted on the transom, not "*Amy Galoshes*." Davis stroked his chin and studied me. He had several days' growth of gray whiskers and his lank blonde hair was shot with gray. His features were finely made but there was a web of lines around his eyes. Where Gottschalk's face had been marked as with a chisel Davis appeared to have been doing battle with overhanging cobwebs, scarred by constant entanglement with silken threads.

"A botanist," he said with an odd light in his pale, blue eyes. "Science comes to the Bering Sea. And who might be sponsoring this expedition?"

"The Marsh Garden, my college's botanical facility."

"Well, we don't normally take passengers; the *Emilia's* awfully small." Davis tapped the boat's hull and stood ruminating for a moment. He looked at Li Po who was working on the seam along the garboard strake. I remembered my grandfather telling me that this seam was called the "devil" and that caulking it gave rise to the expression, "the devil to pay and no pitch hot." Li Po looked a little satanic himself. He had a hatchet-shaped face the color of the keys on an abandoned piano but he did not look up in answer to the unspoken question.

"No," Davis said almost reluctantly. "I hate to disappoint you but I'm afraid it just wouldn't work. We've made other plans and we're a bit stuck in our ways."

"I can pay," I said, a little foolishly.

"Sorry, John. Can't do it. But I wish you luck in your quest."

"Thank you," I mumbled, crestfallen.

"Another time," Davis said. With a polite goodbye to Swenson he picked up his mallet and turned back to his work.

There were a few other schooners floating in the river but they all appeared deserted and we headed back toward town. When we passed the *Seal* no one was visible on deck.

"What about Captain Gottschalk?" I said quietly, "would there be any point in asking him?"

"I wouldn't want to answer to your father if I let you ship with Max Gottschalk."

"Oh."

"I had the impression you knew that man Fitzgerald."

"I met him on the *Victoria*. He was pretty friendly."

"I was surprised to see him with Gottschalk."

"Why's that?"

"Two years ago Gottschalk was brought up on smuggling and bootlegging charges. Fitzgerald was going to be a witness for the prosecution, but just before the trial he recanted and left town."

"So it looks like they've had a reconciliation."

"Max is a lion by nature. Fitzgerald's a jackal. You'll always find the one at the heels of the other."

"Who was the woman on board?"

"Lena, a White Russian. A woman of quality. Why she's with Max I'll never know." He shook his head. We had reached the boardwalk. Swenson looked at his watch. "I'm afraid I have business in town, John. But don't lose hope. I'll ask around the fleet; someone's bound to be heading south."

"Thank you, sir, I really appreciate your help."

"Why don't you join me for dinner tonight and I can tell you what I've found out. My wife and daughter stayed in Seattle this year but I'd like you to meet our local doctor, Alan Macpherson. He's an enthusiastic amateur botanist."

"I'd be delighted," I said, though I was feeling more than a little downtrodden. We parted with a handshake. Behind us I could still hear the ring of the caulking mallet, loud and persistent as an ovenbird.

CHAPTER 6

The etched glass door read "Alaska Steamship Company." The bell tinkled behind me as I left. I had thought to inquire if I could possibly take ship back to Seward and then catch the mail boat, but though the office was smaller than the one in Seattle the information was the same. I was told that the only way to reach Seward would be first to return to Seattle, which would burn up more money and time than I could afford.

I could book passage to St. Mary's on the Yukon, or even Dawson City, two thousand miles upriver. I could book passage north to Point Barrow and points in between but I could not book passage to the Shumagins. I had the impression that nobody much had visited since 1741.

Feeling in need of a friendly smile I decided to look for Natasha. The Nome Native School was in the old courthouse building on Steadman Streeet, near the Catholic Church. The halls of the school were empty, but I found an administration office near the main entrance. A middle-aged lady looked up from her typewriter when I entered. A nameplate on her desk identified her as Miss I. Hutchinson. She wore a blouse with a high, starched collar and a pair of tortoiseshell eyeglasses hung from a ribbon around her neck. She put the glasses on and studied me.

"Can I be of some assistance, young man?"

"Yes, ma'am. I'm looking for Natasha Christiansen. Do you know where she might be staying?"

"I'm afraid not."

"But I thought she was going to work for you."

"Regrettably we had to withdraw our offer of employment. Miss Christiansen was not entirely truthful on her application."

I stood silently for a moment. Although I scarcely knew Natasha I could not picture her lying on an application form.

"Could I possibly speak with the superintendent?" I had some vague notion of telling him about Natasha's care for Mrs. Kelly as some form of recommendation.

"Dr. Westmoreland is still in California. I am acting director in his absence."

"But there must be some mistake."

"Young man, our goal, our mission, is to lead these poor benighted children into the twentieth century, to teach them the values of Christian culture." She tapped her pencil forcibly on the desk. "Our purpose is most definitely not to provide employment for flighty young girls." Two red spots appeared on her cheekbones, bright as rouge. "At this stage in his career Dr. Westmoreland does not need such distractions."

"Yes'm."

"Now do you represent Miss Christiansen in some way?"

"No, ma'am. I just wanted to find her."

"Then I suggest you look elsewhere."

"Yes'm." I backed out the door, hat in hand, feeling like a fourth grader who had been horsewhipped by the principal.

I had no idea where else to look for Natasha. I walked down to the waterfront and stood watching as the *Victoria* took on cargo for the return trip. I would hate to travel back on her with my tail between my legs. When I had finally secured my father's permission I had booked passage immediately, before he could change his mind. He had offered to have his secretary make all the travel arrangements but I was leery of allowing him any semblance of authority over the project. I knew his tactic of opposing something then maneuvering to control it. I had let him pay the extra for a first-class cabin but the rest of the itinerary was my doing. So much for Professor Arbuthnot's reliance on my Alaskan connections. And so much for my own competence. I almost ground my teeth at the prospect of failing so dismally.

I thought of returning to the Snake River to ask Max Gottschalk about chartering the *Seal*, whatever the consequences. Instead I went to my hotel room to lick my wounds and consider my next step. I picked up Steller's journal and read a section dealing with the incompetence and pigheadedness of Bering's officers, about their refusal to listen to Steller's opinions. Under the circumstances Steller's haughty self-righteousness struck a false note.

I turned to the letters and read: "Roaring waves climb the distant rock. The tempests of autumn drive the moon through reefs of broken clouds, but at the back of the tumult I hear your soft voice call my name. I strain to listen but then it fades, scattered like the sea foam . . ."

This sounded even worse, the reverse side of the coin of self-absorption. I lay back on my lumpy mattress and stared at the walls, which met the floor at something other than a right angle. Through the partly open window I could hear the traffic on Front Street—the clatter of wagons and the soft clop of hooves in mud.

"She was called the *Kamchatka*," Swenson said. "An old whale ship, built stout to stand the ice. She'd killed so many whales that her decks and timbers were saturated with oil. Had a wonderful odor, that oil-drenched pitch pine, not rancid like you'd expect. But it proved her undoing. On Friday the thirteenth, of all days, in the middle of the North Pacific, a fire started in the engine room."

He stopped to knock the dottle of tobacco out of his pipe and then packed the pipe again as he spoke. "It was rough, too. Terrible big seas. Once the fire got hold of the timbers there was no chance of putting it out. And if the whale oil wasn't bad enough we had barrels of gunpowder and caseloads of ammunition in the forepeak and drums of gasoline lashed on decks."

"My god, man, you were a bloody fire ship like in the Napoleonic Wars." Dr. Macpherson had thick and tangled eyebrows that he used to punctuate his comments.

Swenson gestured with his pipe. "That was pretty standard cargo for a trader but knowing it was there didn't do much to calm us. When the fire got to the generator all the lights went out. We were on deck in the pitch-black screaming wind with smoke pouring out of every hatch. You could hear the sound of the fire above the waves. Somehow we launched a whaleboat and got in. The *Kamchatka* burned for hours before she sank. Burned with a white-hot light. The standpipes for the fuel tanks shot flames in the air like torches. Ammunition was exploding and then the gas barrels began to explode. The masts and shrouds were burning and finally she sank."

We sat silently for a moment. Captain Swenson drew on his pipe and shifted in his chair. "There was an engine of sorts in the whaleboat. We fought with it for five days, traveling north till we sighted some mountains and headed for them. Came ashore on Chernabura Island in the outer Shumagins. An old Swede was there, caretaking a fox farm. He ran when he saw us. Don't know if he thought we were pirates or revenants. From Chernabura we managed to get to Unga and then Squaw Harbor. Only time I've ever been in the Shumagins."

I looked around the crowded parlor: floral wallpaper, overstuffed chairs with antimacassars, a table with a fringed cloth, a glass-fronted bookcase. Studio portraits of Swenson's family were mounted on the walls. It was much like any middle-class parlor and I found it hard to reconcile its stuffy comfort with the image of a small whaleboat adrift on the North Pacific.

"It's an uncanny place, not much like here," Swenson continued. "Mountainous little islands, cliffs, and sea stacks. There's even a petrified forest."

"A petrified forest?" I asked. "How can that be? I thought there weren't any trees at all."

"There aren't. At least not now."

"It's a strange land, I've often heard," the doctor said. "I wonder what mischance brought Bering ashore there, of all places."

"The hand of Providence, like all else," Swenson said.

"Perhaps so, but tell me, Olaf, we often call Nome the middle of nowhere, yet the Shumagins must be the outermost edge of nowhere. So which is more truly isolated, the center of nowhere or its edge?"

Swenson just shook his head and smiled.

"Could I look at your flowers again, sir?" I asked. Macpherson had brought three albums with approximately one hundred and fifty plants that he had gathered around Nome. His knowledge of the local flora was so extensive that he made me feel like a charlatan, passing myself off as a botanist. I leafed through the album and stopped at the orchids he had collected.

"*Cypripedium passerinum* and *Coeloglossum viride*, the only two orchids on the Seward Peninsula," the doctor said. "I must say I don't understand people's obsession with orchids. A few years ago in England the Pankhursts' gang of suffragettes broke into the greenhouses at Kew and trampled the plants. But only orchids. Can you explain that to me, Nelson?"

"No sir, I cannot."

"To my mind the simple *Dryas* are more lovely," Macpherson harrumphed. He pointed at the album. "You'll find those two orchids in the Shumagins but there'll be stranger plants as well. And stranger doings. I doubt your libraries have prepared you for all that's there."

"If I ever get there at all."

"I'm sorry, John, the *Shuyak*'s the best I've come up with so far," Swenson said, referring to a fish packer that might be going to Unalaska in a week or two. "You may have to get there in segments, like stepping stones."

He poured us all more blackberry cordial. "Jason Davis was a disappointment. I thought he was going to say yes. I don't know what changed his mind."

"I never know what to make of Jason Davis," Macpherson said. "He's a strange duck."

"He's not what I expected," I said. "Very well-spoken, actually."

"I'm sure he's educated," Swenson said. "That's not so unusual up here. It's a strange mix of people. Remember Graham Sutherland, Alan?"

"How could I forget?"

"A couple of years ago," Swenson said to me, "a London solicitor showed up looking for a man who had succeeded to a title. A baronetcy, I believe. He found this Sutherland working as a seal hunter."

"God's mercy on the tenant farmers with that bull loose amongst the heifers," Macpherson said. "But Davis is altogether different. Once I was collecting on Anvil Mountain and I came upon Davis in a meadow on his hands and knees amidst the flowers. He jumped up like I'd caught him with his pants down. I think he's a likely candidate for one of my colleagues in the mental line."

I left soon after that. I walked to the hotel via the waterfront to clear my head of the blackberry cordial. It was a bit disconcerting to see the sun still above the horizon in the north. There was no more than a breath of wind and the sea lay calm. In Swenson's house I had seen pictures of the waterfront locked in ice in winter and of boats swept ashore in the fall storms, but now the sea breathed gently with a susurrant sound as the slight swell ran up on the sands.

I found Jason Davis sitting on the front steps of the Golden Gate. He was wearing a heavy pea jacket and a wool captain's hat. The neck of a brown bottle protruded from one pocket and he was walking a gold coin slightly smaller than a silver dollar arcoss his knuckles.

"The young botanist," he said.

"You were looking for me?"

"I . . . that is, we, Li Po and me, got to talking about how it might be a good idea to take you after all. Are you still interested?"

"I don't know . . ." I hesitated. Swenson's suggestion about the *Shuyak* had been pretty tentative. On the other hand, Davis might have decided I was a pigeon ripe for the plucking. The coin flashed across his knuckles and passed beneath his palm.

"What's the coin?" I asked.

"A ten rouble piece. A woman gave it to me in Siberia. For luck."

"Good luck or bad?"

"Fortune always has two faces." He showed me the coin and grinned sardonically. "Ask Nicholas."

"So how much for my passage?"

"Fifty dollars'd get you to Bristol Bay. After that . . . we've talked about heading for King Cove, we could dicker about a charter."

"I guess that'd be all right," I said slowly, a bit uncertain about the wisdom of the decision. "How soon will you be leaving?"

"Scheduled departure was yesterday, like always. I don't know. We just got the old girl in the water. I've got a few loose ends to tie up but if Li Po gets the engine running we'll have a shot at getting underway tomorrow."

He cleared his throat. "Thing is, it might expedite matters just a wee bit if you could manage a cash advance."

Without a word I opened my money belt and held out a fifty-dollar-bill. His hand moved like a dragonfly taking a mosquito and the fifty disappeared into his pocket along with the rouble.

"*Alea iacta est,*" he said. "Be at the Snake in the morning." With a tip of the hat he walked up the street toward town.

The die is cast, I translated for myself. Caesar at the Rubicon. I watched Jason Davis dwindle into the shadows. Ragtime piano music spilled from the doorway of a brightly lit bar.

CHAPTER 7

A black dog came from beneath one of the abandoned buildings and snapped at my heels. I threw a stick at him and he retreated beneath the sagging front of what had once been McIvor's Gen. Merchandise, according to a faded sign.

The *Emilia Galotti* now lay with her prow against the bank, facing upstream. She was no more than fifty foot overall with short masts and a long bowsprit that appeared to droop a bit. Gray canvas sails were loosely furled along the booms that rested in crutches. There was a blocky, glass-enclosed wheelhouse just abaft the mainmast and a covered companionway that led, I assumed, to the galley and engine room. Tar dripped sloppily from the freshly caulked seams in the stern.

Jason Davis appeared from the companionway wiping his oily hands on a piece of cotton waste. "There you are, Nelson," he said. "Things are going better than expected. Li Po just went uptown to rent a wagon and fetch some of our trade goods. If you catch him you can bring your gear aboard. Quickly now, he'll be at Lindstrom's stables."

I turned to run back uptown but Davis called after me. "Just don't let the old rascal start talking about Lord Byron or we'll never get off."

I sketched a quick salute and ran on, thinking, *Lord Byron?*

I found Li Po leaving the stable in a wagon drawn by an ancient horse. At his invitation I climbed up beside him.

"We have some goods stored in a godown at the far end of town," Li Po said.

The harness jingled as the wagon jolted through the ruts on its iron-rimmed wheels. I glanced at Li Po. At close quarters he looked even more piratical. He was clean-shaven but wore his hair in a long pigtail that almost reached his waist.

"I'm not supposed to ask you about Lord Byron," I said.

Li Po's face broke into a delighted smile. "Do you like poetry, John?"

"Yes, of course," I lied.

"Lord Byron is very good but, you know, I really think William Wordsworth has a more Oriental outlook."

"I never thought of that," I said, more truthfully.

"Think of 'Tintern Abbey': 'For I have learned / to look on nature, not as in the hour/ Of thoughtless youth; but hearing oftentimes/ The still sad music of humanity'."

"Very nice," I said, a bit perplexed. Li Po's voice had a singsong intonation that was quite pleasant and far more intelligible than the affected drawl of some of my college classmates.

We reached the "godown" which proved to be a warehouse with a ridgepole so swaybacked that the building could have more accurately been called a "falldown." The front door was secured with a bar and a huge padlock that was brown with rust. Li Po ignored the lock and simply pried the bar off the door. The horse stood absently grazing on a patch of grass (a variety of *Festuca*, I thought) while we hauled out half a dozen heavy crates and loaded them in the wagon. Some of the crates had Chinese characters stamped on them and some had Cyrillic. Li Po pried the lids off several to check the contents: compressed bricks of tea, rock hard cones of sugar that must have weighed twenty pounds each, and leaf tobacco made up like cabbage heads. "Papushka," Li Po said, hefting a tobacco head. "Left-overs from Siberia. A little hard to get rid of on this side but there are some very poor villages in the delta. They might want some of it." He threw a number of empty quart-sized cans into the wagon. "One more stop, John," he said and boarded the wagon.

A ramshackle shanty stood several blocks beyond the reach of the boardwalk. Li Po drove the wagon around back toward an even more dilapidated stable. The door slid open as if we were expected, its rusty wheel squealing loudly on the rail. A gray-haired man no more than five feet tall appeared.

"Hurry up, hurry up. Ain't got all day," the man said. He looked up and down the street then slid the door closed behind the wagon. Slashes of sunlight penetrated the weathered sides of the barn and dust motes danced in the splintered light. The horse stomped and blew noisily.

"Who the hell is this?" the old man said, staring up at me from beneath a slouch hat. Greasy tendrils of gray hair fell to his shoulders. He appeared to have only two teeth left, both broken and tobacco-stained.

"John Nelson, Lucas. John's traveling with us."

"Jesus Christ. Well, c'mon, we're burnin' daylight." Quick as an eel, the old man unlatched the tailboard and put two planks against the wagon bed as a kind of ramp. He and Li Po began to roll a small barrel up the incline. I sprang to help them. The keg was about the size of a herring barrel—forty-two gallons—and the word KEROSENE was stamped on it. We loaded a second barrel and the old man dusted his hands as Li Po secured the tailboard.

"You sure you're takin' this to the *Seal?*" the old man asked.

"Jason Davis arranged it. We owe Max a favor."

The old man scratched his neck. "Yeah, right. The only reason I'd believe a cock-and-bull story like that is Jason Davis never paid cash for nothin' before." He brandished a buckskin poke suspended by a thong from his throat. "I guess your money's as good as anybody's but fifty bucks gonna seem like pretty slim pickins if Max goes on the warpath."

He stuck the poke back inside his shirt and hopped toward a second large door at the back of the building as we climbed into the wagon. Lucas wheeled the door open and gestured impatiently. "Time to get out."

Li Po clucked calmly to the horse. We rolled forward and the door squealed shut, almost nipping the end of the wagon.

"Good day to you, Lucas," Li Po said as he gathered the reins.

"Anybody asks, I'm visiting a sick aunt in Shaktoolik." With a cackle the old man cut our horse across the rump and the wagon lurched away. I grabbed my hat and looked back. The old man was already gone from view.

We stopped at the Golden Gate and fetched my baggage. I wrote a quick note to Captain Swenson and asked the clerk to deliver it. Watching him pigeonhole it, I realized that if it went astray no one would have any idea where I had gone.

Back on the street a man was talking to Li Po. His thumbs were in his waistcoat pockets and I could see a US Marshall's badge pinned to his breast.

"We're collecting flowers with this young man," Li Po said, nodding at me. "A botanical charter."

"Flowers?" The man rocked back on his heels. His glance flicked across me dismissively then lingered on the wooden barrels. He spat in the gutter. "Just try to keep Davis out of trouble for once." With a curt nod he turned and climbed the hotel stairs. If he intended to check my credentials he was going to be disappointed; no doubt the clerk had already forgotten my existence.

As we rolled away I looked at my trunk and the trade goods piled high in the wagon bed and thought of the clutter already on the schooner's deck. "Will all this stuff fit on the *Amy Galoshes*?" I asked.

Li Po looked at me. "A word, John. You might not want to call her *Amy Galoshes* in Davis's presence."

"Sorry."

Back at the Snake no one was visible aboard the *Seal*. As I suspected, we rolled past it without dropping off the barrels. Davis jumped down from the *Emilia's* deck to help unload. When the wagon was empty Li Po headed back to the stables. Davis and I manhandled my trunk down the narrow companionway. Along the starboard side of the cabin was a small galley complete with a stove and a bit of countertop. In the middle was a table built around the mainmast, which ran through the cabin floor to be stepped on the keelson. There was a bench, or settee, beneath the table on the port side. Forward a door gave access to a cabin with two narrow bunks. What there was not was an excess of space.

"You can take the starboard bunk," Davis said. "Li Po or I will be on the wheel so we can share the other. If we anchor up one of us can doss down in the wheelhouse or on the settee. When you get squared away come lend a hand with the rest of the goods."

Stowing my collecting gear was not easy. I looked with despair at the small cupboard beneath my bunk. I put Audrey's Wardian case on the galley table and touched the glass top lightly, looking for a reflection of green eyes above blue silk. Did mirrors have memories? Images hidden in their depths? I opened the case and picked up a card engraved *Audrey Gould Arbuthnot*. On the back she had written 'Find it for me!' in lilac ink.

Davis came clumping down the stairs and I quickly stuffed the card in my pocket. "How goes the battle?" he said and then stopped abruptly. He picked up the case and turned it in his hands.

"It's a Wardian case," I said, "for transporting live plants."

"I know what it is." He put the case down but his hands lingered. "It's very well made. May I ask where you came up with it?"

"It's Chinese originally but I got it from my professor." I was a little shy of mentioning Audrey.

"And his name is?"

"Arbuthnot. Walter Arbuthnot. He's director of the Marsh Garden at Yale."

"So that's what they call the Yale herbarium. I didn't know." Davis put down the case and briefly touched the vasculum sitting next to it. "Well, Li Po is back. Could you give us a hand with the stowing? I want to get out of here before the weather changes."

We shifted all the crates and boxes into the hold. Li Po rigged a sling and block and tackle and we lifted the barrels onto the deck and lashed them securely to the foremast alongside some steel fuel drums. There was scarcely room to move on deck and there was still a jumble of gear that needed stowing but Davis was in a tearing hurry to be underway. He kept glancing over at the *Seal.* Li Po went below to start the engine. As soon as smoke came from the stack Davis had me cut loose the moorings. I had no sooner jumped back aboard than we were turning in the river's current, outward bound.

Where the Snake met the sea a sand spit nearly blocked the river, creating a lagoon. On the spit several Eskimo families had made camp by using their large skin boats overturned for shelter. I could see the smoke of cooking fires and children running on the beach. The wind was freshening and the *Emilia Galotti* shuddered at the bite of the surf as she crossed the bar.

There were boats in the roadstead but both the *Victoria* and the Coast Guard cutter, the *Bear,* had departed. Davis motioned for me to come inside the wheelhouse. "Here," he said, "take the wheel. We've got to finish on deck. Just keep the compass heading south-southeast."

The wheel was small, scarcely larger than the steering wheel of an automobile, but built of heavily varnished wood with turned spokes. The steering chains were exposed and they rattled as I turned the wheel experimentally. The bowsprit began to fall off downwind and I corrected her gingerly. There was a large black compass mounted in a binnacle next to the wheel and I watched the needle waver first to one side and then the other of SSE. I was disconcerted at being placed in charge of the ship with no charts and only a faint idea where we were bound. About to drop over the edge of the world I knew, that was certain.

Davis and Li Po finished stowing goods in the hold and then put the hatch cover in place. When everything was secure on deck Li Po vanished down the companionway and Davis stood for a moment scanning the horizon, then he turned and studied the Nome waterfront for a long time. I looked back as well. Two days ago Nome had seemed the end of the world; now it was like a last link to civilization. I wished that I had taken the time to at least drop a line to my parents.

I knew so little about my traveling companions and what I did know was scarcely reassuring.

Davis came into the wheelhouse and motioned me aside. I had been standing rigorously at attention but he held the wheel almost negligently.

"Don't you ever use the sails?" I asked. There was a nice breeze directly abeam.

"She's so badly hogged any press of canvas would drive the mast right through the keel. But we'll use 'em if we have to." He fished a tall, brown bottle out of the tiny bunk that ran crosswise behind him, took a drink and then coughed slightly. At close quarters in the wheelhouse he looked older and more haggard.

"Li Po is fixing a meal. He'll eat first then come take the wheel. You can go below if you want."

"Li Po is awfully polite," I said, to make conversation.

"One of nature's noblemen. But if he offers to sell you a horse be sure to check its teeth."

"Has he worked for you a long time?"

Davis laughed. "More like I'm working for him. All the trading stock is his, plus half of the *Emilia*."

"So have you been partners long?"

"I met him in China, donkey's years now, but we didn't hook up till seven years ago in Siberia. The Japanese had a saltery at the mouth of the Oliutorsk River and Li Po ran a small store there. Only his real trade was selling guns to both the White Russians and the Red. A sweet deal till things got a little hot. I happened along just when he decided to cut and run and we took his goods on board and went trading north along the coast. After that we stayed partners in the Siberian trade. We got as far west as the Kolyma a few times but Siberia's pretty much closed off now. The *Emilia's* too rickety to take into the ice walrus hunting so we're just sort of freelancing. Hard times out here."

"Didn't you say you'd been in King's Cove recently?"

"King Cove, yeah." He took another pull at the bottle. "Winter before last we had to get out of Nome so we headed for Kodiak but ended up broke in King Cove. We hand-lined a boatload of cod, split the heads, salted them and put them in barrels. We took the cod to Ugashik that spring. Didn't make any money but then midsummer we took a load of sockeye to Nome to sell and made out all right so we might try that again. Unless something better shows up."

That sounded like a hand-to-mouth existence to me, not much margin for error and a lot left to chance. I looked at the ocean ahead. There was a single ice floe in sight as we headed south across Norton Sound. High cirrus clouds blocked the sun. The wind had begun to die down but it had also veered slightly. Li Po appeared and Davis gave him the wheel, saying, "No sign of the *Bear*. Or the *Seal*." I knew he was not talking about wildlife.

In the cabin we found a pot of rice and one of stew meat. Davis spooned big helpings into two bowls. The only utensils in evidence were chopsticks. Davis took a pair and, holding his bowl almost under his chin, began to shovel food rapidly into his mouth. I chased a few grains of rice around my bowl till Davis noticed my plight and fetched a big spoon for me. He pushed his own bowl aside, took a tobacco can and some papers from a shelf and rolled a cigarette.

"That other schooner, the *Seal*," I said, "is it apt to be going the same way we are?"

"No telling. The ice is still far down the Bering Strait so he's probably not headed north. Could be going to St. Lawrence Island. Or maybe he's going to risk Siberia again, even though he's been sentenced to the mines once already. The devil himself couldn't predict where Max Gottschalk will go or what he'll do when he gets there."

"I gather you'd just as soon avoid him?"

Davis dropped the spent match in his bowl. "A few years ago in the Gulf of Anadyr, Li Po and I bought a boatload of ivory. Black ivory that was going for five dollars a pound in Nome where white ivory got only twenty-five cents. We were headed west to winter on the Kolyma so we sold the ivory to Max for half the Nome price. Only it turns out the Natives had buried the tusks in lake mud to blacken the ivory. By the time Max reached Nome the color had faded and he had a boatload of white ivory."

"Then he should have been mad at the Natives, not you."

"Well . . . ." Davis grinned. "There's a little more to it. Max and I have a habit of bumping into each other."

"But you moored next to him."

"In town is one thing. Out here . . ." He made a little wigwag motion with one hand. "Different story. Funny thing about the black ivory deal is, we'd have been better off heading for Nome ourselves. We ended up caught in the ice."

"In the *Emilia?*"

"No, my old schooner. The ice crushed her and we had to cross Siberia on foot. Tough trip, not that that would get much sympathy from Max."

"Captain Swenson talked of Gottschalk with respect. Said he was a good seaman."

"Respect? I don't know. Recognition of the opposite, more like. Swenson gives everybody a fair shake, even the Natives. But Max, if he can't swindle you he'll plain rob you."

"Why isn't he in jail, then?"

"He has been a time or two, but he's pretty slippery and the Bering Sea's a lawless place at best. Max pretty much goes where he wants and does what he wants."

Davis took a whiskey bottle from the cupboard and with a gesture asked if I wanted some. I shook my head no. He studied me above the rim of his own cup.

"I don't know," he said. "Gets hard to tell right from wrong up here. All the categories blur. It's not like sitting in a pew back in New Haven listening to the college chaplain talk about sin."

"Wait a minute," I said, rising to the bait. "How can it be different? It's the same world, isn't it? The same rules apply."

"No, it's not even the same God. Down south good and evil are enemies, but up here—they're like twins separated at birth, trying to find each other. You're a long way from home, John Nelson."

He put down his cup and climbed the ladder to the deck, leaving me alone in the dim and musty galley. I could not figure Jason Davis out. The pieces did not quite fit together. Behind the mocking tone there was something wounded and a bit of self-hatred. And all his stories were like onions: each layer concealed a deeper and more bitter layer. Maybe at heart he was always a stranger, even in his own land.

I went into the fo'c'sle and lay down in my bunk. Through the thin planks I could hear the Bering Sea rushing by, not exactly a comforting sound.

Much later a movement in the galley awakened me. Li Po was seated at the galley table holding a pipe with a long, thin stem and a tiny brass bowl. A small charcoal brazier was lit on the table before him. I rolled over and pulled the blankets over my head and drifted back to sleep.

Footsteps sounded on the deck above me and I heard someone knock loose the dog on the anchor winch. A few fathoms of chain rattled out. Early-morning light came down the companionway. I dressed and climbed on deck to find that the boat lay in a shallow cove. The wind had veered to the northeast and we had anchored close in to be in the lee of the low dunes.

"Where are we, exactly?" I asked Davis.

"Don't know, 'exactly.' Somewhere near Scammon Bay."

A line of big drift logs lay buried in the sand and above that the blue seagrass rippled in the wind. A small fox picked its way along the drift. "And there's supposed to be a village nearby?"

"A little further down the coast, Hooper Bay. But we've got work to do before we can trade."

On deck there was a charcoal brazier, shielded from the wind by a packing crate. A soldering iron lay in the brazier. A sling was rigged to one of the herring barrels and Davis had me pull on the block and tackle while he and Li Po wrestled the barrel onto a low stand. Davis then took a bung starter and broached the keg. He put a tin cup under the tap and filled it with a clear liquid that he drank off, grimacing slightly. I caught a few drops in my hand and tasted them. It was like a wood rasp at the back of my throat.

Li Po took one of the empty cans and partly filled it from the barrel and then topped it off with dippers full of water from the beaker lashed in front of the wheelhouse. He stirred the mixture briefly and then poured a little into his cupped palm and touched a lighted match to it. It burned with a flickering blue flame. In his thin hand, it looked like a votive candle.

"Just what is that stuff?" I asked, although of course I knew.

"One hundred and eighty proof rotgut," Davis said. "The straight stuff. Dreadful, really. Li Po won't even taste it, that's why he tests the mixture by lighting it. If the flame goes out it's too weak."

"And that's going to be a trade item?"

"Standard part of the Siberian trade. We used to sell one of those tins for five white fox skins."

Li Po took the soldering iron and began to affix a lid to the can. "I can see you have moral reservations," Davis said.

I shrugged noncommittally.

"All the traders sell whiskey. Even your saintly friend Swenson. You can't compete if you don't. The only question is how much you dilute it and what you dilute it with. Some add pepper or kerosene to make the whiskey seem stronger. But the honest trader, he'll sell good, strong whiskey and stop selling it when the customers get violent."

Li Po called to him and they began to argue about how much to charge for one of their carbines. I looked toward the shore. If my money had bought the whiskey did that make me complicit? The fox was gone but the grass still twisted in the wind.

CHAPTER 8

Low, scudding clouds fled before an offshore wind as we followed the desolate coastline. In the distance I saw a flock of geese, their wings flashing white in a random patch of sunlight. We turned into a bay slightly larger than most, then turned again into the shelter of a sandy spit. Davis throttled back the engine as people came running along the shore. I saw several boats pulled above the tide line and realized that some of the piles of drift were actually barabaras—Native houses. As we dropped anchor two or three people began to turn over the largest of the skin boats.

"Umiak," Davis said. "Woman's boat."

Li Po began to put out various trade items while Davis and I carried a huge brass samovar up from the galley and put it on top of the wheelhouse. With the sun hidden it was the most brilliant thing in sight.

"Impressive, isn't it?" Davis said. "Another relic of our Siberian days. We found twenty of them in a Chukchi village, can't imagine how they got there. We traded two carbines for the lot of them. Plus ten pounds of tobacco, I think."

As he talked he opened a box of cartridges and began to fill the magazine of one of the 45-70 Winchester trade rifles. The dull brass of the casings was a pallid echo of the samovar. In answer to my unspoken question Davis said, "Every once in a while things get a little out of hand." He hid the carbine beneath the mattress of the wheelhouse bunk.

The umiak was halfway to the schooner. "Will they have seen white men before?" I asked.

"Of course." Davis laughed. "This is 1924, not 1824. But the area's pretty much a backwater. They'll get to one of the missions on the big river maybe once a year but that's about all. Some of them will speak a little English but they may be reluctant to use it."

When the umiak came alongside I could see that it had a frame of driftwood lashed with rawhide and a covering stitched from pieces of some thick hide, perhaps walrus. The boat held a surprising number of people—men, women and children—dressed in a combination of furs and dirty, patched trade clothing. They had long, straggly hair and their faces were streaked with soot. One or two had ivory labrets.

The *Emilia* tilted to port as they swarmed over the rail. Davis laughingly distributed tin cups of the tea he had brewed in the samovar. A powerful-looking man with wide shoulders and short legs looked at the rifles that Li Po had stacked against a bale of goods. Then he picked up a long knife and tried its edge. Next to him a young woman studied her reflection in one of the small hand mirrors.

Davis kept up a running commentary of polite nonsense as he poured the tea. "I do enjoy this part," he said to me. "Rather like having the vicar round for tea."

I failed to see the parallel. Li Po was counting with his fingers held in the man's face and moving goods into a pile to one side and furs into a matching pile. There were two cans of whiskey in the trade goods pile. A ring of Eskimos surrounded them, constantly reaching out to touch the goods. Trading was obviously a very tactile business.

"Watch Li Po," Davis said softly to me. "He's a master. Don't ever haggle with a Chinaman."

Goods moved back and forth in a pattern that made little sense to me. I soon realized we were going to be there all day. I gathered my sketchpad and collecting gear, launched the *Emilia's* dinghy and rowed ashore. I dragged the dinghy above the tide line and them began to walk inland. Four children rushed from the village to join me as I scouted in the grass above the beach. I stopped and dug up marsh saxifrage, carefully cleaned its roots and placed it in the vasculum slung over my shoulder. As I made a notation in my journal the children knelt by another saxifrage and studied it intently as if attempting to discover the mystery.

The marshy ground was carpeted with cotton grass not yet in bloom, punctuated by clumps of dwarf willow. I also found marsh marigold, arnica, dwarf fireweed, and goldthread. One of the boys accompanying me carried a small bow and several blunt-tipped arrows. He shot at a Lapland longspur but missed. When he saw that I was watching, he drew his bow as far as he could and shot an arrow into the sky. We watched it rise against the gray clouds then hesitate at the top of its arc before plummeting back to earth. All four children ran after it.

We walked north in a long, slow arc, regaining the beach a mile or so from the camp. We sat on a drift log and I folded a piece of drawing paper into an airplane that the wind took a long way down the beach. They wanted me to make more but I did not have paper to spare. We beachcombed on the way back but all I found was an old nail keg with broken staves.

Raucous voices carried across the water from the *Emilia*. Four Eskimos lay stretched on the beach near the dinghy, a whiskey can on its side nearby. The children grabbed the empty can and began kicking it vigorously down the beach. One of the men yelled at them angrily then got to his feet, walked a few steps and urinated copiously in the sand.

I stowed my gear and began to launch the dinghy but the man came over, plucked at my sleeve and gestured at the schooner. I shook my head and he grabbed me and began to speak slowly and loudly as though this would make me understand. I again shook my head and he made a rude gesture and then shoved me. I shoved back and he took a step backward and sat down. I jumped in the boat and began to back awkwardly away, stern first. The man got up and chased me into the water, grabbing the gunwale and yelling angrily but then he stopped and let go of the boat and stared at the water as if surprised to be wet. I spun the dinghy around and headed for the *Emilia*.

There were still nearly a dozen Eskimos aboard the schooner. Several empty whiskey cans lay in the scuppers. The chief, if such he was, was still haranguing Li Po, who stood impassively with his arms folded. Jason Davis stood by the wheelhouse talking to the young girl whom I had seen admiring herself in the mirror. She was now wearing several necklaces of bright blue trade beads, almost the color of gentian, and held a tin cup in her hands. Davis poured a little of his own whiskey into her cup, his hand more unsteady than hers.

I passed Davis without a word. I'm not sure he even saw me. In the galley I poured myself a cup of the breakfast coffee that was still sitting on the stove. While I drank the bitter coffee I took the flowers I had collected and put them between fresh sheets of paper. Then I changed the papers on the flowers I had collected in Nome, put everything in my press and pulled the straps tight. Lastly I took the used sheets of paper and hung them above the galley stove to dry.

I reheated some beans and sat at the table morosely eating them, feeling cold, tired and out of sorts. The deck above was like a drumhead and I could hear footsteps, voices and what might have been song.

The anchor chain ground in the chocks as the boat swung to the increased wind. I opened my eyes. Li Po was asleep in the galley, face down on the settee. His right hand hung down and next to it on the floor lay his brass-bowled pipe. I went on deck to find a blustery day. The wind whipped the brown water of the bay into little wavelets and the *Emilia* tugged at her anchor as if anxious to be underway.

In the wheelhouse I saw a tangle of blankets and two heads on the narrow bunk. The darker of the two heads moved and the girl sat up, swung her legs over the bunk's edge and sat slumped with her long hair concealing her face. Embarrassed, I walked forward. The deck was littered with the debris of the day's trading. I was trying to decide whether I should clean up a bit when I heard a gasping sound behind me. The girl leaned over the rail, retching. She was completely naked, her dark brown breasts hanging over her belly.

A shout came from the shore. Two men were carrying kayaks down the beach—small, graceful craft quite unlike the umiak. I went to the water barrel and brought the girl a dipper full. She took it and drank greedily. I picked up her skin dress which lay on the deck and draped it over her shoulders. She turned a blank gaze on me, her face streaked with tears.

Another shout. The kayaks were quite near, the men paddling fiercely. They sat so low in the water and moved so quickly they were like seagoing centaurs. Behind me the *Emilia's* engine came to noisy life, its exhaust fluting in the stack. Jason Davis was suddenly beside me, barefoot in a dirty gray union suit. He was carrying a rifle.

"Better get behind the wheelhouse, John," he said calmly but I did not move.

The sun had found a rent in the clouds and the sea was suddenly blue. The man in the lead kayak stopped paddling and nocked an arrow in a short, stout bow. Davis stepped to the rail and, so quickly that I could not stop him, grabbed the girl by one arm and flung her into the sea. She screamed desperately as she hit the cold water. The second kayak darted forward and the man in it wrapped one hand in her hair and dragged her half aboard while he hit her savagely with the single-bladed paddle in his right hand.

The other Native had his bow at full draw, pointing at us. Davis levered a cartridge into the rifle's chamber. Sunlight formed a brief arena. The butt plate of the carbine shone brightly and I could see that the Eskimo's bow was recurve and backed with sinew. The moment was frozen, clear and precise, but then broken by the rattling of the anchor chain. I looked forward and saw Li Po bent over the winch. The boat swung slightly at the pull of the chain and the Eskimo relaxed his draw and lowered his bow. Davis gave a slight grunt and walked into the wheelhouse. The sound of the engine changed as we got underway.

I continued to stand at the rail. The kayak with the girl was returning to shore but the other still paddled alongside, easily keeping abreast. In the prow of this kayak there was an odd, decorative hole like the eye of a monster. The paddler was the man I had taken to be their chief. He bared his teeth and shouted at us again. I picked up the girl's dress and threw it overboard. The man stopped, drew his bow and let an arrow fly. I ducked instinctively but it struck the mainmast behind me. The man did not resume paddling but sat and watched us motor away. His boat rocked slightly in the swell as he dwindled from sight. When he was almost gone I pulled the arrow from the mast. It had an ivory point and was fletched with white feathers. An abstract design was carved on the shaft.

A few kittiwakes followed the *Emilia Galotti* despite the rising wind. Li Po and I cleaned the deck while Davis took the wheel. Davis made frequent trips to the water barrel but he also took occasional pulls from one of his brown bottles. We were all locked in silence, islands of solitude. When we finished on deck Li Po went below but I stayed, watching the darkening sky. Li Po reappeared with a pail full of potatoes.

"Would you peel these for me, John Nelson?" he asked with his customary courtesy.

I sat by the foremast in the lee of the barrels and cut long, thick peels that I threw to the kittiwakes. One bird dove and missed a piece which then went bobbing away astern. The bird did not follow it but circled back and waited for the next peel, its stare as unfathomable as that of the Eskimo girl.

When I took the potatoes to Li Po he hesitated and then thanked me. "But I think you cut the peels too thick, John," he said in mild reproof.

He sliced the potatoes and put them in a kettle to boil along with onions and some meat that he said was caribou. When the water came to a boil the aroma began to fill the cabin. I sat at the table silently, trying to come to terms with a world in which you traded whiskey to savages, debauched one of their women, had a confrontation at gunpoint and then fretted about the thickness of potato peels.

By now the wind and sea had increased dramatically. I wedged myself in a corner of the settee, feeling just a little queasy. Davis called for Li Po to come up and lend a hand. As I waited alone I huddled down within myself and slipped into a semi-doze.

I awoke to find that the motion of the ship had eased though the wind had not. I climbed the ladder and poked my head abovedecks. The sky was dark and lowering although it could have been no later than early evening. We were coasting along in the lee of a large island, approaching the head of a wide bay. The schooner rounded into the wind and Li Po dropped the anchor.

Davis came below. "Wind's kicking up a bit. I think it's going to blow hard before morning. Best to anchor and wait till first light."

"Where are we?"

"Tucked in behind Nunivak Island."

Li Po came down the ladder. He lifted the lid of the pot and stirred the contents.

"Ah, stew," Davis said. Li Po served three large bowls and we all bent silently to our food. I noticed that Davis's hands shook slightly as he ate. I stared into the bottom of my bowl and tried to divine my future in the constellation of potatoes and grease flecks there.

"Those furs we took yesterday were pretty poor," Davis said suddenly. "I don't know if there's any future in trading in the delta. What do you reckon, Li Po?"

"I think we should head for Ugashik." Li Po got up from the table, took his pipe and went up on deck. I followed him to fetch some seawater for dishwashing. I dropped the bucket over the side and then hauled it up. In the wheelhouse I could see Li Po bent over his pipe.

Back in the cabin I put a basin of seawater on the stove to heat and began to clear the table.

"Li Po likes to have a few bowls at the end of the day," Davis said. "He claims it helps him maintain philosophical perspective." Davis rolled a cigarette quite neatly despite his trembling hands. "You're quiet today, John," he said as he struck a match. "I take it you don't approve of our trading methods."

"How can I approve of them? Selling the Natives whiskey, sleeping with their women."

"Whiskey's a normal trade item, John. It's one of the things we have that they want. We took some low-grade fur in return. Who's to say they weren't cheating us?"

"That's sophistry," I said stubbornly. "And what if we get arrested? What will my college say?"

"The *Bear* is miles away. Nobody else cares."

"Anyway Natives shouldn't be allowed to have whiskey."

"But that's patronizing. You're taking the missionaries' position, treating them like children who can't make proper decisions. That attitude will destroy their culture more surely than whiskey."

"Well, what about the girl?"

"And what about her? Sometimes an Eskimo will offer you his wife and be insulted if you refuse. Where is your morality then? Do you sleep with the girl or insult your host?"

"You're saying that's what happened?"

"Maybe not quite." He conceded the point as if sacrificing a pawn. "To me it's all just wrong."

"Let me show you something." Davis went up to the wheelhouse and returned carrying a walrus tusk about fourteen inches long. It was elaborately carved and had two series of parallel holes down one face.

"Those Eskimos have had precious little contact with white men. Just missionaries who've taught them they're damned, traders who've taken their furs for whiskey, prospectors who've given them gonorrhea. But they've also gotten this." He waved the walrus tusk at me. "Do you recognize this? It's a cribbage board. Made in imitation of some prospector's board, no doubt. But their shaman thinks it's a tool for divination. He thinks it will prophesy where the deer and seal will be and who will have success in the hunt. The Eskimo doctrine of the elect, I guess. He wanted me to explain how to use it, then was enraged when I said it was only a game. Finally he traded it for a rifle and a can of whiskey. With that madness afoot why care about some Eskimo tart?"

I sat stubbornly silent, unconvinced. Davis fished something from his pocket and tossed it to me.

"Here," he said, "what do you make of this?"

It was a small piece of ivory carved to represent a woman's face. The incised lines made an image that was elongated and very abstract.

"What is it?"

"An amulet of some sort. The girl traded it to me for a necklace. It's very old, generations old."

"It's beautiful." The carving may have been old but the style was strikingly modern. I was in awe of the hand and eye that made it.

Davis nodded. "This is what their culture produced when left alone. After meeting us they're carving cribbage boards. Keep the amulet, John. The God of the Bering Sea is somewhere in that image."

By now the water was hot and I washed the dishes silently, rinsed them in freshwater and then dried them. Davis sat smoking and drinking without saying anything. I decided I was going to kill the next person who told me I did not understand Alaska.

The hour was still early and I took the packet of flowers which I had not yet put in the press and began to examine them at the galley table by the light of a kerosene lamp. I had my notebook and my basic text, Asa Gray's two-volume *Synoptical Flora of North America*. I would have liked to carry John Macoun's *Catalogue of Canadian Plants* as well but that ran to eight volumes. The Gray was particularly useful because his herbarium at Harvard had plants that John Muir had collected around the Bering Sea rim. As I worked I tried to cross reference my findings with the list of the plants Steller had collected. Not an easy job; Steller had worked before the adoption of the Linnaean nomenclature and his identifications were basically descriptions. For instance, one of the orchids he found was listed as *Elichrysum montanum flore rotund ore. Tourn. I.R.H. In Insula d. 1 Sept.* Professor Arbuthnot thought this was probably *Epipactis hellborine*, a common stream orchid, but I had my doubts.

I picked up an arnica with bright yellow petals like a many-bladed propeller and studied it through my magnifying glass.

"What have you got there?" Davis asked.

"It's an arnica. *Arnica frigida*, I think, unless it's *Arnica lessingii*. It's hard to tell."

"Let me see." He took the flower and studied it. "Wrong all around, John Nelson. It's ragwort, *Senecio*. Sometimes it's called pseudoarnica so it's not surprising you were fooled. Where did you find it?"

"Right on the beach almost," I said, checking my notebook. "In sand above the drift pile."

"That's a clue right there. True arnica is a meadow flower. It'll like something wetter. And look at the stem on this. The flowers are similar but this thick white stem is a dead giveaway. In arnica the leaves are basal and the stem is long, almost spindly. Check your Gray if you don't believe me."

He sat back and drew on his cigarette. My jaw had literally dropped in surprise. I took the flower again and thumbed through the Gray.

"You could be right. In fact, I think you are right." I changed the notation in my journal. "But how did you know?"

"I haven't always been a Bering Sea trader, John. I took a degree in botany, seems like several lifetimes ago."

"What happened?"

"Circumstances. Twists and turns. Life is never a straight line."

I thought it was rather a long way from botany to bootlegging whiskey in the Arctic, no matter what the twists and turns. "I don't get it. Did you ever do any fieldwork? How did you end up out here with the *Emilia Galotti*?"

Davis inhaled deeply then considered the glowing end of the cigarette before answering. "I was going to be the greatest field naturalist ever. Better than Bartram, better than Douglas. Better even than Steller. It was my passion." He shook his head. "You're still young, John. You probably don't believe you'll ever turn your back on something you love. Most of us have to; it's the human predicament. But to answer your question, I did field work in China before the war, a plant survey like your own but without a happy ending."

"Something happened?"

"In Yunnan we were attacked by Buddhist monks. Maybe they were bandits posing as monks. Or monks posing as bandits, who knows? We had to flee for our lives. I didn't stop running till I crossed the Amur River into Siberia. I've been in the North ever since."

"Yunnan to Siberia is a long run."

"I was desperate."

Davis pulled the lucky rouble from his pocket and walked it across his knuckles. I tried to comprehend his story. I still believed that life was linear and its path depended upon successive goals set and decisions made, not random flight to unknown lands.

"My boss, Professor Arbuthnot, was in southern China before the war," I said. "You didn't know him by any chance?"

"In fact I did know Walter Arbuthnot. He wasn't a professor of anything then. He was mostly dedicated to furthering his own ambitions."

"Was his wife Audrey with him?" I asked, to steer away from his obvious dislike of the professor. "She's been pretty friendly to me."

"Friendly? Audrey? That's one word for it."

"So you did know her?"

"Know her? Not really." He clenched the rouble in his fist. "No, not at all, except in the biblical sense."

"Hey, wait a minute . . ." I said angrily and half started up from the table.

"She was my wife, Nelson." Davis rapped the rouble on the table, hard. "Still is, so far as I know. Trust Audrey to overlook that fact."

"But . . ." I sat back down, trying to take it all in. "But how . . ." I stopped, nonplussed. Somehow I believed him, implausible though it was.

"That damned box—the Wardian case." Davis spun the rouble. "And Arbuthnot's vasculum. Worse than seeing ghosts come aboard. But I shouldn't be surprised. Objects have lives as improbable as humans. Like seeing a yacht in a regatta in Boston then years later finding it rotting away on a mud flat on the lower Yukon. Things change. I sometimes wonder if objects are as surprised by our own random reappearances and our deterioration."

He had shied away from the personal talk. No wonder; it could hardly be a comfortable subject. I looked at him, trying to find some trace of Audrey. Knowing her must have shaped him, marked him in some way. Palmer had told me that bandits had killed Audrey's first husband but I could scarcely say, "Gee, I heard you were beheaded."

Davis stood up. "Enough of the confessional. Li Po must be asleep by now. I'm going to sit in the wheelhouse and watch to see we don't drag anchor. Poor holding ground here. And maybe everywhere."

CHAPTER 9

Rain beat on the furled sails, on the canvas tarps, on the wooden barrels. Rain pockmarked the surface of the sea. Li Po and I stood in the wheelhouse and watched the gray, humpbacked seas begin to lie down beneath the hammering rain.

"Journeying is hard. There are many turnings. Which am I to follow?" Li Po said. "From my namesake, the poet Li Po."

"Very appropriate." I held my coffee mug against my cheek to feel its warmth. A full day had passed since Nunivak Island. We had run the *Emilia* round the clock, with me sharing the daytime wheel watches. I was not sure at this point whether I was a client, a guest, or just another deckhand. What I did know for sure was that the *Emilia* was much slower than the *Victoria* and Alaska was much bigger and lonelier than I had imagined. Pilot Point was a little more than halfway to the Shumagins and the question of finding my next ride gnawed at my stomach.

A rain-shrouded point loomed in the distance. "Cape Newenham," Li Po said. "We'll change course there." With one finger he indicated on the chart our track across Bristol Bay to the Ugashik River.

"How long till Pilot Point?" I asked.

"Tomorrow, maybe by noon."

Rain flooded the scuppers. Our bow wave pushed a drift log out of the way. Three seagulls huddled on it. I thought they looked disconsolate. Nothing else in sight but the sea.

"Have you been on boats all your life, Li Po?" I asked.

"I wasn't born to it. When I was a little younger than you I went to sea for the first time, on a schooner hunting sea otter in the Kuril Islands."

"The Kuril Islands, where are they?"

"Between Japan and Kamchatka. Very lonely and rugged like the outer Aleutians. The captain, Harold Snow, was a gentleman but the crew was very rough. It was a dangerous business. Ships lost every year and the sea otter fewer and fewer. So I returned to China."

"Jason Davis said he met you in China."

"In Chungking, many years ago."

"Did . . . by any chance did you know Audrey Arbuthnot? Or Audrey Davis, I guess it was, then."

Li Po looked at the deck that was nearly awash. "Both Audrey and Walter Arbuthnot were on that expedition. But I was just a porter. They had little to say to me."

Which told me more than I had asked but less than I wanted to know. And in a way that precluded further questions. After a moment I asked, "You were from Chungking?"

"Shanghai."

"Is that where you learned such good English?" He did not answer at first and I stammered, "Sorry, I don't mean to be rude. It's just that everybody up here has such strange backgrounds. Like Jason Davis. It doesn't make sense. To me, I mean."

"There's no mystery in my life, John. My father had a smallholding outside Shanghai. There were too many children and I was placed in service in a house in the British compound when I was very young. I was a sideboy. I had to stand for many hours listening at dinner. The rhythms of speech came naturally and the butler was kind enough to teach me my letters."

"Did you stay there long?"

Li Po cleared his throat and wiped the mist off the wheelhouse window with his sleeve. "I was fascinated by the many books in the master's library. When I was sixteen they found some of the books in my room and I was let go. I worked for a time in a bawdy house on the Avenue Foch. That's where I met Captain Snow."

"And after that?" I knew I was still being overly inquisitive but there was so much I needed to know.

"I worked for a trader named Jacob Wolf in Chungking, which is how I met Davis. Finally I took my savings and began trading on my own. Mostly wandering north."

"Looking for anything in particular?"

"Just looking to make a living."

We stood silently for a time in the cold and the damp of the wheelhouse. "I can't imagine being completely on my own like that," I said.

"A thousand years ago, when he wandered the Yangtze Valley, Li Po would write poems on leaves of paper and launch them on the rivers like little boats. Not knowing where they would go or who would read them. If anyone. Our lives are like that, John Nelson. Even yours."

"But still . . . have you ever been back to Shanghai, Li Po? To see your family, I mean?"

"The city grew out around our old farm. My brothers and sisters are scattered, I don't know where. But Davis and I go to Shanghai for trade some winters."

"In the *Emilia*?" I was worried about crossing Bristol Bay in the old tub, let alone the North Pacific.

"Once. Two years ago. But mostly in Davis's old schooner, the *Asphodel*."

"The *Asphodel*?"

"She was beautiful. And sea-kindly, but she was caught in the ice near the Kolyma River and crushed. The *Emilia*, I love her, maybe more than Davis does, but she is not trustworthy. And no longer young."

"Davis said she's half yours."

"Now she is. On that trip to Shanghai we had four sea otter pelts. Davis offered me a half share in the *Emilia* for my pelts."

"Two pelts were worth half the boat?"

"Easily." Which might have meant that sea otter fur was worth a lot or the *Emilia* was worth very little.

"What did Davis do with the pelts?"

"I don't know. Probably spent it on women. But he always has some big, complicated scheme going. Simple trading is never enough for Davis."

The *Emilia's* long bowsprit split the rain, carving a rhythmic arc against the gray backdrop. I thought about the name *Asphodel*, about mad schemes and distance and time. "I just don't get it," I said, half to myself.

"'With all this danger upon danger / Why do people come here who live at a safe distance?' That is Li Po again."

"I still don't get it." I shivered and picked up my mug to take below.

Jason Davis was in the galley drinking coffee and smoking. I said good morning but he did not reply. I lay down on my bunk, taking with me the increasingly dog-eared copies of Steller's journal and his letters, one of my few links to New Haven and scholarship. Not that the letters were very scholarly. As Bering's voyage blundered toward its sad end Steller's bitterness and jealousy toward his wife had increased. I read again a letter that was like the dark heart of a flower whose petals had been stripped by the wind: "The endlessly moving sea is a gray mirror to my despair. If I could plumb its cold depths would I be able to fathom your nature? As I stare across the bleak desolation and listen to the cries of the gulls I picture you at a fancy-dress ball, your shoulders milk-white with powder in the light of a thousand candles. Whose arm takes you in to dinner? Who is now beguiled by the seductive trill of your laugh?"

I folded the letter and closed my eyes and felt the gentle motion of the ship—a slow falling, a hesitation, then the roll back. Would I ever understand anything?

Li Po made an evening meal of rice and dried vegetables. He and I ate together then he took the wheel while Jason Davis came below. Davis ate two spoonfuls of rice then pushed his bowl aside and poured a mug full of whiskey. He watched me change the blotting paper on the plants in the press.

"In China one of our coolies would do that," Davis said. "He would put small pieces of paper beneath each petal of a poppy so they would retain their shape and color. Incredible eye for detail, the Chinese."

"My fingers are too clumsy for that."

"Lots of tricks to the trade. For instance, if you want to keep the color bright put the flower in a closed box and smoke it with a sulfur candle."

"The Arbuthnots told me that one."

Davis drew deeply on his cigarette, coughed harshly, and said, "So how are my old friends the Arbuthnots these days?"

"Pretty well," I said cautiously. "The professor is busy with the Marsh Garden and his other duties."

"Is that why he chose not to come on this expedition?"

"Well, that, and of course he's crippled now. He wanted to come but he says his field days are over."

"Crippled? I hadn't heard."

"He uses crutches and sometimes a wheelchair. Something to do with his spine."

"Sounds like the later stages of syphilis."

"No," I said, angry at the slur. "He fell and injured his back. He was hunting orchids in Columbia."

"Trust Walter to still be chasing orchids," Davis said. "When I was in China I was fascinated by asphodel."

"Like the one Professor Arbuthnot named for Audrey?"

Davis reared back as though he had seen a snake. "Jesus Christ, don't tell me Arbuthnot stole that, too."

"I don't know, I guess so," I stammered. What exactly had Audrey said to me? All I remembered was the sweet tone of her voice and the soft touch of her arm.

"Asphodel," Davis said. "So dry and dusty and improbable, like man's own soul. But Arbuthnot would never understand that. Orchids are so obvious. Fleshy and overblown. Are you familiar with Paracelsus's doctrine of signatures?"

"Vaguely. You mean the belief that the shape of a plant tells of its medicinal properties? Like violets have three lobes like a liver and so they're used for liver ailments?"

"Exactly. And orchids have paired tubers that look like testicles. *Orchis* is the Greek word for testicle, but you probably know that." He drank and coughed long and raggedly. "Odd, though, the association of orchids and sexuality. The Greeks used them in Dionysian rites, the Hottentot, Chippewa, Chinese, Hindus . . . They all associate orchids and sex. I think it's the flower itself—the complex petals, that deep, curving labellum. They're sensuous in a way that a primrose or even an iris is not. No one can resist them. Do you know who Joshua Slocum was?"

"The sea captain? Of course."

"Born in Nova Scotia. Raised to a gospel as hard as glacier-scoured granite. But he was arrested for raping a young girl."

"I never heard of that," I said scornfully.

"It's true, John. In Baltimore, when he was an old man."

"But what's your point?"

"He was on his way back from the Amazon with a consignment of orchids in the hold of the *Spray*. Can you imagine sailing alone on the Gulf Stream in a wooden boat haunted by the breath of orchids? The rigging would have coiled like vines."

There was no reply I could make to this madness. Davis raised his whiskey cup with a shaky hand but then hurled it against the galley wall. "God damn all memories. More confusing than dreams."

I looked at the blotch of whiskey dripping down the wall and still said nothing.

"All right," Davis said. "We'll take you to the Shumagins. If I have a role in this I'll stay till the last act, no matter who the players are."

"I can't pay much," I said uneasily. I was desperate for a ride but his offer had a price tag beyond money.

"Pay what you see fit. I don't know what I'm chasing so how can I judge its value?"

He stood abruptly and climbed the ladder to the deck. I could hear his footsteps going forward. The last drop of whiskey slid to the cabin floor. As the boat rolled his cup moved like a bird with a broken wing.

Alyson

"This is getting awfully hard to follow." Alyson frowned.

Talking and smoking pot had given me a dry throat. I drank a little water, then got a bottle of Laphroaig and poured a couple fingers into two tumblers.

"Leapfrog," Alyson said appreciatively, eyeing the bottle. We touched glasses and she knocked hers back in one jolt. My kind of girl.

Alyson poured herself another. "China, the Bering Sea, New Haven? That's quite a triangle. How could they be linked? Thousands of miles and years apart and you just happen to hitch a ride with Audrey's ex? That's a pretty big coincidence if you ask me."

"Plant hunters are a small community. Plus, they go to lonely places, and somehow that makes chance encounters more likely. If you ever need to hide go to New York City, not Alaska. People stand out in an empty landscape."

"Even so, how come . . . ."

"You're getting ahead of the story."

PART III

Ugashik

When I was a boy
        I kept a book
                to which, from time
to time,
        I added pressed flowers
                until, after a time,
I had a good collection.
        The asphodel,
                forebodingly,
among them.

—William Carlos Williams

CHAPTER 10

The tide was ebbing hard as we approached the mouth of the Ugashik River. Sandy shoals were visible in the center of the bay. A
three-masted bark lay at anchor on the deep side of the river bar,
waiting to load the tall cans of salmon. I could see she was the *Star
of Iceland*, one of the square-riggers belonging to the Alaska Packers'
Association.

Ahead of us the sun glinted off the roofs of the Pilot Point cannery. As we entered the river an outbound tender passed, towing a
long string of the small double-ended sailboats that did the actual
fishing. Each of these carried two men wearing oilskins and wool
caps. We tied the *Emilia* to creosoted pilings just behind a tender that
was unloading fish. I followed Davis and Li Po up an iron ladder to a
dock that was a hive of activity. Brailers full of red salmon swayed up
out of the tender's hold and dropped into totes that were taken to the
slime line where Chinese workers gutted and headed the fish.

Davis headed for the office. He claimed the cannery still owed
him money from last year and he was going to leverage credit for fuel.
Li Po stopped and spoke briefly to one of the Chinese then walked
toward the workers' barracks.

I stood alone and looked around. In my childhood the word
"Ugashik" had evoked magic and mystery. My grandfather's northern
realm. The APA logo was now painted on the buildings but some of
the equipment still bore our family's name. I walked over to a wooden
hand truck and ran my hand slowly over the Nelson Packing insig-
nia branded deep in the wood. I could easily picture my grandfather

walking these docks, but my father as a young man? That image was beyond my reach. I had a sudden, vivid memory of my last talk with him:

"I'm inclined to let you go." My father leaned back in his chair and placed his feet on his desk. We were in his office three days after my arrival in Seattle. At first he had been adamantly opposed to my summer plans but I had stuck to my guns and now he almost believed it had been his idea in the first place. His secretary came in and placed some papers on his desk. He did not look at the papers but his eyes followed her backside as she left the room.

"The three summers I spent in Ugashik were the best of my life," he said. "I wanted to stay on but your grandpa Lars insisted I finish college. Then he was disappointed when I chose law school over running the business. Lars never could see that the law was a quicker route to money than canning fish."

"I'm not sure Grandpa would have cared all that much."

"Grandpa Lars' day is past. Try running a business his way and you'd go bust within a year. All those broke-down old Norwegians drawing a paycheck and not doing jack shit."

I remembered those old fishermen as my teachers and friends but I said nothing.

"If things work out like I plan, I made the family more money just by lobbying the White Act last winter. It started out as a tomfool attempt to regulate the canneries, outlaw the fish traps. Might as well give the whole territory back to the goddamn Indians. But I got that turned around to where it favored our side and now the cannery owners are in my back pocket. What would you say if your father was appointed next governor of Alaska?"

"Mother would like it."

"A summer up there will do you good. Toughen you up. You'll need some spine when you start law school. It's not like biology."

My father had been furious when I chose to major in art as a freshman. The switch to biology had only slightly mollified him and he was still determined to have me join his law firm. When I was younger my father had been my hero. I tagged along behind him hunting ducks on Puget Sound and mule deer in the Cascades. But as the rift between him and my mother widened he spent less time at home and more at his club. Or elsewhere. Our conversations shrunk till they were no more than arguments about my future.

"I'm not sure the law is for me," I said now for the umpteenth time. "My mind just doesn't work that way."

"Doesn't matter." Father selected a fresh cigar from the humidor on his desk and with golden scissors cut off the end. "When you sit in this chair the money will come to you."

A deserted storage building the size of a barn sat apart from the other Pilot Point buildings. I went inside and stopped to inhale the musty air. This is what I had liked about our home cannery—not the blood-spattered bustle of the canning lines but the cool quiet of the gear sheds. On the ground floor of this one I found several of the graceful double-ended fishing boats, along with vats for dyeing the linen nets, and pallets carrying nets with wooden buoys that had been soaked in paraffin. Massive fir timbers brought from the Olympic Peninsula formed the frame of this building. In the dim light it felt like a cathedral slumbering between services.

I climbed the stairs to the net loft that I knew would occupy the second story. No one was there. I remembered a winter afternoon I had spent in our Puget Sound cannery, reading a dime novel while cushioned on an old net that smelled of salt and must. Thinking of it now made me feel alone and blue and totally out of place.

My grandfather always wore a three-piece suit with a watch chain across the vest. He kept a bottle of whiskey in his desk drawer and chewed peppermint candies to conceal the whiskey scent when he made his rounds in the cannery. Whenever I saw him I would run and grab him and he would fish a few of the pinwheel-striped candies from the watch pocket of his waistcoat. Maybe the only person who ever loved me.

At one end of the loft a sliding door stood partly open. I looked out over the river at another tender coming upstream towing a few empty double-enders. I could just read the name *Togiak Belle* on her bow. She was making slow progress against the current.

I descended the stairs from the loft. Through different windows I could see successive aspects of the *Belle*. A triptych for the cathedral walls.

Past the cannery offices and the mess hall I came to an open area where a gillnet was stretched over a pair of waist-high rails made of peeled and smoothed logs. Two men were mending the net. Netting needles flashed in the sun as they talked in Italian. An old man came along pushing a handcart laden with boxes. He stopped by me and mopped his brow.

"I seen you come off that schooner the *Emilia* something, didn't I?"

"Yeah, I came in on her."

"Them two, the tall one and the chink, they was in here a year ago, peddlin' a load of salt cod. What in hell're they up to this time?"

"Nothing much. We won't be here long."

"We ain't got the room. We got tenders comin' in reg'ler. I been here since they built this cannery and ya gotta check with me afore ya ties up."

Every cannery or factory in the world must have an old man like this, inhabiting the workplace like a druid. "If you've been here that long you must have known my grandfather Lars Nelson," I said, trying to pull rank. "He's the one who built this place."

The old man narrowed his eyes. "Huh. If'n I was related to that old skinflint I wouldn't be so all-fired eager to admit it. Most miserable tightfisted sonofabitch God ever spawned. Mind, he could teach these idiots something about running a cannery."

He pulled at a tuft of hair that stuck out of one of his ears. "Say, that wouldn't make you Axel's kid, would it?"

"He's my father, yeah. He worked up here a couple summers."

"Work? Axel? Hell, he done everything but work. We had a hell of a time keeping him away from them Indian gals and them Chinese. You probably got a few half-brothers or sisters workin' here now."

I was trying to think of a reply when the *Togiak Belle* nosed into the dock not far from us. The old man pushed his cart that way and began to harangue the skipper but what caught my eye was the figure holding the bow-mooring line, a young girl dressed in gray.

"Natasha!" I shouted and waved. She looked up in surprise and gave me a half-wave. When the *Belle* was secure she put her flowered carpetbag on the dock then climbed the ladder. I took her arm and helped her up the last steps. She smiled a little tentatively and brushed off her dress, which was beginning to look a little the worse for wear. I was surprised how glad I was to see her.

"Where did you come from? And what are you doing here?" I asked.

"From Togiak last night. It's a long story. But what about yourself?"

"Also a long story." I laughed. "Can I carry your bag?" I was already holding it.

"I guess so," she said a little distractedly and then excused herself and went to talk briefly with the captain of the *Belle*. He gave her a friendly pat on the shoulder and then a farewell wave. She rejoined me and said, "I'm not sure just where I'm going next."

In the end we left her carpetbag in a safe corner and walked up the low hill behind the cannery while she told me her story.

"When I got to Nome I went straight to the school district office but the superintendent was gone and this snooty old hen was in charge."

"Miss Hutchinson," I said. "I went looking for you there."

"Well she told me that the position had changed and they now required a four-year degree."

"They can't do that. They can't just change in midstream."

"Miss Hutchinson seemed to think she could. But that wasn't the real reason. She just didn't want to give me the job because I was Aleut."

"But the school's for Eskimos, isn't it? Or Indians. And didn't you say you were Aleut on the application?"

"Not exactly. Well . . . I sort of said I was from Lincoln, Nebraska."

"But . . ."

"Look, John Lars, I was tired of always being 'that Eskimo girl.' I wanted to be just plain Natasha Christiansen. I thought being Aleut would give me an unfair advantage and I wanted to be hired because I could do the job. And then that old biddy looked at me like I was a liar."

She turned and hit me on the shoulder with a closed fist, hard. "And here I finished in the top five of my training class," she said angrily.

"How many were in the class?" I asked, impressed.

"Six." She laughed and picked a blade of grass to chew. I had a hunch that she was not telling me the complete story about her interview. Or about her background. And I was sure that it was her youth and beauty, not her race, that had made the dragon-like Miss Hutchinson breathe fire.

We had reached a small cemetery at the summit of the hill overlooking the cannery. We could hear the steam whistle and see billows of smoke from the chimneys but within the cemetery nothing moved. The graves were marked with white wooden crosses that bore a strange assortment of names. We sat down on a little knoll next to a Slavic cross marked "Veniaminof." At its base was a mason jar holding a decorated Easter egg.

"Actually, I didn't quite finish my degree," Natasha said. "I still owe them a paper for my Bible class. On any book in the Old Testament. What do you know about Lamentations?"

"I'm starting to learn." I looked around the graveyard. More than one cross had a jar and egg. "What's the idea of these Easter eggs?"

"The resurrection of the body. They're Orthodox."

"So what did you do next? In Nome, I mean."

"I was staying with Mrs. Kelly. Her husband has a job on one of the gold dredges. But that didn't work too well. Mr. Kelly was a bit too friendly. I was so depressed all I could think of was going home to Unga."

"But how did you get here?"

"I met this Russian woman, Lena. She liked me because of my Russian blood or something. So I hitched a ride with her on the *Seal*."

"The *Seal*? Max Gottschalk's boat? I thought he was kind of an outlaw."

"Max isn't that bad. Kind of roughhewn but Lena keeps him on a pretty short leash. It's your friend Fitzgerald that gives me the creeps. He was along for the ride and I'd catch him leering at me. Made me want to take a bath to wash off the slime. Ugh." She shuddered. "So anyway I got off in Togiak and caught a ride on the *Belle*."

"What were they going to do in Togiak?"

"Poach walrus, I think. But Fitzgerald had some big moneymaking scheme he was trying to sell. Whenever he talked to Max he'd kind of curve his back like a cur."

"I think he's harmless, just a blowhard."

"Maybe. But anyway, now I'm here. I might have to work at the cannery till I can catch a ride to Port Moller. There's a portage route from there to Stepovak Bay. I can walk it if I have to, and then I'd be almost home."

"You could come with us. We're headed for the Shumagins so we'll be stopping at Unga. It's the only town there, right?"

"Just about." Natasha unpinned her hair and combed it with her fingers. It was thick and dark and fell below her waist and made me want to take her wherever she wanted to go.

"Max knew you were on the *Emilia*," she said. "He doesn't like Jason Davis overmuch."

"Yeah, something about a trading deal that went bad."

"Lena asked me why you were traveling with them. I said I scarcely knew you. She kind of asked me on the sly. I gathered she and Jason Davis were friends a long time ago. In Siberia."

"I can't figure Davis out. He's educated but just a bum, really. A small-time crook. But Li Po's very nice, you'd like him."

Natasha hugged her knees and laid her head on her arms, looking at me. "And you think you can arrange to take me along?"

"Yeah . . . well, maybe. I'm sort of chartering the *Emilia* but it's all pretty vague. But maybe you can help me once we get to the Shumagins. Have you ever been to Nagai?"

"Only once. We were egg collecting on the outer islands and stopped on the way back. It's close—you can see it from Unga—but hardly anybody goes there. It's got a dark feel, like it's haunted or something."

"Shumagin's ghost, maybe."

Late afternoon now, a cool wind in the graveyard. A long blast from the cannery whistle. Shift change?

We found the *Emilia* tied in a shadowed corner of the wharf. When we climbed down the companionway to the lighted galley we found another Chinese man seated at the table with Davis and Li Po. He leaped up angrily when we appeared and began shouting in Chinese. He was short and heavyset and carried his belly like it was a badge of office.

On the table was a box with Chinese lettering. It had many small compartments containing small packets wrapped with leaves. The stranger tried to block our view of the box. With an amused expression Jason Davis chivvied Natasha and me back up the ladder into the cold night air.

"This is Natasha Christiansen," I said. "She's from Unga and I told her we could take her there, if it's all right with you."

Davis gave her an appraising look. "I don't see why not . . ." He stopped abruptly and coughed harshly and repeatedly. Natasha watched him with concern.

"Sorry," he said and thumped his chest. "Yes, yes, of course. Lots of room for a short trip. But listen, the mess hall will still be open. Why don't you get some coffee and something to eat while I tidy the cabin." He watched us climb to the dock and with a wave disappeared below.

"What do you think that was all about?" I said. "They were sure eager to get rid of us."

Natasha laughed. "You've never seen opium before? All the Chinese out here use it."

"Opium? Jesus Christ." Bootleg whiskey and now opium. Further and further into the quagmire. What was next, white slavery?

"Cheer up," Natasha said and took my arm. "Nobody'll care but you and the revenue agents. Out here the Chinese count about as much as us Natives."

The dining hall was brightly lit but nearly empty. There were long ranks of tables covered with red and white checked oilcloth. In one corner three men sat drinking coffee and smoking. I looked around as we helped ourselves to coffee and pie but no one questioned our presence. A Native woman pushed a mop in desultory fashion. She looked to be partly white and I wondered morosely if she were my half-sister. I didn't know how much of the old man's story about my father to believe. My father had little enough respect for the Chinese; for the Indians he showed nothing but contempt. And anyone who looked to have mixed blood he treated like a stray mongrel.

"What do you think you'll do this winter?" I asked Natasha.

"I don't know. I'd like to go back to school and get a proper four-year degree only I need money first. But right now all I'm thinking is to see my father's grave."

"When did he die?"

"Last February. But I hadn't seen him in two years."

"It must be awful, not being able to say goodbye."

"I watched my mother die. One was enough. After Pa lost his job in Unga we bought a fox farm out on Hardscratch Point but he drank more and more and finally I just left. Last February they found him on the kitchen floor. He'd been dead a week or more." Natasha looked down into her coffee cup and then up at me. Her eyes were strikingly gray-blue, evidence of the Russian in her mother's background.

"But I've been lucky," she said. "You should meet Lena, the woman on the *Seal*. She was so beautiful, with these long, expressive hands and huge, somber eyes. But she never smiled, at least not really. She told me her family had an estate near St. Petersburg but they had to flee the Red Army. She got separated from the rest and crossed Siberia by herself, selling her jewelry a piece at a time till there was nothing left. She ended up in Petropavlovsk, singing in a cabaret for tips from drunken sailors."

I shook my head. In my world singing in a nightclub was considered on par with prostitution.

"She met Max Gottschalk there. He'd been sentenced to the mines but somehow escaped. He stole a boat and they ran off together. She's been with him ever since, roaming around the Bering Sea, no idea if her family is alive or dead. At least I've got a grave I can weep over."

CHAPTER 11

"Swan feathers. The shaft is spruce and the head is ivory. Maybe walrus." Natasha ran her hand lightly along the arrow that I had pulled
from the mast back by Hooper Bay. A few splinters of wood were still
caught on the serrated point.

"Why did he use a bow?" I asked. "I know they had guns."

"Arrows are just handier sometimes."

Natasha and I were seated at the galley table, two days south of
Pilot Point. I had been telling Natasha about our trading misadven-
ture. I blamed alcohol for the confrontation, not wanting to mention
Davis and the Eskimo girl.

I had worried about bringing Natasha onto the crowded *Emilia*
alongside Davis and Li Po but she had quickly formed an easy friend-
ship with those two old pirates. They had the land and sea in common and laughed together when they shared stories. Once again I felt
resentful about being the outsider.

The engine slowed to an idle and the boat turned sideways and
wallowed in the trough. Natasha cocked an eyebrow at me and we
went up on deck to see what was happening. The *Emilia* was close to
shore, seeking protection from a fierce southerly that howled down
from the peninsula's mountainous spine. Not far away a small red
buoy tilted in the grip of the current. Beyond it we could see a line of
breakers.

"Cape Krenitzin," Davis said when we crowded into the wheelhouse. "The entrance to False Pass. But there's no hope of getting
past the shoals till the weather lies down a bit."

"How about when the tide changes?" Natasha asked.

Davis shook his head. "Seas will be worse on the ebb. Better to anchor and wait."

The *Emilia* canted slightly to starboard in the grip of the wind. Davis took her to within a stone's throw of the beach. Li Po went forward and when Davis signaled he dropped the anchor and let out about five fathoms of chain. When Li Po dogged off the winch Davis put the engine in neutral. Water sliced around the anchor chain as though we were in a river and the *Emilia* moved backward in a series of jolts.

"No good," Davis said. "Too much current." He put the engine in forward and Li Po pulled in the chain a link at a time against the current. We fell back away from the mouth of the pass and tried again but with the same result. Davis turned the boat till we were running at half throttle back the way we had come, the current giving us a boost now.

"Here, you take the wheel," he said to Natasha then stretched a chart on the bunk. I was annoyed that he had trusted Natasha with the wheel rather than me but I bent over the chart alongside him. With a pair of compass dividers Davis measured the distance back north to a large bay protected by a string of islets called the Kudiakof Islands. "Izembek Lagoon," he said. "Might be the closest safe anchorage, especially if the wind shifts. We can anchor inside and hope it blows itself out in the night."

Li Po took the wheel. Back in the galley I took from my press a plant that had puzzled me and tried to key it out using my Asa Gray. Jason Davis came down the stairs and warmed his hands at the stove.

"False asphodel," he said, looking at the plant. "It's not uncommon out here."

"I was getting there. I figured it was Liliaceae." I looked at the small greenish flower. If asphodel was the plant of forgetting, what was false asphodel? Forgetting what you had only imagined?

Natasha picked up the arrow that still lay on the table and tested the ivory point with her finger. Davis poured himself a cup of coffee.

"I'm curious, John Nelson," he said. "Why are you studying taxonomy? I thought all you young hotshots were doing genetics. Or biochemistry."

"Well, what about you? You did taxonomy. What was in it for you?" Davis's questions always stung like nettles.

Davis studied me for a moment. "The possibilities of form," he said. The boat rolled and sunlight from the companionway glanced off the curving hull. Natasha turned the arrow in her hand. In the reflected light the carved pattern on the arrow shaft moved like running wolves.

A tide-scoured channel pierced a low sand spit. Davis brought the schooner in slowly while Li Po stood in the bow throwing the lead. The surface of the lagoon was a froth of brown wavelets. The *Emilia* threaded her way amongst visible shoals and anchored close to shore. Southeast of us was a mountain the chart called Frosty Peak but it provided little protection from the wind that pummeled the dunes.

Li Po came aft, reddened by the wind and blowing on his hands. "Fine weather," he said. "Midsummer in the Bering Sea." He looked back toward the entrance. "I saw a sea otter."

"Where?" Jason Davis asked.

Li Po pointed. "Only one but there may be more."

"I guess it's the only game in town." Davis took a canvas gun case from a small locker. He pulled out a rifle and worked the lever several times, then picked up a box of cartridges. "Your honors," he said and handed the gun to Li Po.

They unlashed the dinghy and put it over the side, then climbed in and shoved off. The wind took them quickly toward the entrance with Davis rowing and Li Po sitting in the stern with the rifle across his knees.

"It's illegal, isn't it, hunting sea otter?" I asked Natasha.

"Ever since I was a little girl. I've only seen a few of them, in the outer Shumagins. They're virtually gone."

She linked her arm with mine and leaned against me. The low, scudding clouds made it more like night than anything I'd seen since Seattle. The lagoon was a mirror that combined light and dark. Not far away, on the other side of these mountains, Steller had watched an animal he likened to Gesner's sea ape. He shot at it but missed. In the Yale library there was a copy of Gesner's sixteenth-century *Icones animalium*. The woodcut of the ape was completely fantastical, showing a beast with a misshapen head, a long, flowing tail, and elaborate fins rather than arms or legs. If such an animal existed this would be the place it called home, but no biologist since Steller had seen a sea ape. Did this story make the existence of Steller's orchid more likely or less?

I heard the distant crack of a rifle. Two quick shots, a pause, one more shot, then silence.

"They got it," Natasha said.

"How can you tell?"

"Shot spacing." She shivered and tightened her grip on my arm. "Let's go below. I need to warm up."

In the galley I lit a lamp to dispel the afternoon gloom. Natasha stood by the stove, still shivering. The ship was very quiet but the wind sounded both fierce and mournful as if it were bewailing the death of something near and dear.

"Do you think I should talk with them about breaking the law?" I asked Natasha. "I mean, I am leasing the vessel, sort of, and it wouldn't look good for the college if we got caught."

"They're just trying to make a living, John Lars. Nobody follows the rules too close out here. They're not bad men, not really."

Despite what she said I could tell she was upset about the sea otter. We felt the dinghy bump against the hull and went back on deck. Jason Davis climbed over the rail and Li Po handed him the rifle and then the bedraggled corpse of a sea otter. There was a round, red hole in the sea otter's head and a shallow wound across one shoulder. Its fur was long and thick but looked unkempt and ragged in death. Its teeth were worn and one canine was broken.

With his sheath knife Li Po made an incision at the base of each paw. He slit the skin up each leg to join a cut he made from the tip of the tail to the jaw. With brisk little whisking motions he carefully worked the hide free of the carcass, then put a line through the eyeholes and rinsed the hide in the sea. Davis tacked the hide to a board with small copper boat nails while Li Po cut the head and flipper-like feet off the body and threw them overboard. Lastly he washed the carcass in a bucket of seawater.

"Fresh meat for supper," he said.

The sun was barely visible through the clouds. A streak of blood marked the deck. When we were all back in the galley Natasha sat beside me and took hold of my hand beneath the table. Her fingers were icy.

Li Po took a cleaver and cut the meat into thin slices that he put in a skillet along with some onions. "Young sea otter tastes like lamb," he said, "but this one was old. I've never seen one so thin."

The odor of frying onions and meat filled the cabin. Jason Davis sat on the steps with a tin cup of whiskey in his hand. He offered some to Natasha and me, "to cut the chill." Natasha declined but I took half a cup.

"Li Po took only three shots," Davis said.

"I was very lucky," Li Po said. "Sometimes it takes hours and hundreds of rounds. Sometimes the gun barrel gets so hot it won't shoot straight." He turned away from the skillet and gestured with a long fork. "In the Kurils we'd hunt with three skiffs. One hunter and two or three pullers in each skiff. When we saw an otter we'd form a triangle and shoot whenever it surfaced, until it tired out."

He served us plates of otter and rice. The meat was better than I had expected, though stringy. The four of us sat crowded at the table. The mast vibrated faintly where it touched the table, as though it were the wind's tuning fork.

"How could you make money hunting otter if it took hundreds of bullets and nine or ten men to catch just one?" I asked.

"The pelts were more valuable than gold, even back when otter were plentiful," Davis said. "The cornerstone of the China trade, the only thing we had that they wanted."

"Li Po?" I asked a little hesitantly. "When you were hunting sea otter did you ever see anything that looked like a sea ape?"

"A what?"

"My God." Davis laughed. "You're not chasing that will-o'-the-wisp, are you? Steller's seafaring baboon? I thought you had more sense than that."

"The naturalist Georg Wilhelm Steller," I said to Li Po, ignoring Davis, "saw something on Bering's voyage he called a sea ape and he was a great naturalist, one of the best ever."

"No," said Li Po. "There are monkeys on Hokkaido but not farther north. Many strange things I saw in the Kurils but never an ape."

"Steller's pipe dream, more like," said Davis.

"Hey, you're the one always telling me there's things out here I never dreamed of."

"And so there are. But not saltwater monkeys. Doesn't make sense."

"But he watched it for hours."

"Even the best make mistakes. Had to be a sea otter. Or a young fur seal."

"Well, what about flowers? At least there'll be new flowers, maybe even spectacular ones." I felt Davis was belittling me and the whiskey made me reckless.

"New, certainly. Spectacular? Not in the usual sense of the word. This is the tundra, not the jungle."

"Steller found an orchid in the Shumagins. He called it spectacular." I played my trump card. I should have kept it hidden.

Davis slowly stroked his whiskers. "I read Steller's work when I was in Siberia. There was no mention of an orchid."

"It's not in his published stuff. Professor Arbuthnot discovered some love letters to his wife."

"Brigitta Helena? That slut?"

"Slut? How can you say that? Nobody knows anything about her."

"Except that she abandoned him." Davis tipped his cup back and drained it.

"I don't follow," Natasha said. "Just when did Steller write these letters?"

"On board the *St. Peter*. And from Bering Island. We don't know when he mailed them."

"And your professor found them?"

"He bought them from a Russian émigré in Shanghai."

"Shanghai." Davis laughed bitterly. "Everything's for sale in Shanghai. Give me two days and I'll get you a parka made from the fur of sea apes. With unicorn buttons. Arbuthnot's an old China hand; he should know that."

Davis poured himself more whiskey then topped off my cup. The cabin felt stiflingly hot and the kerosene lamp appeared to wear a nimbus of fuzzy light. I thought of the sea otter whose dark blood stained the deck above us. Davis took his lucky rouble from his pocket and spun it on the table.

"How large was this orchid supposed to be?" Natasha asked me.

"About an inch and a half across the labellum. Maybe three inches overall. And bright crimson."

"I've never seen anything like that and I've walked the fields everywhere."

"Well, plant populations can be very small and localized."

"Amen to that," Davis said, coming to my support for a change. "Any plant hunter will vouch for the invisibility of flowers. Particularly the one you're looking for."

He spun the rouble again. It wobbled, slowed, came to rest. The reverse of the coin showed—the two-headed eagle of Imperial Russia. Davis looked at the eagle and frowned, as if questioning the biological possibility. "Never trust orchids, they're too sensuous to be real. In the Middle Ages philosophers believed orchids came from semen spilled on the ground when animals couple. The flowers are supposed to look like miniatures of whatever animal it was."

"But that's just superstition," I said.

"Is it really? Today we know, or think we know, that orchids attract bees by imitating the scent and shape of a sexually receptive female. Is that so very different?"

"Sure it is. It comes from field work, not mumbo jumbo."

"But the point is there's a sense of the sexual nature of the flower. Like I was telling you, all cultures associate orchids with sexuality. Why, in your own neck of the woods young Haida girls eat the corms of orchids thinking it will enhance their bust lines."

Davis took another swig of whisky but his gaze strayed to Natasha's breasts and he spilled a little. He wiped the back of his hand across his mouth. "Tell me, Natasha, in your fine mission education did they ever preach to you about Rachel asking Leah for mandrakes? Thirtieth chapter of Genesis, I believe. Read it for me, I know you have a Bible somewhere."

Natasha regarded him silently and then arose and walked to where her bag was stowed. She returned carrying a small, leather-bound book. The print was very small and as she bent over the book her dark hair shone in the lamplight.

"This must be what you mean," she said and began to read in a soft, clear voice. "'And Reuben went in the days of wheat harvest, and found mandrakes in the field, and brought them unto his mother Leah. Then Rachel said to Leah, Give me, I pray thee, of thy son's mandrakes . . . .'"

"Yes," Davis interrupted, "and what was the trade?"

Natasha kept her head bent and said, "Rachel allowed Leah to lie that night with Jacob."

"And what happened to Rachel afterward?"

Natasha looked up from her Bible and said quietly, "Rachel had been barren but the Lord opened her womb and she conceived and bore Joseph."

"Wait a minute," I said. "Mandrakes aren't orchids."

"It's a mistranslation. The Hebrew word is *dudaim* which is probably salep, an aphrodisiac made from orchids." Davis nodded emphatically and sat back.

"How could you possibly know that?" I asked, mystified.

Davis laughed. "A grand old man named Jacob Wolf told me. A trader in Chungking, but also a Hebrew scholar and an orchid fancier. He was always spouting arcane orchid lore. He was quite smitten with Audrey."

"I thought she only liked younger men." I tossed back the remnants of my whiskey. Davis looked at me, eyes narrowed, and reached out to refill my cup. I tried to move it away but he caught my wrist in an iron grip and filled the cup to the brim.

"Jacob Wolf," he repeated slowly. "He gave Audrey a silk dress. A cheongsam, split high. Made her look like a high-dollar hooker."

"Just how many boyfriends did she have in China?" My turn to feel the cold prick of jealousy. And the spike of lust.

"As many as she wanted. Even one was too goddamn much." Davis relaxed his grip and gestured for me to drink up. "Plant hunters are obsessive by nature. Have to be, to risk everything in pursuit of some rumored flower. Easy prey for someone like Audrey."

"How old was she?" More and more I realized how little I knew about Audrey.

"She was nineteen when we married, three years younger than me. China was our honeymoon, if you can call it that. She'd be forty-five now."

I was startled and shaken. Forty-five? I had thought Audrey ten years younger. And Davis ten years older.

Davis emptied his cup. "The memory of desire," he said. To me or to himself?

Natasha watched with steadfast eyes as though trying to read the undercurrents. "When you find this orchid you'll press it and take it home?" she asked.

"I'm hoping to take a live plant. I brought a Wardian case. Here, I'll show you." I went to fetch the box and the whiskey in me made the floor wobble as though the boat was a dying top.

"Oh, I remember how these work," Natasha said. "We had one in the schoolroom in Unga. But this one is beautiful." She traced a finger carefully along its polished side. In the amber light the wood glowed and the intricate joinery had a shadowed elegance.

"The wood is *ch'un-tuen-shu*," said Li Po, breaking his silence. "I have seen the tree eighty feet tall in Szechuan."

"Rather elaborate coffin for an orchid, I should think," Jason Davis said. "If the flowers spring from putrefied sperm you'd think a coarser wood would be more appropriate."

I looked at Natasha to see if the vulgarity bothered her but she simply stroked the box and said, "It must be very old and valuable."

"Not so old," Davis said. "Twenty-five years. I gave it to Audrey on our first anniversary. If she kept it this long she valued it more than the marriage."

The boat shuddered in a gust of wind. I could hear the rigging tapping against the mast.

CHAPTER 12

Gulls blanketed the beach like an early snowfall. The anchor chain dipped and rose as gusts buffeted the schooner. I drew a bucket of seawater and washed my hands and face, hoping the shock of icy water would cure my hangover. Through the wheelhouse window I could see Davis bent over a chart. He walked the compass dividers over land, like a heron stalking a frog. When he noticed me watching he rolled up the chart and went below.

Natasha stood in the bow with her back to the wind, staring out to sea. From the companionway I could hear Davis and Li Po arguing in Chinese. Natasha turned and walked past me without a word, headed for the galley. The sound of arguing ended.

When I descended the ladder Davis stood close to Natasha with his hand on her elbow. He moved away quickly, almost guiltily, and said, "Li Po has fixed some porridge."

"Thanks," I said though my head was pounding and my tongue felt like a road-killed salamander. Food was the last thing I wanted. Li Po stood at the stove looking as close to anger as I had ever seen him. He handed me a cup of coffee.

"The pass won't be any better today," Davis said. "Maybe the wind will let up by evening but I think we'll do a little engine room work."

"Can I help?" I hoped the answer was no.

"No, no, there really isn't even room for two. If you want you can go ashore while we work. You could botanize in the dunes, then we wouldn't be in each other's way."

Cold though it was, walking the beach was preferable to being cooped up on board. I took my sketch pad and collecting paraphernalia and put them in my rucksack. I also stuffed my copies of Steller's journal and letters into the pack rather than leave them for prying eyes. Last night's conversation had already revealed more than I intended. I tried to find the vasculum in the jumbled fo'c'sle but Davis called and I had to hurry on deck without it.

Li Po held the dinghy's painter while Davis sat at the oars. Natasha stood next to Li Po, a heavy black shawl wrapped around her shoulders. "You could stay aboard if you'd rather," Davis said to her but she shook her head without saying anything, climbed over the rail and took the dinghy's bow seat.

The water in the lagoon was brown with suspended sand. Davis rowed hard but the wind pushed us sideways and we fetched up on a small point some distance from the *Emilia Galotti*. Davis beached the skiff and Natasha jumped nimbly over the bow. Davis took a covert look at her stockings but little was visible beneath her long, gray dress.

"We'll keep an eye out," Davis said. "Just come down to the beach and wave when you want to get picked up." He turned and began the long pull back, the oars dark against the sky. Traveling sideways to buck the wind, the dinghy moved like an ill-designed crab.

Natasha and I crossed the beach through a grounded cloud of Bonaparte's and herring gulls, kittiwakes and terns. There were also geese and brant and some distance away several swans stood on a sandbar. Only those birds directly in our path bothered to fly. The wind drove sand across the beach with a hissing sound and flattened the mass of beach peas at the foot of the dunes. The pale undersides of their leaves flashed as the wind combed the hillside.

A small stream broke through the dunes. Its gully was deep enough to provide a little protection and we began to follow its course. I stopped to pick one of the beach peas and place its reddish-purple flower in a folder but the dunes provided better bird watching than flower gathering. There were a few primula with their petals blown and the first flowering monkshood I had seen. Sparse clumps of grass dotted the sides of the gully.

The stream widened into a small patch of marshland speckled with shooting stars. I found an orchid called a bog candle and showed it to Natasha.

"Most northern orchids look kind of like this. *Cypripedium*—the lady's slipper—is the only one that's flashy. The others mostly have a spike of flowerets on a thick stem with long leaves."

Natasha turned it over in her hands, studying the tiny flowerets intently though she must have seen the plant countless times.

"All these bog orchids are genus *Platanthera*." I fished my magnifying glass out of the rucksack. "If you look close each floweret has three petals and one is enlarged into a labellum."

"It's very complex, like a miniature painting."

I thought of Davis's comment that orchid flowers resembled the animal from whose seed they had sprung. The bog candle looked like nothing, except perhaps a flock of terns seen at a distance. The flower trembled slightly and I took hold of Natasha's hand to keep the magnifying glass in focus. Her fingers were as long and slender as the lanceolate leaves of an orchid. I remembered Audrey's hands teasing the soil from the paired tubers of a *Catasetum*. What was the phrase in the Steller letter—"the morphology of desire"?

"What?"

"Nothing." I had not realized I had spoken aloud. "I was just thinking that nothing out here could ever be sensuous."

"Don't be too sure." She handed the flower to me.

Fine pebbles coated the streambed. They looked almost polished beneath the clear, flowing water. We walked in silence, almost touching when the gully narrowed.

"Orchids have those fancy flowers to attract bees?" Natasha asked suddenly.

"Right, or other insects, depending."

"What about grasses, what do they do?"

"They're wind-pollinated."

"So they don't need to attract anybody?"

"Basically, yeah."

"I like that. All on their own." She drew a deep breath as if tasting the wind. "Why not study them?"

"Too complicated."

"How so?"

"Orchids, they're so dramatic it's easy to tell them apart. But grasses are a nightmare to classify; the differences are so subtle. If you ever got hooked on grasses it'd be like wandering in a hall of mirrors."

We stopped to rest by the creek's edge. Natasha cupped her hand in the water to take a drink, studying the skyline as she brought her hand to her mouth. I knelt and put my mouth to the creek to drink the cold, stinging water. Wasn't it Gideon in the Bible who chose only soldiers who drank from a cupped hand? Lucky for him the Israelites weren't dealing with massive hangovers.

The sky was partly clear now and the sun broke through the clouds, bringing temporary warmth to our sheltered spot. Natasha's hair had been pinned up in proper missionary fashion but the wind had played havoc with the careful coils and now tendrils hung loose in windblown snarls. She took the pins out and combed her hair with her fingers as she had in the cemetery at Pilot Point.

"Were you frightened last night by the drinking and all?" I asked. "It must be a little awkward being stuck with men you don't really know."

Natasha picked a pebble from the creek bottom and considered it. "Why does flowing water make things clearer?" She tossed the pebble back in the creek and said, "My father's drinking cronies were trappers and seal hunters. I'd have to cook and clean for them. By the time I was twelve they were leering at me like I was ready for the pot myself. My father always too drunk to notice. My bed was in the loft and I had to climb the ladder with them staring up my skirt. I used to take a butcher's knife to bed and pull a chest over the trapdoor."

"You don't think Jason Davis or Li Po would try anything like that?"

"No, no, not them. They're both gentlemen in a funny kind of way. Sort of shabby genteel."

"You're kind of taken with Davis, aren't you?" Gentleman was not the word I would have used.

"He's interesting, but I can't understand half of what he says. It's like he learned English from a book."

"I've been accused of that myself."

Natasha braided her hair into two long plaits. When she finished she flipped the braids back over her shoulders and pulled her shawl close. I watched her and listened to the music of the flowing water.

"He's not related to you, is he?" Natasha asked suddenly.

"Who?"

"Jason Davis."

"Are you serious?"

"Well, he looks a lot like you. Or at least what you'll look like if you search for that orchid your whole life and never find it."

"God forbid."

"I don't know, John Lars. Maybe that's your only hope for salvation—wandering forty years in the desert, eating wild honey and orchids."

"Jason Davis doesn't exactly look like he's found redemption out here."

"It's not for everybody." She rose abruptly and walked on. I followed, wondering what wasn't for everybody—this country or redemption?

We left the gully and climbed the haunches of the hill. The wind was dying. A jaeger hunted, hovering above the grass with its long tail quivering. I saw what I took to be brush moving but then three caribou came over the ridge. Seeing us they turned and ran with their heads tipped so that their antlers almost lay on their backs, their hooves lifted in a curiously dainty trot. I heard a bird cry, long and plaintive.

"What's that?" I asked.

"Curlew," Natasha said but she was staring out to sea. Beyond the barrier islands the pencil-thin masts of a boat moved west. Natasha shaded her eyes and said calmly, "The *Emilia Galotti*."

"It can't be." I felt a tendril of foreboding like a cold rill of water.

Natasha headed straight down the hill. I ran after her. When we reached the beach the tide was out and the groove from the dinghy's keel was now well above the water. Shorebirds worked the flats with skittering wings.

"They'll be back, they have to come back." My eyes roved the empty lagoon. "Maybe they're just trying out the engine."

"Have you got any matches?" Natasha asked, already planning the next step. "We need a fire."

I handed her my match safe. She gathered water-blackened driftwood and broke small branches for kindling.

"Can I have some of the paper in your pack for tinder?" she asked.

"No, absolutely not."

She shrugged and then found some almost-dry grass and crumpled it in a ball. She lit a match, shielding it from the wind, then stuck it into the grass. With much blowing she coaxed the fire to reluctant life.

"Those papers are Steller's journal and letters," I said defensively.

"Not the originals?"

"Of course not, but I still need them."

Natasha broke more sticks and blew some more till the fire strengthened. I stared out across the lagoon, not being very useful. I was still dumbfounded by the idea that we might have been marooned.

"Come sit down," Natasha said. "We should probably wait for a bit but wishing them back isn't going to do any good."

"But this is crazy. I thought they were my friends. Why would they leave us here?"

"I don't know, unless . . . Had you told them about this orchid before?"

"No, I wasn't supposed to tell anyone."

"Does that mean it might be valuable?"

"I don't know. Well, yeah, it could be worth a lot. But not up here, you'd have to get it back to civilization. And, anyway, you wouldn't abandon somebody to die just for an orchid."

"Don't be so melodramatic. We're only thirty miles from False Pass. If this kills us we don't belong up here in the first place."

"I'm beginning to think I don't."

"Well, I do. This is just gonna slow us down a couple days. Plus we'll have to find a boat in False Pass. They're probably counting on a week's head start."

"What if they're not orchid pirates? What if they just rifled through my trunks and found my cache of money and decided to cut and run? Doesn't that make more sense?"

"But last night . . . I couldn't follow it all, but it sounded like Jason Davis used to be married to your professor's wife."

"So he says. I don't know if I believe him. I mean, what are the odds?"

"Everything is preordained, John Lars," she said in a deep, sepulchral voice and then laughed. "Calvinism is always handy in a crisis. It makes you feel even worse."

"You're sure taking this lightly."

"Oh, cheer up." From her pocket, she took a pair of sandwiches and handed me one. It was made from sea otter meat and pilot bread.

"Shouldn't we save them?"

"I'm hungry now."

I chewed the stringy meat without even tasting it. All my belongings were gone—my money, my clothing, Gray's *Synoptica*, the Wardian case. I tried to reconstruct the tail end of the evening when Davis and I had sat drinking and talking long after the other two had gone to bed. A typical drunken conversation, both lachrymose and angry. I knew my tongue was loose but what exactly had been said? Davis was hounded by the past. If he figured out that Audrey and I were lovers that might be reason enough for him to maroon us.

I looked at Natasha and remembered Davis's hand on her elbow. The damp wood hissed as it burned.

CHAPTER 13

The cries of the gulls were a cacophony as the light increased. We walked westward until the coast curved back toward the Bering Sea, then we cut inland and followed an old beach line. Midmorning we couold see another bay, one that opened to the south side of the peninsula.

"This must be Morzhovoi Bay," Natasha said. "It almost cuts the peninsula in two. We'll have to go round the top."

We altered our course slightly. Ponds and marshes fragmented the landscape and tussocks of grass made for clumsy walking. Natasha took off her shoes and stockings and slung them around her neck. When we waded small streams she kilted her skirt above the knees.

"Did you always want to be a botanist?" she asked suddenly.

"Actually when I started college I wanted to be an artist."

"Lose interest?"

"Just wasn't good enough."

"How hard did you try?"

"Hard enough." I didn't like the implication that I was a quitter. "When I was twelve I wanted to play center field for the Yankees but that didn't work out either."

We walked in silence for a few minutes. "My freshman drawing class," I said. "When we started doing life studies, everything I drew looked like cut-out dolls. There was this guy in my class, Mark Rothkowitz—he was so good he made me sick. Only I found I could do okay drawing flowers. Barely okay. I'm not in Merian or Redouté's league. Or even Henry Moon. They're as good as Vermeer, if you ask me."

"I don't know any of those people."

"They're not as famous as they should be. Anyway, I started doing illustrations for the museum and somehow drifted into a botany major."

"And now you're going to be like a professor or something?"

"I don't know. I may just end up in the family law firm. My father's pretty intent on that."

"Did you ever tell him what you want?"

"I might if I could figure it out myself."

"That's a problem for you, isn't it?" She swung at the grass with a long stick she was carrying. "So this orchid might be worth a lot of money?"

"Yeah, maybe. The big commercial houses like McBean's or Butterworth's pay a lot for new orchids. And there's private collectors like Albert Burrage in Boston. My professor thinks the fact it's North American could be a big selling point right now."

"Why's that?"

"Oh, I don't know. Upsurge of patriotism after the war, maybe. A year ago Burrage did a big exhibition of only North American orchids and thousands of people attended. Plus, foreign orchids don't do well in American soil. The mycorrhizae—the root fungi—are different or something. Steller's orchid might not have that problem. I mean, this is still North America, after all."

"Just barely." Natasha looked around.

We stopped to rest on a grassy knoll. I took off my shoes. My socks were wet and my feet were beginning to blister. I closed my eyes against the sun and watched fantastic frilled shapes chase each other across the red of my eyelids. What was I really looking for? I had scarcely looked at a flower all morning. I opened my eyes and saw a small blossom, a Chukchi primrose. I picked the bloom and turned it in my hands. How would Asa Gray describe it? Obovate leaves, farinose pedicel, cleft calyx. At the moment it just looked like a flower. I bit the tube end and sucked. Faint taste of nectar. I looked at Natasha. The hem of her skirt was wet and bedraggled.

"So what is it," she asked, "the money or the knowledge?"

"What?"

"Why are you chasing this orchid, for the money and fame or the science?"

"The science, of course. Except . . . well, the Arbuthnots made plant hunting sound so romantic that I kind of got seduced. Only I'm beginning to think I'd be better off back in the Marsh Garden, cataloging plants."

"The Marsh Garden." Natasha looked around at the muskeg and potholes.

"It doesn't have anything to do with swamps. It was named after this guy Othniel C. Marsh who donated the land. He was a pretty famous paleontologist."

"A what?"

"He studied old bones. In fact there's a display in the Peabody Museum of fossil horses he found in Nebraska. At Antelope Springs. Is that anywhere near your school?"

"Never heard of it. But maybe he hired Wesleyan students to polish bones or something. So long as he cleared it with the Scripture Department first."

"Well, this was about 1870. He had a bunch of Yale students along. With a military escort and Buffalo Bill, believe it or not, to protect him from the Indians." I laughed at the picture of Buffalo Bill amongst the Yalies but then stopped short at the thought that Natasha's sympathies might lie with the Indians.

"Buffalo Bill wouldn't do you much good out here." She stood up and brushed her dress. "You're lucky you've got me instead."

"You know," I said as I put on my shoes, "I sometimes feel like I need a guide in New Haven. I don't really fit in there, either."

Natasha pulled me to my feet. "First we gotta get you to Unga. Then we'll find someplace you belong."

I tagged along after her. More sand and scruffy vegetation. Blueberry bushes and what I took to be salmonberry. Steller had been the first to describe the salmonberry, I was pretty sure. The flowers were gone but the fruit was still pale green, inedible. My stomach growled uncontrollably and I picked a leaf of burdock and chewed it. Hunger made me irritable and I thought again of how intently Natasha watched Davis that night on the *Emilia*.

"There's something about you and Davis I just don't get . . ." I started to say but Natasha stopped suddenly and grabbed my arm. Immediately ahead of us a brown bear climbed out of a little swale, his huge hindquarters propelling him effortlessly.

Instinctively I turned and started to run but Natasha arm-tackled me so hard she knocked the breath out of me. "Stay put," she whispered.

The bear stopped, tilted his head and sniffed the wind. The fur along his back and shoulder was faded to a light brown that was almost blond. He was so close that I could see, and even hear, the sand dislodged by his paws trickling down the slope. I had never seen anything half as big and menacing. "Oh, my God," I said. Natasha shushed me again and the bear turned our way as if sensing something. Natasha slowly stood up and faced the bear. The bear took a step in our direction and Natasha also took a careful step, but toward the bear rather than away. The bear took another step and so did she, locked in an ominous dance. I felt like a fool, crouched behind her. On the other hand I didn't feel like interposing myself.

The bear huffed audibly and Natasha slowly raised her arms and began to sing. The bear rolled his head as if he did not understand, then turned in a half circle like a dog about to sit down. Luckily he changed his mind and began to walk slowly along the ridge away from us. When he dropped out of sight I stood up and we quietly walked in the opposite direction.

"Wow," I said when we were some distance away. I gingerly touched the elbow that had been scraped when Natasha tackled me.

"Sorry about that," she said, "but the worst thing you can do is run away from a bear."

"But did you have to walk towards it?"

"I'm not much good at backing down."

"I guess not." I shook my head. "What was it you were singing?"

"A Russian hymn, from my mother. I don't even know what the words mean."

I looked back. I could see the bear again, topping a distant ridge, still too close for my comfort. "Grizzlies aren't Methodists?" I asked.

"It was just the first thing that came to mind. Closer to the heart, I guess."

For the remainder of the afternoon we kept as close to the south shore of the isthmus as we could. Late in the day we reached a gut through which a large tidewater lagoon drained. I collapsed on the bank and looked at the dark, slow current. Natasha stared inland at the salt marshes and sand flats.

"What a mess," she said. "It'd take us hours to work our way around, plus we'd be headed back toward that bear. I'd rather swim. It's nearly slack water."

I simply shrugged, too tired to argue.

"Me first," Natasha said and wrapped her shawl around her head like a turban and waded into the water holding the hem of her dress gathered in her right hand. I took off my shoes and pants and shirt and stuffed them in my rucksack. Dressed only in my skivvies I waded gingerly into the water after her, glad that she wasn't looking back.

The water was piercingly cold. When it reached Natasha's breasts she flopped forward and swam in a kind of breaststroke but only for about ten yards before she regained her feet and dashed ashore, laughing.

I followed without laughter, holding my rucksack aloft in one hand as I swam. Once ashore I sat down and began to pull on my pants. Natasha stood a little distance away, twisting her skirt into a knot to wring it dry. She looked up, caught me staring at her and ducked her head shyly and dropped the hem.

"I think we should stay here," she said. "It's getting too late to cross the hills and we won't find any firewood once we leave the shore."

"Whatever you want," I said almost inaudibly, embarrassed at being caught watching her.

Driftwood was more plentiful than in Izembek Lagoon and soon we had a fire going. Natasha stood close by it trying to dry her dress. After a few minutes she said, "You'll have to excuse me, John Lars." She unbuttoned her dress and pulled it over her head and then held it over the flames. She was wearing a white cotton shift that was scarcely less modest than her dress. It too was wet and clung to her body. I could see two places where the shift had been darned with white thread. It reached almost to her knees and below that her legs showed welts from the grass and willow scrub.

"Chukchi primrose," I said, half to myself.

"What?"

"Nothing."

"You've got to stop mumbling all the time, John Lars."

"Sorry."

She pulled on her dress and studied me as she buttoned it. "You look awful."

"I feel awful, don't you?"

"Just a little hungry. I'm going to get some firewood. You sit there and keep warm."

I sat close by the fire. The wind had died and the evening sun illuminated the dunes but I was bone-weary, my clothes were damp, and my throat was sore from drinking brackish water. I was wind-battered and sea-leveled. I poked the fire with a stick. The only sound was the crying of the gulls and the crackle and hiss of the fire. How was I going to explain to the Arbuthnots that I had lost all my gear before I even reached Nagai? If they actually knew Davis that would only make it worse.

Natasha dropped an armload of wood by the fire. "By any chance did you know Jason Davis before this?" I asked her.

"What makes you say that?"

"He spent time in King Cove. And, I don't know, you seem awfully familiar."

"I've known men like Jason Davis all my life." She picked up a short stick and headed inland. Half an hour later she reappeared with a handful of plants.

"Aleut potatoes," she said, showing me a small white tuber. "They're not full-grown so I don't know how good they'll be. A bear was digging some."

"A bear?"

"He was long gone, just the ground was all torn up."

"You sure these aren't camas bulbs?"

"What's that?"

"Death camas. A type of lily with a bulb that looks like an onion. Very poisonous."

"Trust the bear if you don't trust me."

We tried roasting them on a bit of wood placed near the fire. They were no bigger than radishes and quite bitter.

"My mother died before she could teach me much about gathering but I remember in the fall for a treat us kids would look for caches of seeds and tubers the mice made. *Anlleret*, we called it. Mouse food."

"Doesn't sound too appetizing." I threw a half-eaten bulb in the fire.

"You're kind of squeamish for a scientist, you know that?"

"I'm supposed to classify what I find, not eat it."

"The people at Nebraska Wesleyan weren't much into wild food, either. Once I found a clutch of eggs and took some to the kitchen, only the cook acted like I was worshiping graven images or something."

"Maybe she just didn't want you disturbing the nest."

"No, because they had some blown eggs in the parlor. For decoration. To them food was from farming and anything wild was unclean. Which is pretty comical if you've ever seen a chicken coop. Yuck! But they thought I was a savage anyway. Every time I skipped chapel to walk on the prairie they'd just shake their heads." She made a face like a prune and mimed a prim, churchy nod and said in a lugubrious tone, "Blood will out, poor child."

"You do seem like unlikely root stock to graft Methodism on to," I said cautiously.

"Boy, you got that right. Too much Bering Sea in my blood. Too much Orthodox Church in my early years. Those priests with long beards and tall hats and heavy crosses on their chests. It all made a deep impression."

Long shadows crept out from the dunes to hesitate at the fire's edge. The surface of the bay was silver and overhead a few stars were visible, including one that was particularly bright. *Venus, I thought, the evening star.*

"I can't remember that much of St. Paul," Natasha said. "I was so young when we left. But I have these few vivid memories that have a kind of power, almost like magic. Of Christmas, especially. We had this custom called 'slavying' where they carried a star in procession from house to house. A huge star with lots of points. It was so amazing in the dark with the drifted snow. People in masks tried to capture the star. King Herod's men, they were supposed to be. They always lost but it was very scary for a little girl."

"This was supposed to be a Christmas celebration?"

"Orthodox Christmas, January seventh. But it also had something to do with the new year. You have to wear a costume and chase your shadow. If you don't you might lose part of your soul."

"Sounds primitive."

"Primitive?"

"Well, superstitious."

"John Lars . . . ." She stopped and shook her head. In the fire a long piece of wood had nearly burned in two. Natasha snapped it and pushed the fire together. I felt a sudden blast of heat.

Alyson

"You're too hard on yourself, Uncle John,"

"How so?"

"This guy you're describing, he's kind of a dweeb. A nebbish, whatever you want to call it. And completely full of himself."

"I was twenty years old that summer. I thought I knew everything, was smarter than anybody, but at the same time I was completely awkward and self-conscious. Plus, I was a bit of a prig. Know any twenty-year-olds like that?"

"All of them." Alyson laughed.

"Right. Egotism and naivety are a messy combination. Always have been. Sometimes I wish I could go back and grab my twenty-year-old self by the throat and throttle him. For all the mistakes made, all the opportunities wasted. For the wrong words said and the wrong things done."

"Don't you think it's high time you forgave yourself?

"Not quite yet."

"Anyway, I can't picture you trailing after Natasha. Doing field work with you is like the Bataan Death March. Nobody can keep up."

"Natasha was on her home ground and I wasn't, but it was more than that. Following her was like chasing a shooting star."

"The celestial kind or the flower?"

"Both."

CHAPTER 14

A wisp of smoke rose from the charred end of a burnt stick and bits of ash whirled in a slight eddy of wind. I rolled over and sat up. Natasha sat by the cold fire reading from my Steller typescript.

"Hey," I said, "that's mine." Without comment she handed them back, stood up, and waited while I laced up my boots. They were iron-hard after drying by the fire and I hobbled after her. The land was no longer flat and sandy but climbed steadily toward a sky roofed with high, thin clouds.

"I think if we cut across this hill on a long diagonal we'll reach False Pass," Natasha said. "The village is across the water but there'll be boats around. I can't remember for sure but there might be a cannery on this side."

The hill in question was something more than a hill and less than a mountain. My feet were sore and I kept lagging further behind. Natasha finally stopped and waited for me.

"John Lars," she said when I reached her, "there's no possible way the same person wrote the journal and those letters."

"How would you know?"

"They sound completely different. Steller only thinks about himself and his science. But whoever wrote the letters, he sees the woman in everything."

"Professor Arbuthnot thinks they're genuine. And so do I."

"Wait," Natasha said and pointed south. A flash of sun glinted on metal. I shielded my eyes and saw something rectilinear.

"I can't tell what it is," she said, "but it's gotta be man-made. We'd better take a look—it's a lot closer than False Pass."

We headed south, giving up our hard-won altitude. As we walked I thought about the letters. Audrey had translated them but not the journal. Wouldn't that explain the discrepancy in tone? How much of the language was hers and not quite Steller's? Problem was, the letters did not sound at all like Audrey. They were intense and beseeching, torn from the writer's heart, the kind of letter Audrey might get but never write.

"The letters have to be real," I said. "What would be the point of forging them?"

"Aren't they valuable?"

"Maybe a little, to a rare book collector, but the Arbuthnots didn't pay anything for the letters. They found them in the frame of a Chinese painting. So what kind of bunco scheme would that be?"

"You ever play the stick game?"

"That's an Indian game, isn't it.?"

"One guy takes two sticks. He holds his hands behind his back then brings them forward. The other guy has to bet which hand holds the short stick."

"Sounds easy."

"If anybody ever asks you to play, better say no."

As usual I had no idea what she meant. By now we could tell that we were approaching a trap barge—a moored barge with a caretaker's house for tending a system of stationary salmon nets.

"I never heard of a fish trap in Morzhovoi Bay," Natasha said. "I thought they were all out in Ikatan Bay, at the mouth of the Pass."

Smoke came from the chimney of the house but no one was in sight. We shouted hello and almost immediately a figure appeared at a door on the second floor of the house. Even at a distance we could see his surprise and discomfiture. He hurried down the exterior staircase, climbed into a battered dory with a tombstone transom and rowed ashore. He was a heavyset older man wearing denim overalls. He was unshaven and his white whiskers were as bristly as a boar's—too short for paintbrushes but stiff enough.

"Jesus H. Christ, where did you two spring from?" he asked.

"We walked across from the Bering Sea side, over by Izembek," I said.

"On foot?" he asked, incredulous. "Why in hell'd ya do that?"

"We went ashore from a schooner and there was a bit of a misunderstanding and we got left."

"A bit of a misunderstanding, I'll bet." He rubbed his hand through his short hair. "Well, you'd better come aboard."

He rowed us out to the barge. The deck and the walkway to the pens were slick from age, rain, and fish slime.

"I didn't know there was a salmon trap in Morzhovoi," Natasha said.

"Just the one. Travelin' fish get pushed into the bay on the flood, 'specially if there's a southerly. They come out along this shore and we get a few. Not many but enough for the cannery to keep it going, I guess. You from around here?"

"Unga," Natasha said. "That's where we're going. Any chance we can get a ride from here?"

"I dunno. The tender ain't due for a few days. He can give you a ride back to False Pass but after that it'll be chancy. Somebody'll be goin' to Unga but no tellin' when. They're all busy fishin' now."

Moored to the inshore side of the barge was what appeared to be a slightly smaller version of a Bristol Bay double-ender in which the mast and sail had been replaced by a small inboard engine. Two long oars were lashed to the seats. On the bow in faded white paint was the number 67.

"How well does the motor work in that gillnetter?" Natasha asked, obviously thinking about begging a ride.

"Runs like a top, missy, but it ain't mine. Belongs to my friend Gus. He uses it for handlinin' cod but he's got a bigger boat for salmon. He's out there now."

I looked around. The trap was moored to driven pilings much like the ones in Puget Sound. Nets were suspended from huge logs that were chained together to form the inner and outer "hearts." The inner net funneled the salmon into the pot, which was a large pen of webbing with a spiller at one end for concentrating the fish. There was also a net buoyed with scraps of wood like shingles that stretched all the way to shore to lead the fish into the hearts. Two long nets stretched at right angles to the lead net.

"I thought jiggers were illegal now," I said, staring at those two long nets.

"What are you, some kind of fish cop?" the man asked, bristling.

"No, no . . ."

"The last thing we need is a bunch of goddamn outsiders messing in our business."

"It's just . . . Well, my grandfather used to run a trap," I said lamely, neglecting to mention that my grandfather had in fact owned the cannery. Silver flashed in the pens as blue-backed salmon turned together like shorebirds wheeling quickly in unison.

Lard sizzled in the cast iron skillet as the bargeman sliced potatoes. His name was Clyde Glover and his living quarters on the second floor of the barge were scrupulously clean. The wood floor was scrubbed and shining; the stove was polished and there were curtains at the barn sash windows.

Clyde turned to us and said, "I ain't got runnin' water. I got to haul it from the creek. But there's a hip bath in there." He gestured at a narrow door like a ship's door. "I expect you'd like to get clean. Take this kettle off the stove, there's cold water and soap already in there. But wait a minute now."

He stopped as if he had remembered something and went through another door that obviously led to a bedroom. He came back carrying a canvas bag with a drawstring top.

"Had a guy workin' for me last summer for a bit but he went up to Naknek gillnettin' and got hisself drowned on Deadman's Sands.

Maybe some of his gear'll be of use." Clyde gave the bag to Natasha then carried the kettle into the bathroom for her.

I sat at the table nodding with drowsiness. I stared at the floor, which was pockmarked from the caulked boots of some past resident less meticulous than Clyde. There was a soft thump as a cat jumped down from a windowsill at the far end of the barge, then stalked into the kitchen. He was large, gray, and scarred. He rubbed against Clyde's legs and then came over and regarded me with an unblinking gaze.

"You're not from Unga, are you?" Clyde asked.

"Seattle."

"Thought you looked like a city fella. What takes you to Unga?"

"I'm supposed to be studying plants there. Flowering plants. For my college."

"Flowers?" Clyde said with obvious disbelief. "Shore is a marvelous world we live in. So, what about this schooner that marooned you?"

"It was the *Emilia Galotti*. Captain Jason Davis?"

"Never heard of him. Why d'ya figure he left you?"

"Haven't the faintest idea."

"Huh."

A door clicked and Natasha came out of the bathroom. She was barefoot and wearing a pair of faded dungarees much too big for her and a white jersey made of a coarsely woven fabric almost like burlap. Her hair was shining wet and she was carrying her old clothes over her arm. She looked at the stove and I thought her cheekbones sharpened as she sniffed the air but she said nothing. She sat at the table and began to braid her hair. She and the cat regarded each other solemnly.

In the bathroom I found a sink and a toilet that must have drained straight into the bay, a small bathtub, and the now half-full kettle of hot water. I stripped and washed and then looked in the duffle bag. I felt a little strange handling the clothes of a dead person. Had they recovered his body or was it still on the bottom of Bristol Bay, rolling over in the storm waves, its mouth full of sand? Pushing the image away, I put on a pair of dungarees and a work shirt, combed my wet hair and tidied the bathroom.

Back in the kitchen Clyde was saying, "I spent a year in Akutan myself. Long time ago. Never could get used to the stink of the blubber from the tryworks, but comin' from St. Paul you must be used to slaughter."

"It's not my favorite thing," Natasha said.

Clyde put a loaf of bread and a tin of butter on the table, wiped his knife on the end of the loaf and then cut generous slices. "Made this bread yesterday, but I'm out of yeast so it's salt-rising."

He put three tin plates and spoons on the table and then ladled out fried potatoes and baked beans. He sat down with us and to my surprise bent his head and mumbled a brief grace over the meal. The beans had been cooked with salt pork and molasses and I ate a second plate and then a third and several slices of bread and butter. Clyde sat back, took a kitchen match and whittled it to a point, and began to clean his teeth.

"Yeah," he said as if continuing a conversation, "after I left Akutan I ran a store for a spell out in Atka. Lonely sort of place. Then I drifted back to King Cove. Had a hankerin' to see a tree again and they got two or three there must be a good five foot tall."

"Are you from this country originally?"

"Nah. Upstate New York. We had a small farm there but the soil give out and after Pa died I headed west and then north. But now I'm stuck in an eddy, kinda like. I just drift from one end of the chain to another. Happens to people out here, like it's some kind of Sargasso Sea. Expect I'll leave my bones on one of these beaches."

While he was talking Clyde lit two kerosene lanterns and placed them in the kitchen windows. By now it was early evening but it was scarcely dark inside the barge. We offered to do the dishes but he declined and washed them himself, talking all the while. I drank more coffee in an effort to wake up sufficiently to ask about the sleeping arrangements. Natasha sat with her chin cupped in the palm of one hand, her eyes nearly closed.

A soft knock on the door startled me. The door opened and two men walked in without waiting for word. So tired was I that I had not heard them on the stairs, nor had I heard their boat. The first man was of medium height, stocky and bearded. He wore a heavy black sweater and a black watch cap. His companion was Aleut, taller with lank, unkempt hair that fell to his shoulders. One side of his face was hollowed as if all the teeth were missing.

"A little company, I see," the first man said, looking at Natasha and me and smiling with strong, white teeth.

"Castaways, Gus. This here is John and Natasha. And this is August Masek and Sam Dementieff. These two young 'uns got left on the Bering side, Gus. By a boat called the *Emilia* somethin'. They walked across."

"The *Amy Galoshes*," the man named Gus said. "I seen her headed north early yesterday."

"The *Emilia Galotti*," I said in defense of something, I wasn't quite sure what, and Gus nodded. He filled two plates with beans and handed one to Sam who sat down on a wooden box next to the stove. Stenciling on the box indicated that it had once held two five-gallon tins of kerosene; now it held kindling. Sam took a drink of coffee and then spoke to Natasha in a language that I assumed was Aleut. When she replied he laughed softly, showing that he was indeed missing quite a few teeth. I looked at Natasha with raised eyebrows.

"Sam's my third cousin or so," she said. "Says he met me when I was six but I don't remember."

"How's the fishing been?" Clyde asked Gus.

"Poor. I'm thinkin' of headin' out to Sanak. Or maybe up to King Cove but it's a little early for them mainland streams." He scraped the last of the beans from his plate. I could see the letters H A R D L U C K tattooed across his battered and flattened knuckles. There was scar tissue on his eyebrows as well—an old boxer, by the looks.

"Is there any chance you could take us as far as King Cove?" I asked.

"Nah. Bad luck to take a woman on board." He grinned at Natasha as if to imply he was joking. "I don't know how soon I'll be headed that way. But what I want to know is, what brings you out here?"

"I'm doing a botanical survey," I said yet again.

"On your own hook?"

"For Yale College, more or less."

"Yale, isn't that where John Reed went to school?" Gus said, speaking of the famous, or notorious, Communist.

"He went to Harvard, actually."

"I thought they were the same place."

"Not exactly. Leastways they have different football teams." When you were stranded on a fish trap in Morzhovoi Bay, Harvard and Yale did in fact appear indistinguishable.

"All the way from Yale to get marooned in Izembek," Gus said musingly. "And all your gear still on the *Emilia Galotti*, I'd guess."

"And my clothes," Natasha interjected and fingered her coarse shirt ruefully.

"What I can't figure out is why Jason Davis stranded you."

"Do you know Davis?" I asked.

"A little. Him and Li Po both. Over in Siberia. I was doing a little prospecting till the Bolsheviks threw us out. Can you imagine that? Me, a better Red than any of 'em. First I get run out of Ketchikan for organizing a strike at a sawmill, then I'm run out of Siberia for being a capitalist tool. Ain't no justice, now is there, Clyde?"

"None this side of the grave," Clyde said sententiously.

"And I ain't real confident about the other side, neither. Rich folks probably got that bought up, too. But Jason Davis, now, I never could figure out how an educated man like him wasn't a socialist. And I sure can't fathom why he'd drop you off that way."

"You'd have to ask him," I said.

"Can't till I catch up with him. For now, I aim to drink coffee and whip Clyde at cribbage. Sam"—he nodded at the Aleut who sat grinning—"thinks crib is beneath him so I drop in here for some all night games."

Clyde's eyes lit up at the mention of cribbage. From a shelf he took an old board with broken kitchen matches as markers and a greasy pack of cards. Gus took the cards and began to shuffle them, glancing briefly at me. As if taking a cue Clyde said, "I expect you two are about played out. I ain't got but the one bedroom but it's got a trundle bed in it."

He took me by the arm and steered me toward the bedroom. Natasha followed, yawning. I protested taking his room but Clyde said he would probably be up late and the talk would bother us if we slept on the sofa. He pulled out the trundle bed, puffing heavily as he bent over. The bed was already made up with sheet and blanket. Like the rest of the house the bedroom was scrupulously clean. Clyde bade us good night and closed the door. Without further ado Natasha lay down on the trundle bed and folded her arms.

"Wait a minute," I said, "you sleep on the big bed. Let me take the cot," but without answering she rolled onto her side, her arm covering her eyes.

There was a kerosene lamp atop a chest of drawers but it was not lit. The single window let in the twilight. I sat down on the bed and heard the satisfying twang of bed springs. As I took off my shirt I realized this was the first night since the hotel in Nome that I was to sleep in an actual bed. I lay back and looked at the bright slash of light beneath the door. I heard the scrape of a chair and a low voice saying, "fifteen-two, fifteen-four and a pair is six . . ."

CHAPTER 15

The room was completely dark. Someone was moving. I spluttered a question and a cool hand covered my mouth. I could tell it was Natasha from the scent of her hair. She took my arm and beckoned me to the window. Nothing was visible but very faintly I heard a squeal of metal, the working of a rusty cable on a drum. After a moment I could make out the shadowy outline of a boat tied alongside the pound at the end of the trap.

"They're brailing fish out of the trap," Natasha whispered and headed for the door. I grabbed my trousers, struggled into them, and followed her through the dark kitchen. She very cautiously opened the outside door and we crept down the stairway and partway along the deck. A wind had come up out of the southwest and small waves lapped against the barge. The boards felt slick and cold beneath my bare feet.

There was a faint blush of light to the north where the sun hid beneath the horizon but the trap lay deep in a pool of shadow. The dark seemed to eddy around us with the gusts of wind; nonetheless I could make out the shape of a fishing boat with a small wheelhouse. The trap's spiller had been lifted to concentrate the fish and the boom of the fishing boat swung outward as we watched. There was a brief explosion of, if not light, then an almost phosphorescent darkness as the brailer dropped in amongst the fish. We could hear the faint mutter of the boat's engine and the splashing of the fish. The brailer lifted and swung inboard, the fish dropped in the hold and then the net bag again dropped into the pen—variations in the dark like shadows dancing.

Natasha touched my arm and led me back to the stairway. Once inside the kitchen she lit one of the kerosene lamps and placed it where the faint light would not be visible through the window. She then opened the firebox of the cook stove, stirred the coals, and added a stick of wood.

"It's cold," she said. "They'll want something warm when they come in."

"Shouldn't we go back to bed and pretend we didn't see it? Then we can report it when we get to False Pass."

"Report what?"

"Why, robbing a fish trap. They can't do that."

Natasha was looking in the cupboard for Clyde's five-pound tin of coffee. Over her shoulder she said, "All the traps get robbed, usually by bribing the watchman. Nobody cares. They all belong to a bunch of rich outsiders."

"Everybody doing it doesn't make it right." Having been raised in a cannery family, my sympathies were definitely not with trap robbers.

"But I thought you said they were fishing illegally anyway with those jiggers."

"That's just fisheries' regulations. Theft is theft. What kind of ethics did they teach you at that Methodist college?"

Natasha turned around and looked at me, holding the red coffee can against her shirt. "How would you have painted that trap-stealing scene?"

"Paint it? What do you mean, 'paint it?' It was pitch-black out there; what kind of painting would that make?"

"You could see it, couldn't you? At least a little. If you can see it you can paint it. If you could understand what you were seeing you could paint it even better. What kind of art did they teach at that Congregationalist college?" Natasha asked. With a toss of her hair she turned to the now boiling pot. She spooned coffee into it and moved it to a cooler part of the stove.

I looked at the kerosene lamp. Its chimney was cloudy and the light a pearly yellow. On the ceiling directly above the lamp there was a single bright disc of light surrounded by a penumbra of shadow and then a band of diffused light. I couldn't paint that either.

"Anyway," Natasha said, "do you want to get to the Shumagins or not?"

Quiet footsteps sounded on the stairs and the door was opened by someone turning the knob very slowly so the latch would not click. When they saw us in the kitchen, however, Gus laughed and said, "You youngsters are up a little early."

"Coffee?" Natasha asked, indicating the pot. All three helped themselves. When done she said, "Looks like we just arranged passage to King Cove."

Gus turned one of the chairs around and sat on it backwards. "We'll be taking our fish to King Cove all right."

"And," Natasha continued, "we're going to rent your double-ender to take us to Unga. You can pick it up after salmon season and we'll pay you then."

Gus looked at me and stroked his beard. A faint grin played across his lips. "Your college got an official policy on blackmail, kid?"

"It's fine, just so long as it's done in pursuit of knowledge." I figured I was entitled to Jesuitical reasoning like everyone else.

"All right. I was gonna take ya anyway but we gotta hurry. I want to be well out of here before the sun gets too high."

Clyde organized a box of provisions for Natasha and me while Gus and Sam rigged a towing bridle for the 67 and fastened it to the stern of the larger boat, which I could now see bore the name *Black Cat*. The black cat symbol of the IWW was painted on the side of the wheelhouse.

Gus leaped aboard the *Black Cat* and Natasha followed. When the engine started Sam and I cast off the bow and stern lines and climbed aboard. Clyde waved goodbye and the boat backed away from the dock as the first rays of the sun broke over the mountainous northeast side of the bay.

The *Black Cat* headed in a long slant toward the point at the east end of the bay. There was a stiff chop now that we took on the beam and the boat rolled wickedly in the trough. All four of us were crammed in the tiny cabin that served as both wheelhouse and galley.

"Natasha tells me your granddad owned the cannery at Pilot Point," Gus said conversationally.

"He built it but we sold it when he died."

"I didn't know he'd passed. I'm sorry to hear. Everybody said he was an honest man."

I said nothing but scoffed inwardly at the idea of a trap robber passing judgment on my rigidly upright grandfather. Gus was at the wheel, watching the waves, but he must have sensed my scorn.

"Us fisherman tried to get Congress to outlaw the traps but the canneries blocked it," he said. "Last year twice I loaded my boat but had to pitch the fish overboard 'cause the canneries had all the trap fish they needed. You call that fair?"

"But if the canneries don't have the capacity to handle your fish how can you blame them?"

"Hell, they do it just to keep the independents under their thumb. APA's a fuckin' octopus. Law says they gotta shut the traps down a couple days a week. Think they do that? First the canneries fight every law, get it changed the way they want it, then scoff at it anyway. And piss and moan when some little guy breaks the law. They're rapin' us, kid. Ain't no two ways about it. That's why I strike back any way I can."

I figured I had better not tell Gus about my father's role in shaping the White Act. A gust of spray hit the wheelhouse windows with a sound more like the rattling of hail than rain. The boat lurched sickeningly away from the wind and then dipped its starboard rail as it rolled back. Suddenly I did not feel argumentative.

"It's going to be rough for a couple of hours till we get across," Gus said. "You can lie down in the fo'c'sle if you want."

I waited a moment to see if Natasha would accept the offer. She made no move but my stomach was queasy and with a quick thank

you I headed down the narrow companionway on the starboard side
of the wheelhouse. In the dim light I saw two narrow box-like bunks
that met in the bow. They were unmade, each a tangle of blankets
with no sheets. The engine was louder down below, separated from
the fo'c'sle by only a thin bulkhead. I lay down on the port bunk and
fell into an almost-sleep, a troubled state between waking and dream-
ing where images coiled and twined and separated—Jason Davis and
Li Po and waving fields of grass and Natasha holding an elaborate
orchid, all linked and transformed into a whirling pinwheel of images.
At one point Sam came down the ladder and went into the engine
room. The brief explosion of light and noise entered my dream like a
jagged step in the spiraling dance.

When I awoke the motion had eased and the sound of the water
through the planks was a companionable hiss. I climbed the ladder
and emerged blinking into the brilliant light of a sunny day. Natasha stood at a small Shipmate stove, frying bacon. Through the open
door I could see Sam sitting on the hatch cover, splicing a bit of line.

Gus still stood at the wheel. The galley was hot and he wore a
sleeveless cotton singlet. On his right shoulder was a tattoo of an
upraised, clenched fist. Without even a nod to acknowledge my presence he continued talking to Natasha, holding up one finger at a
time. "You got the Red Army. You got the White Army. You got the
Czech Legion. You got the Japanese Imperial Army. You got General
Graves and the US Eighth Division." He waved all five fingers. "All
of 'em. Carvin' up Siberia like a Christmas goose. Not to mention
half of Russia runnin' east. And here's Mother Masek's favorite son,
barefoot, penniless and a hundred miles from Anadyr."

Natasha laughed merrily. She handed a plate of fried potatoes and
bacon to Sam. "You want some?" she asked me, waving the spatula.

"In a minute." I stepped out on deck. Behind the wheelhouse I
found a canvas deck bucket with a rope tied to its handle. I tossed
it overboard and hauled it back. Sam watched me from the corner of
his eye, probably expecting the drag of the bucket to snatch me over-

board but this much, at least, I knew from Puget Sound. I took off my shirt and washed my hands and face in the cold water.

Above the drone of the engine I could hear Gus's booming voice and Natasha's answering laugh. She sure liked to hear old men spin yarns. I could not imagine why. Looking up I saw that we were running in the lee of an island with grassy hills.

"Where are we?" I asked.

"Deer Island." Sam speared a ketchup-coated potato with his jack-knife and pointed forward. "King Cove just ahead."

Natasha came on deck with two plates of potatoes and she and I sat together and ate. When she finished, Sam reappeared and with a flourish opened a chessboard. "Okay, little sister," he said, "finally somebody to play me chess."

He rattled the box like dice and then began to set out the pieces. I was a little surprised that he would be a chess player but I moved in close with half a mind to challenge the winner. However, the game proved to be different from the one I knew. Sam placed the pieces in a confusing order with the pawns arrayed in staggered ranks. In the back rows, the black and white sides were not quite the same. The rules of play might have been different as well but they moved the pieces at such lightning speed that I could not be sure. Natasha sat on the hatch cover with her legs stretched out to the side as if she were doing a ballet exercise. She kept her arms straight and her hands on her knees when not moving a piece. She frowned intently and chewed the end of one of her braids. They played two games in rapid succession and she won both.

Sam practically rolled on the deck laughing at his plight. "You much too good, little sister," he said. "You been away so long I thought you'd forget."

He looked at where I sat kibitzing, grinned and said something to Natasha in Aleut. She blushed and looked a little flustered. Sam challenged her to another game and this time he won. He nodded, satisfied, and as if on signal the engine noise changed and the boat began to slow.

Sam pulled the 67 alongside, jumped in, and began to bail her with a partially flattened coffee can. Gus appeared on the back deck with a chart that he unrolled on the hatch cover.

"We've just about come to parting of the ways," he said. "This here is the beginning of Deer Passage. You just take a bead on this headland"—with a pencil he indicated Belkofski Point on the chart and then pointed ahead to a jutting shore—"then if you're feeling bold you can make a break for Archadean." Again he indicated a point, which was named, despite his pronunciation, Acheredin.

"Howsomever," Gus continued. "I figure the wind's gonna lay down then veer nor'west. If'n it was me I'd cross Pavlof and anchor by Tolstoi for the night, then come round the top of Unga, down Popof Strait."

Natasha nodded. "That's how I planned to go. I know these waters."

"Good. I didn't think ya'd have any trouble. Now let me introduce you to 67."

As usual I felt a little left out but I followed Gus into the skiff. He offered his hand to Natasha but she leaned on my shoulder as she jumped down. Gus lifted a box off the engine that was mounted amidships.

"These make-and-break engines can be fickle as a woman, beggin' your pardon, Natasha." Gus pinched her arm familiarly. "Ya gotta prime the engine with this distillate and then wrap this line around the flywheel like so. Now she ain't got a true reverse. Ya gotta get the crank turnin' the other way. If you slow the engine down and retard the spark she'll backfire, then open the throttle and if you're timing's good you're goin' backwards fast, which's been handy a time or two in my life."

I was confused but Natasha nodded. "I know Atlantics. Our skiff on the fox farm had the same engine. I can run it."

"Shoulda known. Could of saved me breath to cool me porridge, as mother used to say."

Sam had stowed several five-gallon gas cans in the bow, along with our food box. Lastly he brought a canvas gun case and a box of shotgun shells which he handed to Natasha, saying, "You might need this."

"I thought there weren't any bears in the Shumagins," I said in surprise.

"There aren't. It's to protect her from you," Gus said, and he and Sam laughed boisterously.

Natasha pulled the gun out of the case. It was a double-barreled twelve-gauge shotgun, so old that all the bluing was worn from the barrels. One of the hammers was partly broken and the stock had been badly cracked and repaired with tightly wrapped copper wire. She shoved it back in the case and stowed it carefully alongside the engine.

"The *Black Cat*'ll be in Unga come September," Gus said. "There'd better be a check from Yale College for the rental."

"I expect they're good for it," I said.

Gus threw his head back and laughed. "You're all right, kid. Forget about flowers. Come back next summer and you and Natasha can fish the *Black Cat* while Sam and me go huntin'. We'll all get rich if we just have sense enough to put Natasha in charge."

"I already got that much figured out," I said. Gus tossed me the bow line and I coiled it down. With a sharp pull on the starter cord Natasha brought the engine to noisy life She took the tiller and opened the throttle. The stern settled a little and the bow began to throw spray as the gap between the two boats widened. Natasha looked back and waved. Sam stood alone on deck, one hand raised in salute. A puff of smoke came from the stack and the *Black Cat* swung on a course at right angles to our own.

Despite the sun it was cold in the open boat and Natasha wore a peacoat and cap that Clyde had given her. She turned up the collar against the wind. I tried to say something but the engine noise hammered, then scattered, my words and Natasha shook her head in puzzlement. I put my lips to her ear and shouted, "Call me if you get tired."

I crawled forward and hunkered down behind the bit of foredeck with a bedroll for a pillow. I pulled my head down inside my coat like a turtle and a wave of exhaustion swept over me. I had not had a full night's sleep almost since leaving Seattle. I felt as though I had fallen off the edge of the world into a pack of wolves. No one ever needed to sleep, or eat regular meals, or stop and think before acting.

Natasha sat with the tiller tucked beneath her right arm and her left hand in her coat pocket. She stared ahead and her lips moved slightly as if she were softly singing.

Alyson

"Back up a minute. I'm getting more lost. So you were still on the hunt for the orchid but Natasha figured the letters were fakes?"

"At least different from the journal."

"Do you still have the letters?"

"My copies, yeah. I look at them from time to time."

"Can I see one, just for a minute?"

"Sure." The letters were in the bottom drawer of my desk. I brought the sheaf to Alyson along with a recent reprint of Steller's journal, then headed for the bathroom.

Another task that took longer with age. I washed my hands and studied my reflection in the mirror. I looked awful. If everything else was falling apart, what about my mind? For fifty years now the voyage had bounced around in the prism of my memory, reflected off every facet. How trustworthy could my account be? Memory was always part imagination. How much of this story had happened and how much was a dream born of my own hopes, needs, fears, regrets? I stood there and tried to picture those lonely shores in detail. The driftwood, the sand, the grass that rippled endlessly in the wind. The smell of salt and fish. The cry of the gulls and the hammering sound of the Atlantic engine. Maybe placing myself there would ground my memory.

"I think Natasha had a pretty good bullshit detector," Alyson said when I returned to the front room. "Even at just a glance these letters sound way different from the journal. They're kind of off the wall."

"But they were love letters, not a scientific journal. And Audrey translated the letters but not the journal. And the journal was translated from a copy. Lots of different voices."

"So you believe they're real?"

"Back then I did. You're right the letters are florid but even in his journal Steller could be pretty intense. He was always criticizing Bering's decisions, confronting him. Once Bering had the trumpeter play a fanfare when Steller went ashore. To mock him."

"Bering sounds like a doofus."

"Steller thought so and when I first read the journals I sided with him. But now that I'm older my sympathies have shifted. I mean, think about it. Bering had a leaky ship in uncharted waters with a crew dying of scurvy and winter coming on. The last thing he needed was a know-it-all ship's doctor challenging him. Some greenhorn kid who'd never been to sea."

"Point taken, but still . . ."

"Hush, now. We've got a ways to go."

CHAPTER 16

"Pavlov Bay," Natasha shouted as she cut the throttle. "That's Long Beach."

She shut the engine off and the boat slid slowly to a stop. We were running close inshore along a sandy beach. I could tell by the sun that I had been asleep for some hours.

"Wow, I'm stiff," Natasha said, massaging her right arm. "That's Cape Tolstoi over there. I think we should refuel before we cross."

Together we lifted the engine cover. The fuel tank was located just forward of the engine. I found a large galvanized funnel and carefully filled the tank from one of the five-gallon cans while Natasha flexed her arms and twisted at the waist. She shivered violently.

"Sorry I overslept," I said. "You should have awakened me."

"You looked so vulnerable I didn't have the heart." Natasha grinned and picked up the starter cord.

"Let me." I took the cord from her and wrapped it around the flywheel the way Gus did, primed the engine, and gave a sharp pull. Nothing happened. I tried again and then again. The flywheel spun sluggishly and I could hear the valves pop as they opened and closed, but nothing more. A little dark engine oil began to drip from the exhaust. I pulled hard again and the engine backfired and started in reverse, throwing me flat in the bilge. Natasha quickly killed the engine and put her hand over her mouth to hide her laughter.

Angrily I tried again and yet again. The engine would not even fire. I sat down on the gunwale, disgusted.

"Maybe it's flooded," Natasha said. "Maybe you don't have to prime it so much when it's already warm. Tell you what, let's row ashore and build a fire. I'm cold and hungry."

"Do we have the time?"

"I don't see why not. We've made good time so far. We got a big push from the tide. And we have to anchor by Tolstoi no matter what, so we just have to leave enough time to cross Pavlov before dark."

We lowered the engine cover and I unlashed the two oars while Natasha found two sets of thole pins and mounted them on the gunwales. The oars were more than ten feet long and very cumbersome but sitting side by side on the engine cover we managed to work our way toward the beach, our elbows bumping all the while.

"All together now, John Lars." Natasha laughed and then after a few more strokes the skiff struck ground. She kicked off her boots and rolled up her pants and jumped overboard. I followed her lead and together we pulled the heavy bow partway on land. Natasha took the bow line and tied it to a drift log and then walked up to the grass at the beginning of the dunes. She came back with some small sticks and a handful of dry grass for tinder. Soon a fire was going and a kettle next to it. Sam had given us a salmon from the *Black Cat's* hold and Natasha cut two bright red fillets from it. She greased the skillet with a piece of salt pork and began to fry the fish, kneeling on the sand and humming softly.

I watched her work. Despite my sleep I felt tired and out of sorts. My throat was scratchy and my entire body had the sort of damp, misfit feeling of an oncoming cold. There was a dusting of sand on Natasha's trousers and for some reason looking at it irritated me.

"Where do you get all your energy?" I said waspishly.

She glanced at me, her brows knitted. "I'm nearly home, John Lars. Every step takes me closer to what I know."

I picked up a stone and tossed it toward the water.

"Look at those mountains," Natasha said, pointing westward at a series of jagged spires that could have been a Paleolithic cathedral. "The Aghileen Pinnacles. In Nebraska sometimes we'd sing this hymn, 'From Greenland's Icy Mountains,' and I'd always picture this. The rest of the hymn is about missions in the jungle but I never heard that part. After the first line I'd be miles away, somewhere out here."

I threw another stone and listened to it clink across the shingle and plop in the water. Ducks and drakes.

The salmon was delicious. We ate it straight from the pan with our fingers, accompanied only by pilot bread and butter. Natasha ate very daintily despite the lack of utensils. When she finished she thrust her hand into the sand to clean the grease from it and then washed by the water's edge. She had made a pot of tea as well and as we sat drinking it my mood improved. Natasha unbraided her hair and then began to brush it with her fingers.

"Long hair is such a nuisance," she said. "Maybe I should just chop it all off. What do you think? Isn't that the way girls are wearing it back east?"

"Lots of them are. At least the jazzy ones, like my sister Alyson. And the skirts are getting shorter and shorter. Do you know the illustrator John Held?"

"Not unless he does Methodist devotional literature."

"No." I laughed. "He does stuff for *Collier's*. Girls in short skirts and guys in raccoon coats. Flapper style."

"Once, my girlfriend Anna and I sneaked off to downtown Lincoln. We went to see a moving picture show, then we put on makeup in the powder room. We belted up our skirts so they were almost to the knee and walked around window-shopping, hoping somebody would flirt with us. But we kept seeing our reflections and breaking into giggles. We had these horrible gray church stockings on. They looked so silly."

"Did you meet any boys?"

"Nope, the only one who noticed us was the church organist. She was downtown getting her dentures filed to points or something. Boy, did we ever get in trouble. But I just hated those long, drab dresses. Problem is, with short skirts you couldn't run. It wouldn't be ladylike."

I thought that in my upbringing running even in long skirts would not be considered proper.

"How about dancing?" Natasha asked. "Do girls wear short skirts to dances?"

"If they're going to a speakeasy, sure. But not at a formal dance like a college prom. They still wear fancy gowns for those."

"Did you go to your college prom?"

"Nope."

"Why not? I wouldn't have missed it for the world."

"Oh, I don't know. Didn't really want to. Didn't have a date. But my mother used to make me go to cotillions and debutante balls at home in Seattle. Not to mention Miss Marian's dance class in grade school. Learning to waltz when I could have been playing baseball. I hated all of it."

"Hated it? We used to have dances at Unga. There was this dance hall, an octagonal building from the Apollo mine. We'd dance till daybreak, even us kids. I'd give anything to go to one of your cotillions."

"Nah, they're terrible. I'd try to hide but I'd end up having to sign the dance cards for all the wallflowers, all my friends' ugly sisters."

I thought of Natasha wading in a stream with her dress kilted up around her long brown legs, of her smiling at the tiller of a skiff, and even facing down a grizzly bear. I could not imagine her wild and blithe spirit at something so stiff and dreary as a formal dance and I laughed aloud at the incongruity.

"I just can't picture you at a fancy dance," I said.

I instantly knew I had said the wrong thing. An odd look compounded of shame and anger crossed her face and she picked up a stick and stubbed it savagely in the fire.

"John Lars," she said, "if you even think of turning Gus and Sam in for robbing that trap I'll never speak to you again."

"What . . . ?" I said, caught wrong footed as always. I tried to think of a way to explain what I meant but my stupid remark was gone irretrievably downriver.

"Let's go." Natasha picked up the skillet and kicked the fire apart.

The tide had fallen and we had to struggle to launch the boat. Finally it floated and I hopped in over the bow but Natasha continued to push until the water was halfway up her thighs before she climbed aboard. She took the starter rope, wrapped it around the opposite way and gave a vicious pull. The engine roared to life and she ran the skiff in reverse in a long arc away from the beach, then cut the throttle till the engine stuttered and backfired. She instantly opened the throttle wide and with a jerk the shaft began to spin the opposite way. Natasha put the tiller hard over and 67 spun so quickly that a little water from our own wake slopped over the bow. She set a course for Cape Tolstoi, sitting at the tiller with her pants soaking wet and her jaw set in a firm line. Once she looked back over her shoulders at the Aghileen Pinnacles.

I thought about the series of drawings of seed dispersal mechanisms that I had made for the museum. Some were coiled like catapults, some bristling with spears. They looked more like mechanisms of warfare than reproduction. Maybe plants know something we don't.

The crossing did not take long but it was early evening as we coasted along in the lee of Cape Tolstoi. Sunlight slanted across the water. We followed the curve of the shore to the back of a shallow bay. Natasha cut the engine and without a word went to the bow and rummaged around till she found the small anchor, which she then threw overboard.

In the wake of the engine noise the silence was almost preternatural. I could hear the whistle of duck wings and the quiet call of some inland bird. I watched a flock of what I thought were phalaropes turning together, the sun flashing on their wings. They alighted on the shore nearby and worked along the water's edge, jerky as marionettes. I could hear a ticking sound as the motor cooled.

Natasha was making up the bedrolls in the bow. Since the night was clear she put them on the floorboards aft of the cuddyhole formed by the decking. First, she spread an old sail as a groundsheet, then she unrolled the blankets. I thought it best to keep out of her way.

I assumed that we were sleeping on the boat rather than the beach because of bears but I was afraid to ask.

When we lay down together we were practically touching but I felt like a medieval knight with a naked sword in the bed between him and the lady. Natasha pulled the blanket over her head. She must have been very tired but I was wide awake now.

"Just how does that game work you were playing with Sam?" I asked.

"It's chess," Natasha said, her voice muffled by the blanket.

"I know, but the pieces were arranged differently. How does that go?"

She pulled the blanket off her face and spluttered as if blowing out a piece of lint. "Let's see, in the back row I had my corners empty and then went knight, king, rook, bishop. Sam took black and he had the right corner empty then the rook and king, then three blanks, then the knight. I can't quite remember how we laid our second rows. I'd have to draw it out to be sure."

"But the pawns are different, too."

"Yeah, you put four in the third row and three in the fourth row, staggered. After that the rules are pretty much the same, I guess, only you have to play real fast. Playing slow is almost worse than losing. I don't know; we borrowed it from the Russians but it suffered a sea change somewhere."

"Have you ever played real chess?"

"That is 'real chess.'"

"I wish we had a chessboard right now," I said peevishly.

"I would annihilate you, John Lars. I know how your mind works. You're way too timid."

"You ever play a Queen's Gambit?"

"Yes . . . no . . . I don't know."

"How about the King's Indian?"

"Whatever are you talking about?"

"Chess, the way it's supposed to be played."

"Find us a board, John Lars. I'll leave your bones scattered on the tundra."

"Can't scare me," I taunted back and we both laughed, the tension gone. In truth I had never tried a Queen's Gambit—too risky. Natasha was right: I played a very conservative game, developing a strong middle and trading pieces grudgingly. My roommate Palmer would have liked Aleut chess. He kept his knights moving like jitterbugs while his rooks made headlong dashes into enemy territory, but he rarely beat me.

"So what was it Sam asked you in Aleut before the last game?" I asked.

"None of your business."

"Come on."

"Well, if you must know, he was making a joke about you being my boyfriend."

"Oh, great."

Natasha was quiet for a moment and then added, "Actually it was a little vulgar, but it sounds a lot more rude in English."

"I'll bet." I needed to change the subject. "So do you think any of those stories Gus told were true?"

"Why not?"

"They were pretty extravagant."

Natasha laughed. "Gus was a bit much. He was like the prairie chickens back in Nebraska. The cocks like to fan their tail feathers and strut in front of the hens with their chests all puffed out."

"Sounds like Gus all right."

"Maybe all males are like that. I remember on the Pribilofs the old bulls were the first ashore in the spring. They had these huge necks and shoulders and they'd roar so loud you could hear them above the surf, even on the windiest days. Each one tried to grab as big a harem as possible. You never saw such pushing and shoving and bellowing. The young males had their own area behind but they'd have to run the gauntlet past the bulls to get to the water."

"But sooner or later the young ones grow up and replace the bulls."

"Some of them. But it's the young males they kill for pelts. The workers drive them overland to the killing grounds and they go like sheep. They don't resist at all. But the old bulls attack anything that comes near."

"Well, you sure fall for the old bulls," I grumbled.

"John Lars . . . in chess we call the king *alix*—old man—but the pawns are *layakucan*—little boys."

"So do you call the queen a crone?"

Natasha turned toward me. "Do you know how appropriate it was the first time I met you, you were falling overboard with your shoes on the wrong feet?"

"Wait a minute . . ."

"You remind me of this young minister at my college. He was good on homiletics but sure didn't know much about girls. I used to flirt with him, mostly out of boredom. Flutter my eyelashes at him while he was lecturing, stuff like that. He'd get completely flustered and forget what he was saying."

"What happened in the end?" I was not flattered by the comparison.

"Nothing, of course. Well, he did have a heart-to-heart talk with me, all sheepdog eyes and earnest looks. He told me about his 'expectations' and about his responsibility to the lower races. Which included me, I guess. What a drip. And his Adam's apple sort of perched on his collar and gulped when he talked, like a heron swallowing a fish. I bet he ends up married to somebody like Miss Hutchinson back in Nome. Talk about the white man's burden."

That made me chuckle, picturing the ironbound Miss Hutchinson.

"What's it like being a boy, John Lars?" Natasha asked in a more conciliatory tone. "I mean . . . there's never been anybody I could ask. But how do boys feel when they meet girls?"

"I don't know." I stared into the darkening sky and listened to the night sounds. "Terrified mostly. Like at a cotillion when you're supposed to ask some girl to dance and then make polite conversation? I'd rather deal with that grizzly bear back at Izembek."

"But do you ever . . ." She raised up one elbow and looked at me but then lay back down. "Oh, what's the use? Boys never understand. The teachers were always telling me my talk was too bold and I guess it is." She rolled onto her side with her back toward me. I stared into the deepening blue of the sky. A few stars were shining, more every minute. I tried to catch the moment at which a pinprick of light became visible against the darkening sky. Somewhere a flock of birds landed on the water with a sound like tearing silk.

CHAPTER 17

"Tide's turned, we're starting to drag," Natasha said. "Time to pull the anchor." Fog lay thickly along the surface of the water and the shore was barely visible but directly overhead I could see blue sky. Together we raised the engine cover and this time I succeeded in starting the engine. Natasha took the tiller while I hauled the anchor. When it broke the surface dripping wet sand she turned and headed out the bay at half throttle.

"We'll have to take it easy till the fog lifts," Natasha said. Conversation was just possible at this speed. "We'll be okay if we keep the shore just in view on the portside. Here, you take her awhile. I'm going to make some coffee."

I took the tiller. I could tell from her voice that her anger was gone, washed away in the night, lucky for me. Nothing was visible forward but unruffled water and cottony fog. Off to port the shore was an indistinct gray line. Natasha took a brass Primus stove from a locker, pumped its little plunger handle, poured methylated spirits in the burner, and put a match to it. When the burner was cherry-red she opened the kerosene valve and bright yellow flames flared. I could hear the stove roar in counterpoint to the engine. Natasha balanced the coffee pot on the burner using the hem of her shawl as a potholder. Still kneeling she looked around at the fog-shrouded water. There was a ghostly triad of rocks to port but I had already seen it and altered course.

When the water boiled she added grounds and turned off the stove. She stirred the coffee then poured two cups and handed me one. She sat beside me on the stern seat, allowing me to keep the tiller. I was grateful for the warmth of the cup and the touch of her shoulder.

"Thank goodness this boat belonged to Norwegians," she said. "All the Italian fishermen use little coal stoves. They're a disaster." She tossed the dregs of her cup overboard and started to pour another but looking to starboard she stiffened suddenly and then reached over and cut the engine. Following her gaze I saw the topmasts of a small schooner barely visible above the fog, like the faintest of pencil marks against gray paper. The boat was a ways offshore, headed east but at a greater speed than our own. We could hear the distant mutter of its engine.

"What is it?" I asked in a low voice although we could not possibly be heard on the distant deck. Natasha shook her head and continued to stare until the other boat faded from view.

"Nothing," she said. "Just another boat."

Within an hour we left the fog bank to find the sun shining and the sea empty of all but birds. Across the open water to the south an island was visible. "Unga," Natasha said. She put her hand over mine on the tiller and turned the boat till it pointed at a distant headland.

The crossing took several hours. Despite the strong coffee Natasha's eyelids began to droop and she dozed for a time, leaning heavily against me. I liked the pressure of her shoulder. I was ever more fascinated by Natasha though I did not feel free to say so. Or even feel so. Being enchanted twice on the same voyage was a bit excessive, especially when still spellbound by the first. That did not say much about my constant heart.

Natasha was a never-ending surprise. I was embarrassed to admit, even to myself, that at first I had condescended to her because she was part Indian. Everyone I knew took Indians' inferiority for granted, it was what we were taught from the cradle on. But here on Natasha's home ground I realized how smart and decisive she was. I was dazzled by her speed, and her beauty. She was fearless and straightforward where Audrey was all spin and angles. Audrey would lead me on and then slide away, always out of reach until suddenly she wasn't. Thinking of her now awakened the never completely dormant desire. Five times we had made love and I remembered every touch and every soft word. *Ensorcelled*, a word and feeling I had never known before that spring.

I shifted uneasily. Natasha opened her eyes, stretched, and looked around. "Unga Spit," she said, pointing ahead at a long, sandy spit. "Let's land there. I need to stretch."

She took the tiller and when we reached the spit she ran us gently up on the shore. We dragged the boat a few feet inland and set anchor. By the drift line we built a fire and made a late breakfast.

"I didn't sleep much last night," Natasha said. "I was afraid the wind would come up and we'd drag anchor. I kept waking up to watch." She looked up and down the beach then pointed east. "There's a creek mouth over there. I'm going to go wash up. It's still early. We've got time to rest a bit."

She left her coat and boots behind and walked down to the water's edge. For want of anything better to do I began to walk the drift line in the opposite direction, then turned and headed inland, climbing the first wave of dunes. From the crest I looked back and saw Natasha. She had taken off her clothes and was wading in the water. Embarrassed, I looked away despite the distance.

The back slope of the dune was covered with a tufted grass that was probably a type of brome. Behind the dune was a freshwater pond with wild iris growing along its edge. Amidst the marshy tussocks I found adder's tongue and cow parsnip and an orchid I had not yet collected—a *Spiranthes* called "ladies' tresses." I picked one of the convoluted blossoms.

Despite the extravagant shape it fit my notion of a Linnaean world, one as sharply delineated as the squares of a chessboard.

Yet Aleut chess had shown me that the game was not as fixed and immutable as I had believed. And maybe the Linnaean system was no more than a convenient naming system that had very little to do with the wild sprawl of life. It might be time to reconsider my beliefs.

I walked back across the dune and fetched my drawing pad from the skiff. I began to sketch the ladies' tresses but my hand felt a little clumsy and I cursed beneath my breath. I heard a footstep in the sand and looked up to see Natasha, her pants folded over one arm. Her coarse linen shirt nearly reached her knees.

"Look," she said and held out a small rock. It was petrified wood. I could see the grain and a small knothole perfectly rendered in rust-colored rock. "When I was a little girl we used to come here for picnics and collect bits, but this one's nothing. A few miles from here there are whole petrified stumps."

"But how'd they get here?" I looked around at the barren hillsides and tried to imagine what cataclysm could strip these hills bare of trees and change the wood to stone.

"Noah's flood?" Natasha said, grinning.

She had rinsed her hair but the sun and wind had already dried it and it hung heavy and loose on her shoulders. She turned to tend the fire and I had a sudden desire to kiss the backs of her knees. Looking back Natasha caught my gaze and knelt down, smiling shyly and tugging at the hem of her shirt.

"I know that flower," she said. "Is it another orchid?"

"Yup. Ladies' tresses. I like the shape of the petals. I've been trying to catch the exact curve but my hand's a little rusty."

"I wish I could draw." Natasha spread her peacoat over her legs and leaned back against a piece of driftwood and stifled a yawn.

"I wish I could." I was annoyed that my one talent, my sense of line, had deserted me. I flipped to a new page in the sketchbook and began again. I could hear the distant cry of gulls. I looked at a nearby blade of grass and noticed that as it had danced with the wind its tip had drawn a perfect circle in the sand. I stared again at my drawing pad, intimidated by the blank page.

Natasha had fallen asleep, lying back with her hair shielding her face. Her chest rose and fell almost imperceptibly in a gentle rhythm. The peacoat had partially slipped from her legs. I turned back to my drawing and tried again to catch the curve of the petals but my pencil carried the line till it became a throat and the sepals became the collar of Natasha's shirt. It was not a new drawing but a transformation of the old and for once my hand and eye did not stumble over one another.

The fire snapped and a burning ember flew out to glow briefly on the sand. Natasha opened her eyes and sat up.

"Spruce makes the noisiest fire. It'll pop and hiss like it's talking to you." She stretched her coat on the sand and sat on it with her legs tucked beneath her and began to braid her hair. This time she gathered it in a single loose braid which she pinned on top of her head, exposing her neck. Each time I watched her braid her hair she seemed to do it a little differently.

When she finished she came over and knelt beside me and looked at the drawing. She put an arm across my shoulders and studied the sketch for a long time. "I thought you only did flowers," she said, finally.

"Mostly. The flower wasn't working and this just sort of happened."

"Will you give it to me?"

Without comment I tore the sheet out of my pad and handed it to her.

"Thank you," she said and carefully rolled it. "We'd better go now. We stayed a little long."

The flooding tide had partially floated the skiff and turned it sideways. As we pushed it free the shallow water felt warm from the sun.

"Almost home," I said and Natasha flashed a quick grin.

"Think people will be glad to see you?" I asked.

"Some of them will."

"Only some?"

"I was a bit of a problem child till the teachers took me under their wing. Pa and I weren't what you'd call stellar citizens."

She hopped in the skiff and quickly pulled on her dungarees. Still barefoot she started the engine and we headed out. Beyond Unga Spit there was a deep bay. Pointing into it Natasha yelled, "Zachary Bay. There's a bluff with a seam of coal. We used to gather it for the stove."

After we crossed the mouth of the bay we turned south into the strait that separated Popof and Unga islands. The first bay on Popof contained a few buildings with metal roofs.

"Sand Point," Natasha said with a big smile, indicating the only village other than Unga in the Shumagins. "And that's Egg Island ahead." She pointed at a small island still a few miles away. She had to speak with her hand cupped next to my ear and through her hand and her warm breath I felt the bright spark of joy that animated her.

We passed Egg Island on the Unga side. Natasha steered close inshore near a cluster of small cabins and outbuildings. "Hardscratch Point," she said. "That's the Sobergs' place." I could see a cow standing in a pasture, its head turned to watch us pass. Natasha waved at it merrily.

Beyond the Sobergs' farm, however, she steered even closer to shore and slowed the engine to an idle. We coasted along, slowly losing way as she stared at a collection of weathered buildings. The shingled roof of the main cabin was thick with moss and one of the outbuildings had collapsed.

"That was home," Natasha said. "For a while, at least. I'm surprised nobody's moved in. It looks like somebody salvaged the wire from the fox runs, or maybe Pa sold it before he died."

"Do you want to go ashore?"

"Not today. I'm not ready for it. Wrong kind of memories."

She stared somberly at the cabin as we drifted. Grass stood high in the dooryard. The faint clang of a cowbell came from beyond the hill.

"Just beyond this is a place they called Valhalla," Natasha said. "The man who lived there always had a big vat of homebrew and the Norwegian men would gather there all winter."

She bumped the engine to just above idle and we slowly motored past. "Time to move on. I need a bath and a change of clothes." She plucked at her dungarees. "I'll have to borrow something to wear in Unga till I catch up with my carpet bag."

"I thought you were tired of those mission dresses anyway."

"I am, but I spent practically my last dollar in Seattle on a nice piece of flowered muslin I was going to make into a dress. I'm fixin' to get it back."

"Come on," I scoffed. "Those two are probably halfway to Kodiak by now. Or back in Nome."

Natasha opened the throttle wide. "Nagai," she shouted above the engine. "We'll find them on Nagai." She pointed southeast. Beyond Unga, across an expanse of water, I could see the long, dark outline of what had to be Nagai Island.

PART IV

Unga

The wind bloweth where it listeth,
And thou hearest the sound thereof,
But canst not tell
Whence it cometh, and whither it goeth:
So is every one
That is born of the Spirit.

—John: 3:8

CHAPTER 18

A collection of small frame houses lay situated near the mouth of a bay that opened to the southeast. The bay was Delarof Harbor and the village was Unga.

Natasha brought us into a landing place at the base of a small hill, alongside a row of beached skiffs. An old skin-covered baidarka sat on a rack nearby. Three small boys stopped playing ball and helped us haul the skiff ashore, then stood regarding me solemnly.

Two elderly white ladies appeared at the top of the knoll, waved uncertainly to Natasha and began to walk carefully down the hill holding their long skirts. I assumed they were Natasha's schoolteacher friends, alerted to our presence by small-town telepathy. Natasha ran to them and gave them each a hug but I stood awkwardly by our boat. I could not make out the words as their voices fluted and trilled. Natasha gestured in explanation and the shorter of the ladies touched her high collar with a nervous gesture. She gathered her skirt and kneaded it with her fists unconsciously. Natasha called me over and introduced me to Miss Devlin and Miss Dennison. Miss Devlin was the taller of the two and appeared to be the one in charge.

"Pleased to make your acquaintance, Mr. Nelson," she said. "I believe we can put you in old Hjalmar's spare room for the night. Natasha will stay with us, of course." She signaled to the small boys and said to them, "Take this young man to Mr. Mork's house, boys, if you please, and ask for his hospitality."

Natasha went off without a backward glance and the three boys led me through Unga. There were no true streets; the houses appeared to be scattered almost randomly but in a short time the boys deposited me at the door of a tidy bungalow with green shutters. They knocked on the door and then ran, laughing, which left me to explain the situation to the white-haired man who answered the door.

His name was Hjalmar Mork and he was an almost-retired miner. My sudden appearance at his door did not faze him in the least. He showed me his spare bedroom and then laid out a supper of soup and bread on a table covered with checked oilcloth. His kitchen windows overlooked Delarof Harbor.

"So Natasha's come back," he said as I ate the soup greedily. "I had half a mind she'd stay outside in the big city and never see Unga again. Or maybe them Nebrasky missionaries would clip her wings. Not that I was so worried about that. I'd back Natasha against the whole Methodist Church, and give good odds to boot."

He laughed as though pleased at the thought and poured himself another cup of coffee. His hands were bent and gnarled and he could scarcely hold the cup. He was so much like Clyde Glover at the trap barge that they could have been formed in the same mold. Or perhaps this country was the anvil and the wind the hammer that forged these twisted, bright, garrulous old men.

"The minute I seen your skiff come 'round the corner I knew it was Natasha by the set of her head. Many's the time I watched her comin' in from the farm in their old power skiff. Her maybe fourteen years old with her mother dead and old Karl probably drunk on the kitchen floor and her not afraid of nothin'. Her head up like she was the goddamn Queen of Sheba instead of a halfbreed livin' on charity." He shook his head. "Place seemed about half dead when she left."

"So you've known her a long time?"

"I remember the first day she showed up for school. Barefoot, in coveralls two sizes too big, and no lunch bucket. The girls laughed at her and she ignored them, but when the boys teased her she beat the tar out of poor Alex Soberg."

"I thought she was some kind of teacher's pet."

"Well, she was that, too. She's smart as a whip and she ain't got no quit in her. Doesn't even know the word. That goes a long way with Miss Devlin. And me, too. But it's gonna get her in trouble one of these days, sure as God made the grass green."

Hjalmar would have willingly talked all night but I was tired and begged leave. As I got up from the table he looked hard at me and said, "Natasha, if she's your friend she'll do anything for you. Stick her hand in the fire, needs be. Best be sure you're worthy of it."

The next morning I woke early and slipped out the front door without waking Hjalmar. No one was afoot in the village. High gray clouds covered the sky and a fierce wind blew in from the southwest. A few drops of rain hit me, hard as buckshot. I walked along the path that meandered amongst the houses till I found a white clapboard building with a sign by the front door saying "U.S. Post Office." There was a flagpole by the front door but no flag flying. I tried the door only to find it locked. I knocked softly, tentatively, and was about to turn away when a woman appeared pulling tight the belt of a housecoat.

"Excuse me," I said. "I wasn't sure if you were open or not."

"We don't usually get anybody this early," she said. "If you want to mail something the mail boat's not due back for two weeks."

"I just wanted to see if I had any letters. General delivery for John Lars Nelson?" I stepped into the foyer. There was a wooden counter and a shelf with a series of pigeonholes. From the interior of the house came the smell of bacon frying.

The woman grabbed a sheaf of letters from one of the pigeonholes, riffled through them, and handed me two envelopes: one from my mother, one from Audrey Arbuthnot.

"Thank you, thanks very much. Sorry to disturb you." I said and the woman gave me a wan smile as I slipped back through the door.

I sat on the front stoop, opened my mother's letter, and scanned it briefly. One of the upstairs maids had quit; father was back in Washington; my sister Alyson had a new beau—a junior partner in father's firm—for whom Mother harbored great hopes. I folded the letter and put it in my pocket. I looked at the lilac envelope from Audrey, feeling the pull of the marionette strings, then tore it open:

> My Dearest John,
> Walter has asked me to write and tell you that we've been thinking of you. I hope this finds you well, if it finds you at all—I remember from China how dreadful the rural post can be! I hope your travels have not been too taxing. At least your weather must be cool. New Haven has been so beastly hot that even the lightest silk frock is a burden. But my garden is doing splendidly in all this heat. I wish you were here to walk with me among the roses, or that I was out there searching for orchids with you. At least if I was there I could rescue you from whatever tedious companions you've found. I hate to be so brief but I really must run. My new friend Ned is waiting. Walter is so dreadfully busy but Ned has been an absolute angel about taking me shopping. He says that he knows you. Please think of me often and bring the orchid back to me speedily.
>
> In haste but with much love,
> Audrey

Light blue ink on lilac paper, handwriting coiled as fine as a seashell, a trace of perfume, but despite the coy, even flirtatious tone the letter seemed oddly impersonal. I crumpled the letter in exasperation and then smoothed it out and read it again, seeking something that wasn't there. Ned? Who the hell was Ned? The only Ned I knew was a tall, dark-haired senior, a member of DKE who rowed in the varsity boat.

I stood and headed back the way I had come. If Audrey was a flower 'capreolate' would be part of her description. A term for plants with tendrils, and the ability to entwine and entangle. And sometimes, like bittersweet, to strangle.

In the open roadstead a small schooner pulled against its anchor like a dog fighting a chain. She looked a little longer than the *Emilia* overall and her masts were raked aft. I was pretty sure she was the *Seal*.

Two women stood on the knoll above the landing place, their long skirts flaring in the wind. I walked toward them and found Natasha talking with a woman whose long hair was shot with gray.

"Lena, this is my friend John Lars," Natasha said, "the flower hunter I was telling you about."

Lena extended her hand. She was very lovely but like all Bering Sea women her hands were rough and her grip was firm. There were fine lines around her eyes like the craquelure in an oil painting. Though she smiled at me I thought her eyes were the saddest I had ever seen.

"Flowers," she said. "What a lovely thing to hunt."

"Yes'm, only we haven't found many so far."

"Natasha told me a little about your troubles."

"I guess you know Jason Davis," I said.

"I met him years ago in Petropavlovsk."

"Siberia?" At the far end of town I could see a man chopping wood outside his house. By the time the sound of the blow reached us he had already raised the axe for another swing.

"Siberia," she said and smiled again. "Where all dreams go to die. Or all dreamers."

A boisterous shout interrupted us and Francis X. Fitzgerald came walking along the path carrying a box of groceries. Behind him came a tall, bearded Cossack wearing a baggy gray sweater, woolen pants and greased leather sea boots. He carried an even larger box. Fitzgerald put his box down beside us but the Cossack continued down toward the landing.

"Young Jack, me erstwhile shipmate," Fitzgerald said. "And Natasha, the belle of Unga, which ain't saying overmuch. I heard at the store you two had hooked up. Where's Jason Davis?"

"Headed north," Natasha said brusquely. "Kodiak."

"Well, ain't that a happy chance. We was talkin' about headin' that way ourselves. And where might you be bound, Jack?"

"Andronica," Natasha said before I could get a word in. "And then maybe over to Pavlof on the mainland."

"She callin' the shots now, kid?"

"It's her home; she knows the best places for flowers." I was a bit annoyed at Natasha for assuming I would be dumb enough to blurt out my plans. I was equally sure Lena would never tell Max Gottschalk that Jason Davis had marooned us, though for my purposes I cared not one whit what the *Seal* and the *Emilia Galotti* had to do with one another.

I heard a clatter of oars as the Cossack launched a dory. He stood knee-deep in the slight swell that broke around the point, looking up at us.

"Time to go," Fitzgerald said. "Max ain't the man to be kept waitin', now is he, Lena?"

Lena said nothing and Fitzgerald shouldered his box and started down the grassy slope, calling back, "Good luck with them posies, Jack."

Lena stared out at the *Seal*, which dipped and rolled as if impatient to be gone. A single figure was visible on deck, leaning on the after-rail. Lena turned toward us and said, "My pleasure to meet you, John Lars." She gave Natasha a hug. "Try to be at least a little careful. I don't want anything to happen to you."

"Not a chance," Natasha grinned.

Lena touched her again and then walked down the hill to where the Cossack handed her into the dory. We watched them pull toward the *Seal*.

"Bit of a surprise running into those guys," I said, as we turned and began to walk towards the house.

"That was the *Seal* we saw back at Tolstoi. I thought so at the time but didn't want to believe it."

"What do you think they're up to?"

"No good."

Natasha's hair was clean and shining and pinned severely in place. Looking down I could see that she wore black lace-up boots beneath her long dress.

"You look all proper and schoolmarmish this morning."

"Protective coloration. Besides, there wasn't much of a selection."

The wind flattened the dress against her legs, producing an effect very unlike when Miss Devlin wore it, I imagined. I looked around. The man chopping wood had gone back inside. There was smoke from a dozen chimneys but the only person in evidence was an old man leaning on a cane as he made his way slowly along the path.

"Where is everybody?" I asked.

"They keep late hours in the villages, I don't know why. People stay up all night and don't get moving till afternoon."

"Then what got you up so early?"

"Visiting my father's grave."

The cemetery was not far off. An iron fence enclosed the weathered headstones. Two stunted spruce trees twisted in the wind. Someone must have imported them from the mainland to keep the dead company.

"Were your friends glad to see you?" I asked.

"I think so, but what's better they offered me a job at the school. Miss Dennison wants to retire and spend part of the winter back home in Kansas, only they haven't been able to find a replacement. It's not much money but at least it's a job."

"That's lucky."

"But I told them I was committed to take you to Nagai first."

"How'd they take that?"

"Not very well." Natasha laughed. "Not hardly. Traveling alone with a strange man? But I said you were a gentleman and I leaned pretty hard on your association with Yale. Not that Miss Devlin seemed overly impressed with that."

"Maybe she has doctrinal differences with the Congregationalists."

"Or maybe she met a Yalie somewhere." Natasha took my arm briefly and then let it go. "Anyway, you and Hjalmar are invited to dinner tonight. Be sure to bring your best manners. You'll be under close scrutiny so don't ask why the ketchup bottle isn't on the table."

Natasha wanted to visit Hjalmar Mork. We found him in his tidy kitchen drinking coffee and staring out the windows at Delarof Harbor.

"Flowers," Hjalmar said after we talked a little about our plans. "I never paid 'em no mind. They was just the frosting on the overburden, so to speak. But if you're going to Nagai you'll have to wait for the wind to die."

"We need to come up with food and some other gear," I said.

"No problem." Hjalmar poured us more coffee from a graniteware pot. "I got a tent and tarp I can let ya have. And more bedding and camp gear. Gas and grub can get charged to my account at the store. I know Natasha at least will be good for it."

Hjalmar found a map of Nagai to replace the one still on the *Emilia Galotti*. The map was nearly worn through at the creases and cracked slightly as he unfolded it on the kitchen table.

"Nagai," Hjalmar said meditatively. "I spent part of a summer there, prospectin'. Didn't find a damned thing. I worked around Wooly Head, here"—he pointed with a twisted forefinger—"and Eagle Harbor and then toward the north end some. Kind of bleak country to my way of thinkin'. Nobody goes there much. You plannin' to hunker down in one spot or range around?"

"Both, I guess. I'm supposed to survey the whole island but I'll do extensive cataloguing at different sites, in different terrains."

"But why Nagai, I can't help askin'."

"Oh, historical interest. Because Bering landed there." I evaded the question for the umpteenth time.

"Hmm," Hjalmar said skeptically. He folded the map and handed it to me. "I best lend ya a pick and shovel. Sometimes you find somethin' a little different than what you think you're lookin' for."

Natasha had been looking at a small collection of rocks and minerals on a shelf. She picked up a large black rock and tossed it to me, saying, "Hey, catch, John Lars."

I grabbed the rock but nearly threw it over my head in surprise at its lightness. It felt like a solidified piece of sea foam.

"Tuff," Hjalmar said, laughing. "Lots of it on the beaches around here. And pumice, too, from the volcanoes. Took me a long time to get used to the idea of a rock that could float."

That afternoon we visited the village store. We purchased odds and ends of gear from a list Natasha and Hjalmar had compiled. As Natasha rummaged through the pile of goods on the counter the storekeeper said to me, "There was a couple of gents off a schooner asking after you."

"Yeah, the *Seal*. We ran into them."

"They was looking for charts of the outer islands but we're out of them. I told them Hjalmar might have some but I guess they didn't go there?"

"Nope," I said.

I took a bath that afternoon in a galvanized tub and then, dressed in new canvas pants and a flannel shirt, I walked with Hjalmar to the small house behind the one-room schoolhouse. Dinner proved to be something of an ordeal, an ordeal conducted with impeccable manners as we ate corned beef and cabbage off china plates with a willow pattern. Miss Devlin asked polite questions about my family, about Yale, and about the plant survey. Small talk, but something of an inquisition as well and I barely tasted the meal.

Hjalmar's table manners were severely correct, almost stiff. I assumed that he rarely came to the house but I found out later that he was in fact a frequent wintertime dinner companion for the ladies. To give myself relief from the questioning I asked him about the sample of tuff in his home.

"Probably from the explosion of Mount Katmai," he said, "But there's other volcanoes along the chain. It's a pretty lively place."

"You were somewhere nearby when Katmai erupted, weren't you, Mr. Mork?" Miss Devlin asked.

"Yes'm, but not too close. I was prospecting on Kodiak with my partner Ben Turnipseed. June 1912, it was, but for all we knew it was the end of the world. We didn't hear the explosion, mind, and had no idea what was goin' on. First thing we knew was this ash fallin' from the sky. It fell for three days, heavy, fine ash. It piled up and drifted like snow and even avalanched on the hills. Terrifyin', dark, chokin', stuff, but not hot. Second day we decided we'd best walk into town. Dark as Hades at midday, beggin' your pardon, ladies. We was wadin' through ash, chokin' on ash. The trees was coated with it. On the outskirts of town we found buildings collapsed from the weight of the ash."

"It must have been horrifying."

"It sure enough was. I had a bandanna across my nose and mouth but old Ben, he just knew the end had come and all through the walk he kept yellin' out this one Bible verse till finally it was burned in my brain: 'And he opened the bottomless pit; and there arose a smoke out of the pit, as the smoke of a great furnace; and the sun and the air were darkened . . .'"

"That would be the ninth chapter of Revelations," Miss Devlin said.

"Yes'm, I believe it was. In Kodiak, now, it weren't so dark but people was in a rare panic. They was shelterin' in saloons and old Ben, he goes in one and gets up on a table and commences to preach, readin' out of his Bible. Let me see if I can find it."

Hjalmar took a Bible from a bookshelf and a pair of reading glasses from his pocket and began to look through Revelations, muttering beneath his breath. "Here it is." He cleared his throat and read, " 'When he had opened the sixth seal, and, lo, there was a great earthquake; and the sun became a sackcloth of hair, and the moon became as blood; and the stars of heaven fell unto the earth . . .' There. I never seen no stars fall but the rest about fits. Old Ben was up there preachin' away and people was prayin' and babies was cryin'. I had half a mind to take up a collection."

"You are such a joker, Mr. Mork," Miss Dennison said reprovingly.

"Yes'm. Well, there was a revenue cutter in town—the *Manning*, I believe it was—and it took us all on board. We all thought we'd seen the last of Kodiak at the very least. But, don't you know, two years later the island was greener than ever, like the ash was fertilizer or somethin'. But old Ben Turnipseed, he never come back. Decided the

country was bewitched and moved back south and took up preachin'
in earnest."

There was a small, cut-glass condiment bowl on the table, much
like the one my mother had at home. The table was neatly set and the
room was scrupulously clean and somehow familiar. Yet I could hear
the wind fluting in the chimney and sense the windowpanes trembling beneath the weight of the wind. The flame in the kerosene lamp
wavered with each gust. The facets of the glass bowl cut the reflected flame into geometrically correct slivers but even these danced to
the rhythm of the storm. The house felt as frail as an eggshell and I
thought of the swirling chaos of the oncoming winter.

The conversation reminded me of my night in Nome with Captain Swenson and Dr. Macpherson. At home in Seattle at my father's
table any discussion would center on politics and business. Out here
people created fables. Swenson and Hjalmar twined their storylines
like a cat's cradle, using them as nets to catch some mythological
beast, or as a woven barricade to exclude the formless dark.

"Could be, Ben was right," Hjalmar said. "This country's almighty
strange. Rocks that float and mountains puffin' ash. Bears as big as
houses and rivers choked with salmon red as strawberries. And a
wind like the devil's own dragline. I don't rightly know what God
had in mind when He pieced this ground together."

"Doubtless it was meant to teach man his own insignificance,"
Miss Devlin said dryly, "like much of Creation."

"Amen to that," said Miss Dennison. "I'm sure I never properly
understood humility till I lived here. The weather alone is a lesson in
God's wrath and the atonement for sins."

"It's just home to me," Natasha said and we all looked at her, this
lovely daughter of chaos and turbulence.

CHAPTER 19

Once free of the loom of the land both wind and waves increased. Our course was slightly south of east, which kept us in the trough of the waves that swept up the channel. Natasha and I sat shoulder to shoulder on the narrow stern seat as the skiff wallowed along, occasionally shipping water.

Bering had made his landfall on the east side of Nagai but with the seas so high we would have little chance of rounding Mountain Point at the south end. Natasha thought we should come into the lee of Wooly Head and make our first camp in Eagle Harbor.

We were both wearing borrowed oilskins and sou'wester hats but the spray found its way down my collar. I could feel a yoke of dampness and cold spreading across my shoulders and down my chest. Natasha sat on the windward side with her face averted from the spray. A few tendrils of hair escaped from her hat and I could feel them whip my face, cold and tasting of salt.

I pulled my coat tighter. On the charts the Shumagin Islands had looked small compared to the awesome sweep of the Aleutians but now from the stern seat of our skiff Nagai loomed above us—windswept, desolate, and immense.

Natasha elbowed me and pointed at the bailing can. I knelt in the bilge and scooped water from a small well in the floorboards and sent it over the lee rail. The tide was now ebbing fast against the wind and the seas were steeper. Natasha pointed the bow a little more into the wind. I listened to the laboring engine and prayed it would not quit.

When we drew near the island we were a little south of our intended landfall and Natasha turned carefully and we ran with the sea on our stern. Each wave lifted the stern and there would be a dizzying moment as the skiff started to broach. Her bow would point momentarily at the gray sky, then the crest would slip beneath us and the dark-backed wave would roll on without a backward glance, leaving behind the faint hiss of water sliding on water. Every time the stern skidded sideways my heart climbed into my mouth.

The sea was even more turbulent at Wooly Head, which did not appear at all like fleece, but rather convoluted and hardened as a ram's horns. Two small birds, dark with long, pointed wings, swooped sharply on the skiff and then as quickly were up and away.

"Peregrines," Natasha shouted. "Nesting." She pointed at the cliff face. The sea broke jaggedly in a welter of foam at its base.

Once we turned the corner into Eagle Harbor the seas quickly subsided, dying into a fan-shaped pattern within the confines of the bay. Natasha throttled back to an idle, adding to the feeling of a sudden relief of pressure.

"Cold," she said and laid her hand against my cheek. Cold though I was, her hand felt like something from the grave. "A little lumpy out there, once the tide started to run."

"A little lumpy?" I had been ready to compose my death song.

"Just a bit."

"Doesn't anything ever frighten you?"

She stuck her hands inside her oilskins and shivered. "In St. Paul we had the last house in the village, by the killing grounds. At night I could hear the foxes cracking the bones. I'd lie in bed alone, terrified of what was out in the dark. But I was pretty young." She opened the throttle wide and headed up the bay.

Eagle Harbor was perhaps five miles long and funnel-shaped. On either side the hills rose steeply but at the head the ground was low and somewhat marshy. We beached 67 on a small stretch of sand and climbed out, ashore on Nagai at last. I nearly fell to my knees, not in exultation but from cold-induced clumsiness.

Natasha took off her sou'wester and shook out her long hair. "So what do you think of Nagai now that you're finally here?"

"Kind of forlorn. I'm beginning to understand why most orchids grow in the tropics. Sensible plants."

Actually now that we were off the water the weather was not too bad—windy and overcast with brief bursts of rain, but not bad. We pitched the tent Hjalmar had lent us. Its canvas was stained by smoke and mildew and several spark holes had been patched with old oil-skins and netting twine. For my sleeping area we made a lean-to from two poles and a tattered tarpaulin.

"You know you really should have offered to pay Hjalmar something for the use of all his gear," Natasha said.

"He seemed pretty happy to lend us the stuff." I was already worried about justifying expenditures back in New Haven.

"John Lars, he's an old man trying to get by on a couple of pickle jars full of gold dust."

"I'm pretty poor myself right now."

"Poor? You? Poor is a winter day without a cup of oatmeal in the cupboard and not a stick of wood for the stove." She walked over to the skiff and perched the anchor on the bow on top of its coiled line. "And no oil for the lamp," she said, more to herself than to me. She tied a shore line to one of the flukes, then summoned me to help. We pushed the boat till it floated. When it had drifted a little way offshore Natasha tripped the anchor and then tied the shore line to a log in the drift pile.

"Pa always called this 'siwash anchoring,'" Natasha said, "but I don't think my mother cared for the term."

We gathered wood and kindled a fire. Natasha heated a can of beans that we ate straight from the skillet, sopping up the juice with thick slices of bread. "Luxury living," she said as she poured us more coffee. Flecks of ash floated in my cup. "So what's the plan, chief?" Natasha asked.

"I guess the best would be for us to split up. I'll take the south side of the bay, you can take the north."

"Just what am I supposed to look for?"

"I'm going to try to do a pretty thorough survey but you should just keep your eye out for anything unusual. The orchid should be pretty recognizable if it's anything like Steller's description."

We left camp early the next day. I looked back once and saw Natasha dip from view in a swale. The morning passed quickly and enjoyably but was also a little disappointing. Like any treasure hunter, I had a secret expectation of instant success. But everything I found was exactly as expected, and in fact much of what I gathered matched plants I had already collected and left on the *Emilia Galotti*.

By noon I had worked my way to Wooly Head. I saw the peregrines again but could not locate their nest. I made my way back along the ridge top and found Natasha already in camp, sitting by the fire eating a piece of pilot bread with butter. She had spread a few specimens on a flat piece of drift: lupine and monkshood, both of which I had collected on Unga Spit, but also a nice cinquefoil and an androsace I had not yet seen.

"I couldn't resist picking a few," she said. "It's impossible to spend a whole morning looking at flowers and not pick any."

"*Androsace chamaejasme*," I said, picking up the pinkish flower. "Rock jasmine."

"It's kind of sweet and unassuming, don't you think?"

"Scientists don't talk like that. It's against the rules," I said and Natasha made a face at me in reply.

We had borrowed a few old textbooks from the school and some tissue paper for pressing flowers. While Natasha made an early supper I worked on saving our few specimens.

"Monkshood," I said. "*Aconitum*. It's actually quite poisonous."

"I know. The Aleuts used it to poison arrows and lances. I think they pounded the roots to get the poison."

"It's a ranunculus, actually. A buttercup."

"Poisonous buttercups, now there's a plant I can identify with." Natasha sat down beside me and began to leaf through one of the borrowed geography books.

"Morocco," she said, "I've always wanted to go there. Maybe I could be a harem girl." She fluttered her eyelashes at me.

"To think when I first met you I thought you were all proper and ladylike."

"Some of the time I am, just not very often. I'll have to work on my act a bit, though. The only way I'll get to Morocco will be as a lady missionary. Unless you take me, John Lars. We could hunt exotic plants together."

"But you just got here. I thought you were so happy to get home and now you're talking about leaving."

"Oh, relax, John Lars, I don't expect anything from you." She tossed the book aside and picked up the monkshood and bit one of the petals. "I know I'll never leave this place."

"You got as far as Nebraska, that's a start." I tried to pull my foot back out of my mouth where it seemed permanently lodged. Natasha did not reply. She hugged her knees and watched the blue flames play across the salty wood.

The wind increased in the night. I had intended to spend the day working in the meadow behind camp but on impulse we decided to cross the island and visit Larsen Bay, the site of Bering's landfall. We climbed a steep ridge that was about a thousand feet high. At the top Natasha touched my arm and pointed at a fox trotting along with its head held high, a ptarmigan in its jaws. We watched the fox till it disappeared in the brush, completely unconcerned with our presence.

Striated wave patterns marked the water far below us. The outer islands were a maze of windswept passages receding in the blue distance. Nothing moved other than the wind; not a single boat was evident, not even near Unga. The complete emptiness gave me a feeling of vertigo, as though I was teetering on the edge of a cliff. From where we stood I could see along the spine of the island. There were deep bays, twisted headlands and narrow spits. If the sea were to rise only fifty feet Nagai would become a collection of a dozen or more islands rather than one. I looked at the hills, marshes, lakes, and salt chucks and for the first time truly understood how a plant could elude discovery for generations.

We descended the ridge and spent the afternoon botanizing along the eastern shore. We found the charcoal remnants of a beach fire. Natasha knelt and broke one of the blackened sticks. "This is pretty recent," she said.

"Like maybe the *Emilia*?"

"Who knows?" She dropped the stick and looked out to sea.

"It's not just your muslin, is it? You really want to see those guys again."

Natasha only shrugged in reply.

"I don't get it. What's so interesting about Jason Davis?"

"He's awfully fragile."

"Fragile?"

"Well, wounded."

"Because his wife left him? That was years ago." But maybe it would take more than a lifetime to get free of Audrey.

"His wife," Natasha said slowly.

"When I find the orchid we're going to name it after her," I blurted out and then wished I hadn't.

"How's that work?" Natasha stood up, her brows knit in a frown that I had learned to be wary of.

"Whoever discovers it has the honor of naming it," I said cautiously.

"Wouldn't that be Steller?"

"He never described it scientifically so it doesn't count."

"But you could still name it for him. Or his own wife, not somebody else's. Or if you're the one to find it why not somebody you know?"

"I do know her, and Audrey's a pretty name."

"Is it?" Natasha touched the remnants of the fire with the toe of her boot. "I doubt it's what the flower calls itself."

"But Audrey—Mrs. Arbuthnot—has always wanted an orchid named for her. And this is kind of her expedition." I tried to back away from trouble.

"I don't think I'd like that woman." Natasha kicked apart the remnants of the dead fire.

We walked south without talking. Somewhere not far away was the pond where Bering had drawn water, despite Steller's objections that the water was brackish. Shumagin's grave would be nearby as well and maybe even the orchid. I pulled my watch out and wound it. The hour was already late.

"We should probably head back," I said, breaking the silence.

"We could carry the tent over and make camp here, if this is the side you're interested in," Natasha said.

"Too much work. Anyway we don't know for sure just where Steller went on the island. The *St. Peter* anchored here for a couple days and Steller went off collecting but the journal is vague about distance and direction. The orchid could be almost anywhere, but I don't think Professor Arbuthnot realized how tough the country is. Or how nasty the weather gets."

"The wind will die down. We have a saying, 'The wind is not a river, sooner or later it will stop.' But it can sure take a while."

We made it back to camp very late. On our third day on the island we made a foray south to Falmouth Harbor but found nothing new other than a stand of avens—*Geum rossii*, I thought—and a Greenland primrose. *Primula egaliksensis*, I knew that one for sure. It was difficult to classify flowers without a text to guide me. This whole trip was warped by layers of uncertainty.

Traveling back by a slightly different route we came to a meadow in a little dell that was protected from the winds. The soil was damp to the touch and the grass grew high and lush. There were galaxies of flowers. I could see lupine and blue flag, both a little past their prime, but also wild roses and columbine. Cow parsnips hovered above the grass, their tall stalks holding white blooms nearly the size of pie plates. Tucked lower in the grass, almost like an understory, were dark brown chocolate lilies and throughout the meadow cranesbill flowered like a cloud of spring azure butterflies.

I wandered the meadow entranced, looking for a crowning flash of crimson. I thought about running a transect—marking out a perimeter and cataloging the plants—but it seemed almost sacrilegious to impose a grid on this tumult, a riot of colors and shapes so vivid and complex that it made Audrey Arbuthnot's garden back in New Haven almost insipid by comparison.

Flattened grass marked my spiraling path. Natasha lay asleep, her head pillowed on the rucksack. I picked a stalk of wild barley and tickled her nose with its tasseled frond. Without opening her eyes she grabbed my wrist and pulled. We mock wrestled for a moment but then I broke off. She sat up and looked at me.

"No orchid?" she said.

"No orchid."

Alyson

"No orchid. Why am I not surprised?"

"Hey, it ain't over till it's over."

"Yogi Berra probably wasn't even born when you were in the Shumagins."

"It was true even before he said it."

We had moved out to the front porch. I live in a Mission-style bungalow in the University District, so close to campus that I can bicycle to my office. The yard has room for only a small garden but the students walk, jog, and bicycle past, creating a colorful second garden that I can watch in all seasons, at all hours.

Though it had been a warm spring day, the night air was cool and Alyson and I sat on the porch swing sharing a blanket. We had brought the bottle of scotch with us but not the glasses. I took a swig and handed the bottle to her. In turn she handed me a joint she had just lit.

"When's the *Emilia* gonna reappear?" she asked.

"Natasha thought it was still out there, that Davis would come back, but I thought he was just gone."

"He has to come back, otherwise the story doesn't make sense."

"It's a story now but back then it was just what was happening. And I had no idea what was going on. Still don't for that matter. Am I remembering something real? Or if it was only a dream, whose dream was it?"

"You keep saying things like that but if the story changes in the telling then it also changes in the listening."

"Believe me, it changes in my memory as well. I stay awake some nights wondering just what was going on. You know the saying: when you're playing cards, after fifteen minutes if you don't know who the mark is, then it's you?"

"I don't play cards."

"Thing is, we were all marks. We were all looking for something, even Natasha. Something different for each of us and nobody wanted to hear that it didn't exist. We were all puppets and maybe we all took turns as puppeteer as well."

"I still want the *Emilia* to come back."

"Why?"

"I like those guys."

CHAPTER 20

The headland shielding Sanborn Harbor was troubled by an ugly cross sea. We had decided to shift camp toward the northern end of Nagai but it was not easy going. Rounding the headland the skiff shipped water and I had to get down on my hands and knees and bail. When she was finally dry I stayed kneeling in the bilge. I felt exhausted and scratchy and had the sort of heightened, fragile perceptions that came with the onset of a fever. By the time we reached the calm water of Sanborn Harbor I was shaking with cold and beginning to cough.

We made camp by a small stream that drained a large meadow. I went quickly to bed but lay awake listening to the tarpaulin flap in the relentless wind. I arose very early and built the campfire, one skill that was improving on this journey. I felt terribly low. My feet were blistered and my face wind chapped and I no longer believed that Steller's orchid would be just around the next corner.

Natasha came out of the tent, yawning and rubbing her eyes. "Still blowing," she said by way of good morning.

"Are you sure the Aleuts say the wind has to stop?"

"We have another saying that if you talk about the weather it will only get worse."

The flames of my fire were so flattened by the wind they looked like a creeping flower. I held my hands over it, trying to draw a little warmth. "I just don't get this place. Not the land, not the people, not anything."

"If you understood it you'd like it better."

"I don't get that either. I'm sick and tired of being told I don't understand stuff. So what if the weather and the plants are a little different up here? It's still the same world and people have to follow the same rules. Right is still right and wrong is still wrong."

"Not really."

"How can you say that? Did Miss Devlin teach you that?"

"John Lars, the thing is, I know it's the same but you don't know it's different."

"That doesn't make any sense at all." I grabbed my rucksack and we set off in opposite directions. I remembered my resolve to kill the next person who told me I did not understand Alaska. It still sounded like a good idea.

I walked until I found a grassy spot out of the wind where I sat and rested. A raven perched on a granite boulder, its glossy black feathers ruffled by the wind. Circular patches of bright orange lichen marked the rock and at its base bloomed an arctic harebell—a delicate blue flower with a stem so slender I could not imagine how it withstood the ruthless wind.

I felt cut adrift, lost without my collecting gear and my copy of Asa Gray. All along the idea of the orchid had been my lodestar but now the quest was losing focus. I thought of Steller, his drive for knowledge, his arrogance and impatience. I knew I lacked that intensity. Natasha had asked if Davis and I were related. Maybe I was becoming more like him, a perpetually lost soul on a forlorn quest, tangled in past desires. Not a pleasant thought.

But I had to find the orchid. Had to. I did not want to return to Seattle and New Haven empty-handed. I had something to prove, and the more elusive the orchid became the more I had to believe in its existence.

I looked up as if seeking divine intervention. Overhead the clouds swirled in distinct strata. The highest layer of cirrus clouds was streamlined but with rolling shapes unlike any I had ever seen, contoured as though shaped on an immense potter's wheel. In this country even the sky was different.

I did not pick the harebell. I walked back to camp and collapsed by the fire. Exhaustion and the futility of the search had pushed me close to the edge. In the distance I could see Natasha working her way back toward camp. She stopped to pick a flower which for some reason annoyed me.

"No flowers at all?" she asked when she reached camp and saw my empty hands and the rucksack turned inside out.

"What of it?" I snapped.

"Well, excuse me, but I thought we were running a plant survey here."

"I am, not 'we.'"

She pushed the fire together and sat back on her heels. "Do you have any idea what you're looking for?"

"God damn it . . ." I started.

"Don't swear at me."

"God damn it!" I was practically shouting now. "You may know about boats and stuff but let me do the botany." I grabbed my gear again and walked to a nearby meadow. I knew that my anger was pointless but I was still fuming as I took a ball of string and marked out the perimeter of a square twenty-five feet per side, intending to run a transect. I broke the string viciously while knotting it but once I stepped inside the square my anger began to ebb. I quickly collected the more conspicuous flowers but then the grasses literally slowed me to a crawl and this tempo brought my temper to earth. More and more the actual work of botany brought me a feeling of peace, a way of making order out of tumult. Maybe this was what I was meant to do.

I pulled a wild barley plant and carefully shook the dirt free. Root, stem, flower. So slender and simple yet the entire mystery of the seeded earth was there. How had I been seduced into chasing something so gaudy as an orchid?

From somewhere I caught a fragrance akin to lavender. No more than a whiff but somehow it brought Audrey to mind. And the scent of the sheets on her bed. Every time I thought I was free of her, from out of nowhere came a faint tug on the line. I sat back and straightened my legs. The knees of my canvas pants were wet and grass-stained.

"Peace offering." Natasha handed me a fried cake that she had somehow cooked above the wind-harried fire.

"What is it?" It was more like a biscuit than a pancake.

"Bannocks, we call them. Camp bread." She smiled at me. Her braids were pinned up in thick spirals and there was a faint dusting of flour along one cheekbone.

We broke the steaming-hot bannocks and ate them with butter and jam. While we ate, Natasha looked at the grasses I had collected. She picked up the stem of wild barley.

"*Tatyux*, my mother called this one."

"*Hordeum*," I said with brisk authority, though in truth it might have been an *Elymus*.

"My mother used to pick lots of it and dry it. The long fibers make it good for baskets. In the winter she'd sit in the kitchen and split the grass with her fingernails. She could make threads as fine as silk."

"Did she teach you?"

"Only a little. I was kind of a tomboy. That last summer in Akutan I picked all the grass for her but she died in December and Pa just threw the grass away."

I finished the last of the bannock, licked the jam from my fingers and sat back. The heat from the fire made me drowsy and my head began to nod.

"You don't look too good," Natasha said. "You better move into the tent with me, you'll sleep warmer and drier there. We can't have you getting all run down."

"You might catch my cold."

"I've never had a cold in my life."

"But what would the Miss Ds say?"

Natasha glanced away, out across the shifting water. "'Thine own wickedness shall correct thee and thy backslidings shall reprove thee,'" she said, almost inaudibly.

"More Bible?"

"Lamentations." She rolled the word on her tongue with a rhythm like a dirge. "Or maybe Jeremiah." She poked at the fire till the coals burst into flames and I wondered what memory or image crossed her mind when her spirit wavered so suddenly. A candle guttering when the wrong door opened.

But then she laughed. "I got an honorable mention in the school scripture contest. For almost memorizing the second chapter of Jeremiah and then forgetting it."

"Almost?"

"Enough sermonizing." She jumped to her feet. "Tomorrow maybe I'll save your worthless soul. Right now I'm going to tuck you in bed."

With a firm grip on my elbow she guided me to the tent. I stretched out on her bedroll while she fetched my blankets and made up a second bed.

"When I was young, if I had a cold my mother rubbed camphor on my chest," I said.

"We do not have any camphor, John Lars," Natasha said sternly.

"No, no, that's not what I meant. I was just thinking of that strange smell. It's from a tree, you know. A cinnamon, which is actually a laurel."

I knew I was babbling. I watched her spread and smooth my blankets. They smelled a little damp and musty. "When I was about eight," I said, "there was this infestation of earwigs in Seattle. My mother made me wear gauze earmuffs to bed. Lots of mothers did. She was afraid one of the earwigs would burrow into my brain and drive me mad."

"I think one got past her defenses," Natasha said and slipped out of the tent. I closed my eyes but I could hear her tying the tent flaps. Behind that I could hear the crackling of the fire, and behind that the wind's own lamentations. I remembered that our housekeeper Annaliese was the one who fashioned the gauze earmuffs and rubbed the camphor on my chest. Annaliese was quite young, the daughter of one of Grandpa Lars's fishermen. She had long, blonde braids and blue eyes. All one summer I followed her around like a puppy dog. She liked to sketch and she bought me a box of watercolors and gave me my first drawing lessons. The cool touch of her hands when I was sick brought sleep quickly, as did the memory now.

I awoke much later when Natasha came quietly into the tent. She sat on her bed and began to untie her boots. I could hear the rasp of rawhide laces.

"It's late," I said. The tent was dark.

"Shhh, you weren't supposed to wake up. I was sitting by the fire, communing with ghosts and memories."

She slid beneath her blankets. I could hear and feel her wiggling to undress. I shifted restlessly and cold air seeped into my bed like a finger of the tide. I remembered a dressing table covered with cosmetics, the light through a blue perfume bottle, lace curtains moving in the wind. I shivered then coughed.

"They say a cold is only suppressed tears," Natasha said. "Some sorrow you can't face."

"Who are 'they'?" I grumbled. "And how come you've never had a cold? Your life's been full of sorrow."

"Out here sorrow is a constant. Tears are a luxury you save for the dying."

I lay staring into the darkness trying to fathom this. I could not even make out the weave of the tent's canvas.

Natasha rolled toward me. I could feel the warmth of her breath. "I was trying to remember my mother. I was still pretty young when she died. I can picture her sitting in the kitchen in Akutan, the dried grass piled on the table. I can remember the slippery sounds the barley stalks made as she split them but I can never remember much that she said."

"You must remember your father pretty well."

"Oh, sure. But mostly I remember that last winter on the fox farm when he was drinking so much. He'd have the shakes so bad he couldn't light the kitchen fire. He'd be ornery and foul-mouthed, but then he'd start crying and apologizing and that'd be even worse."

"It's sad the way bad memories can drive out the good."

"'Can a maid forget her ornaments, or a bride her attire? Yet my people have forgotten me days without number.' See, I still remember some of Jeremiah, chapter two. Only I don't think memories have much to do with what really happened. I think they create their own world that we're sort of looking through a window at."

CHAPTER 21

"There's a change coming; I can feel it," Natasha said. "I think we should go round the top of the island and anchor in Northeast Bight. That way if the wind lays down it's a short jump to Larsen Bay."

"But what if . . ." My voice trailed off as my mind ran through a litany of possible disasters.

"But what?"

"Nothing." I felt too listless to care who made the decisions.

Once again we loaded the skiff. Natasha insisted that I wear every stitch of clothing I owned, including two pairs of pants and two shirts. If we had capsized I would have sunk like a stone. I sat huddled next to her in the stern as we rounded East Head and began the long traverse of Porpoise Harbor. The engine stuttered momentarily and Natasha and I crossed glances but then it smoothed to its normal clamor.

In the strait a few miles north a row of tall pinnacles called the Haystacks split the sea. They looked like gigantic, rough-hewn chess pieces, abandoned in the middle of a game and awaiting resumption of play. Beyond these stacks I could see Andronica Island. Natasha suddenly stood up and braced herself with a hand on my shoulder, staring intently north. Following her gaze I saw the masts of a boat catching the sunlight for a moment against the shadowy bulk of Andronica. One of the sea stacks intervened and the boat disappeared from view but it had not been very far away.

"The *Emilia Galotti*?" I asked.

"The *Seal*," she said. I looked again toward Andronica but saw only the play of light and shadows across the rocks. Natasha turned the skiff toward the shallower water alongshore but the engine, faltered, caught, faltered again and died.

"Shit," Natasha said and quickly raised the engine cover without waiting for my help.

"What's wrong?"

"Don't know. Probably bad fuel; that last can was a little cruddy. I should have strained it, or cleaned the filter." She glanced quickly toward the Haystacks. The *Seal* had reappeared and was heading our way, throwing a fine bow wave. Natasha took a screwdriver from our small tool kit and bent over the engine.

There was nothing I could do to help. I huddled on my thwart watching the *Seal*. Now that we were dead in the water the skiff turned broadways to the swell and rolled heavily. Natasha pulled the fuel line loose from the engine and an iridescent sheen spread across the bilge. I thought of the leaded glass windows in my parents' home: the beveled edges of the glass would split the light and cast flattened, captive rainbows across the hardwood floor. I wished I was there.

Natasha knelt and began to suck on the fuel line. The *Seal* came at us full bore then backed down and turned hard to port so that her starboard rail dipped and rolled above us. Her wake nearly capsized 67. Natasha slipped and cracked her elbow on the engine block but she just spat in the bilge and kept sucking.

Gottschalk and Fitzgerald and the Cossack lined the rail staring down at us. The woman Lena stood a little apart. No one said anything but I had an impression that being adrift alone on the open ocean might be less menacing.

"I thought you were headed for Kodiak," I said, after a moment.

"We got as far as Chignik but decided to come back," Fitzgerald said. "Just on a whim, you might say. You folks need a hand?"

"No, we'll be fine," I said and Natasha spat copiously into the water between 67 and the *Seal*. Without a word she put the fuel line back in place and quickly tightened the screws.

"We seen the *Emilia* out between Bird and Chernabura but she didn't hang around to visit," Fitzgerald said. "Not very neighborly. You talked to them?"

"Nope."

"You want a tow?"

"I don't think so." Gottschalk's silence was more unnerving than Fitzgerald's blather. Out of the corner of my eye I watched Natasha wrap the cord the wrong way round the flywheel.

"Get a line on 'em, Fitzgerald," Gottschalk said, obviously impatient with the small talk. I did not take the line Fitzgerald offered, so he stepped over the rail, balanced momentarily on the rub rail, then sprang into the front of our skiff. As he did so Natasha gave a sharp pull, opened the throttle wide and cranked the tiller over. The engine roared, Fitzgerald teetered briefly then fell backwards into the water cursing loudly. To my surprise I heard Max laugh out loud. Natasha cut the throttle, the engine stuttered and my heart nearly died with it but then with a loud backfire it started in forward and Natasha spun 67 toward shore so sharply that she almost dipped one rail. Looking back I could see the Cossack fishing Fitzgerald out with a long boathook. Natasha took the skiff almost to the beach, into shallow water, all the while watching the *Seal* over her shoulder. Once Fitzgerald was aboard, the *Seal* shadowed us for a few minutes, just offshore, but then abruptly turned and headed southwest away from us. Natasha throttled back and the engine ran smoothly at an idle.

"So the *Seal's* back," I said.

"If she was ever gone."

"What do you think they're doing?"

"Playing cat and mouse."

"With us or the *Emilia?*"

"I wish I knew." She opened the throttle again but continued to hug the shore. An hour later we rounded the northernmost end of the island and tucked into Northeast Bight to avoid the swells in the east strait. At the bottom of the bight we came ashore and made camp as a light rain began to fall. So deeply indented were the bays that our previous camp at Sanborn Harbor was not much more than a few miles overland, though we had taken the better part of a day to round the top of the island.

"So it was that fuel filter thing?" I asked her.

"You don't know much about engines, do you?"

"Everything around our house always works."

"What a deprived life." She laughed.

"Well, what would you have done if it hadn't started when we needed it?"

"Something, I don't know what. Look, we don't know what those guys are up to so let's forget about them for now. I want to take a walk."

Crossing a narrow isthmus brought us to Mist Harbor. Beyond we could see the waters of the east strait. Waves still broke on the headlands.

"This place never lets up," I said. "It just beats and beats on you."

"Tomorrow, I promise." Natasha took my arm and drew me away. We walked back in the general direction of camp, following an outcropping of rock. Natasha stopped by a little pond and picked a bouquet of blue-eyed grass.

"*Sisyrinchium*," I said.

"I know these aren't rare or fancy but I like them. They're like God was trying his hand before he created the iris."

The outcropping of rock extended into the saltwater. Below the tide line it was coated with blue-black mussels all aligned in one direction like a church congregation. We walked out to look at a tidal pool. Its crystalline waters were like a saltwater Wardian case. Bright sea anemones flourished and small crabs scuttled across the fissured granite bottom. A hermit crab in a conical shell stopped directly beneath us, standing on a white band of quartz as if on a target. Natasha reached down with one of her grass stalks and touched the crab, which instantly shot sideways into a crack. Faint concentric rings spread across the pool from the grass stalk.

On a nearby bit of shingled beach I saw a cluster of mistmaiden plants with their star-like white flowers. I wished that I could draw them. Draw them together with Natasha as she bent over the pool in the light rain.

We walked back to camp and despite the rain Natasha quickly had a fire going. The evening was prematurely dark. I felt lightheaded from fever and both cold and hot simultaneously.

"Maybe in two nights we'll be sleeping on a bed of orchids," Natasha said as if sensing my mood.

"I don't know. I still believe it exists but I'm not sure I'm the one who's going to find it."

"Maybe it's like the Holy Grail. Maybe you have to be in a state of perfect grace if you want to find it."

"If orchids are anything like Jason Davis says maybe you have to be in a state of perfect sin."

"Perfect sin." She laughed. "Now there's an idea I didn't hear much of in Nebraska. But if Steller found the orchid, what was his sin?"

"I don't know. Pride, maybe."

"Then how about you, what sin will qualify you?"

I watched the flames that played across the damp wood. "Penance," I said, avoiding the question. "This whole trip is penance for past sins."

"I think you're looking too far inside yourself."

"What do you mean?"

"If all you want is to find that fancy orchid to prove something about yourself, it's like looking in a mirror wondering if you're pretty. You'll be so blinded by your own reflection you'll never find anything."

I digested this for a moment while Natasha undid her braids and combed her hair. "That's hocus-pocus," I said finally. "Either the orchid exists or it doesn't and either I'll find it or I won't."

"Maybe so. But the real question, John Lars, the real question is whether I should cut my hair."

"No, don't. I like it long."

"Then how should I wear it?"

"I've seen Scandinavian girls kind of braid the two sides together into a roll on top of their head."

"I know how to do that." She divided her hair into three strands and then took two or three of the stems of blue-eyed grass and began to braid them together with her hair. Watching her I tried to picture the orchid somewhere in the night, its petals dark with rain. Then I thought of the hermit crab and how it could not live without a rigid structure to protect it: how vulnerable it must feel when it has outgrown one shell and is seeking another.

Natasha was working with her hands up behind her head. Her shirt was pulled taut across her breasts and she caught my gaze and held it expressionlessly until I flinched and looked away. The rain continued to pebble the surface of the water.

"There," she said. "What do you think?" She turned her head to show her profile. The flowers were woven into her dark, glossy hair.

"Beautiful."

"So maybe you could take me to a dance after all." She punched me in the shoulder.

"Only it's like, whenever the music starts, I'm ready to waltz but you take off in a tango."

Natasha laughed and then tangoed off to gather another armful of firewood. She built up the fire till it was properly ablaze. I basked in the heat. The rain had slackened but the evening was still cold and gloomy.

Natasha twined a bit of string around her fingers, forming one pattern after another.

"Cat's cradle," I said.

"We call it a string story. Watch." She formed a complicated set of triangles, using her teeth to help hold the twine. "This one's called *qalgagim ukata*—raven's basket."

"Very nice."

She took the string off her fingers. "I shouldn't be doing this. We're only supposed to play it in autumn. If we do it in summer it'll bring a cold winter."

"You sure have a knack for courting disaster."

"That's what the sisters in Nebraska always said. Too restless, I guess."

"*Hvileløs.*"

"More Latin?"

"No, it's an old Norse word my grandpa Lars liked to use. It means restless, only a kind of deep-seated restlessness of the soul."

"Well, tonight feels like autumn anyway."

A stray cat's paw of wind ruffled the water. I shivered and coughed. Natasha moved closer and put her hand on my forehead. "You're burning up. You should be in bed."

"No, I feel much better, really. Almost human."

Without a word she grabbed my collar and shoved me in the direction of the tent. As I undressed the clammy canvas felt like kelp against my skin and I dove beneath the blankets. The bedroll was cold and my skin was morbidly sensitive to the touch. I lay shivering. Outside I could hear the clink of dishes as Natasha tidied the camp. I fell into a half doze for what seemed like a long time till she entered the tent.

"What time is it?" I asked.

"Almost tomorrow. Wind has shifted northwest and the sky is clearing. I could see a star."

She pulled off her trousers and sat on her bedroll. By the motion of her arms I could tell she was unplaiting her hair. She shook her head to free her hair and I could smell woodsmoke and rain and blue-eyed grass. She reached beneath my blankets and placed a hand on my chest. I flinched away from her cold fingers but she kept her hand there.

"Wow, you're like a furnace." She drew her hand slowly down my stomach and then took it away. I could still feel the imprint of her fingers on my skin.

"Once in Lincoln," she said, "my friend and I snuck away to a music hall to see a show. They had a magician and he hypnotized this lady and balanced her between two chairs. Her head was on the back of one and her feet on the other. She was stiff as a board. He even sat on her, she was so rigid. You're just about as relaxed."

"I'm trying to think of what to say."

"Just tell me this blue-eyed grass is pretty." She traced my cheek with a sprig and I caught a faint scent of cut greenery. She gently drew her fingers across my lips. "Go on, say it."

"It's beautiful. My favorite flower."

She sighed and swung across and straddled me with her knees gripping my sides. I could feel the strength of her slender legs, lithe as willow. Her hands were on my shoulders and she bent and kissed me lightly. Taste of salt and something like wild strawberries.

I slipped a hand beneath her shirt and felt the gentle buds of her backbone. Her skin was cool and very soft and I thought of the wildflowers that slumbered between the pages of the geography books. She kissed me again, hard this time, but a strand of hair tangled in the kiss, which made me splutter and her giggle. She sat upright, still straddling me, and stripped off her shirt and I wondered if she had learned this in her scripture class in Nebraska but that made me think of the Song of Songs and of Solomon's beloved whose breasts were like two roe deer that fed among the lilies but in the darkness of the tent it was more like the chocolate lilies we had found in the Aleutian marshes. I reached up and cupped her breasts that were small but firm as apples and then I kissed her stomach tasting again the sharp slipperiness of salt. The tent flapped in a sudden gust of wind.

She took my hand and drew me into her and then began to move, gently at first, like the rocking of the skiff that night we slept alongside each other in Tolstoi Bay. I closed my eyes and thought of orchids—the voluptuous curve of the labellum, the convoluted throat, the vivid colors. I saw again the light in the conservatory, my hand on the polished banister that led upstairs, the curtains moving in the wind. Then the image dissolved and I could see only grass twisting in the wind and islands scattered like seeds beneath a swirling sky.

Natasha lay beside me, one knee on my stomach and one hand slowly rubbing the hollow of my collarbone. "When you drew that picture of me back at Unga Spit, that's when I decided we'd be lovers," she said. "I wasn't sure till then."

"At least I finally got something from my art." I felt oddly distant and petulant. Decided? She decided? I remembered Miss Marian's dance class and little Imogene Dickinson who had insisted on leading when we learned to waltz. Natasha's skin was cool against mine but for some reason I had to fight the desire to flinch away from her touch. Which was odd because I now knew how much I wanted her. And even needed her.

"Why do I always fall for blondes?" she said. "You'd think I'd know better, growing up around those crazy Norwegians. Alec Soberg was my first love. I had this huge crush on him when we first moved to Unga. I tried to get him to teach me how to milk their cow." She giggled at the memory.

"Hjalmar said you beat the tar out of him."

"That was earlier in the relationship." She tugged at a lock of my hair. "Now tell me about your girlfriends. There must be somebody."

"No, not really. Just, you know, the girls I had to escort to those boring dances." I remembered the slow tick of a clock in an empty house and the gold clasp of a blue necklace.

"No special sweetheart?"

When I did not reply she rested her hand on my chest. "Okay. If you won't tell me about your lady friends tell me about your family. I told you about mine."

"There's not much to say. My father is a lawyer, prominent in the business community, I guess. My mother does society things. My sister Alyson runs around in her roadster."

"What's your home like, then?"

"It's kind of big. Three stories with a mansard roof. Made of quarried stone. My grandfather John built it, my mother's father. He was a lawyer, too. A judge, actually."

I turned on my side and faced her. "Funny thing, when you asked me about the house the first thing I pictured was the stairway that starts opposite the front hall. The first-floor rooms are really tall, more than ten feet, so it's a long stairway. All mahogany, with polished treads and balusters. The bottom tread curls around the newel post. I have this vivid memory of standing at the top, clutching Annaliese's dress, terrified of going down. It was so dark at the bottom and the banister glistened and curved like a snake."

"I knew it wasn't much like Hardscratch Point," Natasha said, more to herself than to me.

"But at least your parents loved you."

"My parents never even bothered to get married." She pulled her knee away and rolled on her side, facing away from me. The tent trembled beneath the wind's hand.

"Who's Annaliese anyway?" Natasha's voice was muffled.

"Somebody. A friend. It doesn't matter." Annaliese had worked for us less than a year. In the heat of that summer I heard whispered arguments between my parents that quickly rose to anger and one day Annaliese was just gone. In November I asked if she could come to my birthday party but my mother told me we did not fraternize with the help.

Natasha and I lay still, back to back. What should I have told her—that I feared my father, that I scarcely knew my mother, that I mourned my grandfather? That I was mesmerized by my professor's wife? Those chambers of the heart were still out of bounds, even to me.

I would have liked to tell her about Grandpa Lars and the peppermint candies he carried—surely that was innocent enough—but the words had not come. Now I stared into the dark and listened to the quiet rhythm of Natasha's breathing. I wanted to put my arm around her but I didn't.

Back in Unga I had mentioned to Hjalmar how sad Natasha was that her father had passed away. He snorted in reply. "More'n once I seen her come to town with her shirt buttoned high to hide the bruises. Some days she could barely sit from the whippings Karl give her." Hjalmar shifted uncomfortably in his chair. "I got reason to believe it was worse even than that. But what scared me most was that Natasha, she'd finally have enough and just slit Karl's throat. Don't you ever think she couldn't. Or wouldn't."

At last I fell asleep and dreamed that I was on an icy mountaintop, miles above the tree line, caught by night and a fierce wind. Then I found a door in the summit, a heavy wooden door with iron strap hinges. I passed through the door into an absolutely quiet, windless space that smelled of must. A faintly lit staircase led down in darkening stages and far below I could barely discern a figure in white holding something crimson.

The crack of canvas awakened me. I was drenched in sweat but my fever was gone. The tent flapped hard again and I realized that the bed beside me was empty. I struggled into my pants and boots and crawled outside. A fierce wind blew from the northwest, the clouds were gone and to my surprise the moon was full. The sky had been overcast so long that I had lost track of its phases. The moonlight was brilliant on the water though the camp lay in shadow. Natasha was nowhere in evidence but looking east I could see a faint patch of white approaching the crest of the ridge.

I walked after her. When I gained the moonlit top I found her standing there dressed only in her white shirt. Her arms were folded across her chest and she was staring at the brilliantly lit strait. A crisscross pattern marked the water—the remnant of the southwest swells now overlaid by the north wind. In the midst of this a whale breached. He jumped three or four times, a great plume of water exploding around him, then put his head down and smashed the water repeatedly with his huge flukes.

The whale leaped again, twisting in the air to form the dark heart of a ghostly fountain. Beyond the whale were the twin peaks of Spectacle Island. So bright was the moonlight that I could see the white hull of a boat anchored close beneath them. I touched Natasha's arm and pointed at the boat but she did not respond.

The wind poured across the island like a river out of Siberia— cold, clear, implacable. The tall grass moved in waves, flashing light and dark as the blades bowed and twisted. Natasha's shirt rippled in the wind.

CHAPTER 22

The crackling of the fire brought me out of the tent. The wind had died and a thick fog blanketed the bight. Natasha sat by the fire, a cup in her hands. I was not sure whether I should act any differently toward her. Something had obviously shifted in the night. I poured myself coffee and said, a little formally, "Was that the *Emilia Galotti* over by Spectacle Island?"

She nodded.

"And the *Seal* has to be around somewhere."

"Downright crowded." She threw the dregs of her cup in the fire. "Let's go. If we get to the *Emilia* before she moves we might get our stuff back."

"Isn't it too foggy?"

"It's always like this when the weather breaks. Mist just hangs in the bays till the sun burns it off. It may be clear out in the strait already."

We broke camp and then felt our way slowly out of Northeast Bight, staying close to the rock-strewn shoreline. When we rounded the headland we found that the strait was indeed clear, an alleyway of blue water amongst the fog-shrouded islands. The peaks of Spectacle Island stuck out above the fog.

We were nearly across the strait when the *Emilia* suddenly appeared, her white hull catching the sun's rays. "Headed north," Natasha shouted, "but we can cut 'em off!"

The *Emilia Galotti* held her course for a few minutes and then suddenly turned and headed back into the foggy pass between Spectacle and Bendel Islands. Natasha grabbed my arm and looking back I saw the *Seal* a few miles away, headed in our direction. We continued to hold our course until we, too, entered the thick fog bank. For a few minutes we ran at reduced speed then Natasha killed the engine and sat listening. Straining my ears I heard the faint creak of a block some distance away.

"Sails," Natasha whispered.

"There's no wind."

"Enough for steerageway, maybe."

Water lapped faintly against the hull. The distant hammering of the *Seal*'s engine grew louder and then slowed to an idle as they entered the fog. Natasha bent to wrap the starter cord around the flywheel then whispered to me, "I'll bet the *Seal* didn't see us, we're so low in the water. Maybe we can decoy them away."

"I don't get any of this. Why help the *Emilia*?"

"Sympathy for the hunted, I guess."

"But they marooned us."

She shrugged and pulled the cord. Knowing that people out in the fog were listening made the engine sound louder than usual. Natasha put the compass on the floorboards in front of us and headed east. Within a few minutes a sheer cliff face appeared and she turned and ran alongside it at half throttle. The cliff stretched into the mist, its face speckled with perching birds. With the engine running we could not hear the *Seal* but looking back across our wake I thought I could see her topmasts ghosting east toward Big Koniuji Island.

"I've gathered eggs on this island," Natasha said in a nearly normal tone of voice. "I remember it a little."

After about twenty minutes we had to steer out to avoid a cluster of rocks and then the cliff seemed to fall away into a large bay. The fog thinned and suddenly we could see the northern half of the island. Natasha put the tiller hard over and the skiff turned back into the sheltering fog. She killed the engine and we could hear the soft mutter of the *Seal*'s engine offshore. I strained to see her outline through the swirling fog. There was now a faint, pebbled texture to the water as the breeze strengthened slightly.

We sat drifting and listening. The *Seal's* engine stopped as though they, too, were listening. With an impatient motion Natasha freed her long hair from the collar of her oilskins., The *Seal's* engine started again. As the sound gradually faded I judged she was headed north and east.

"Let's double back," Natasha whispered. She carefully pulled the oars free and mounted the thole-pins. As we began to row the *Seal's* engine stopped again. I concentrated on rowing very smoothly with no splash as I lifted the blade. The engine restarted and the sound gradually faded away.

"What I like about rowing," Natasha said suddenly, "is watching the oar leave the water. That little whirlpool at the end of each stroke and the line of dripping water as you bring the oar forward, it's mesmerizing."

"I don't get it," I said, irritated as always by her nonchalance. "Are those guys chasing us or what? They couldn't still think we're the *Emilia*." When she didn't reply I said, "It doesn't make sense anyway. The *Seal* gives you a free ride from Nome while Davis and Li Po abandon us and steal our stuff. Seems like you're helping the wrong side."

"You don't know those guys, John Lars."

A puff of wind leavened the fog and I could see that we were midway in the pass between Spectacle and Big Koniuji islands. "How'd we get out here?" I was disoriented as well as confused but at least I could not see or hear the *Seal*.

"Tide's pushing us more than I expected," Natasha said. "I thought the fog would be gone by now. Pretty cold day, I guess."

We continued to row. Fog still filled the narrow passes and bays as though someone had spilled a gigantic cotton sack over the mountainous islands but the strait was an alleyway of light filled with seabirds. A puffin surfaced next to us, his multi-colored beak crammed with so many small fish that he seemed to have a silvery moustache. He scuttled away, too stuffed with food to fly.

"The *Seal* must still be headed north," Natasha said. "Question is, where'd those other two get to? And what are they doing out here in the first place?"

"I thought you were the one who was so sure they'd be here."

"Oh, I knew they'd be here, I just don't know why. Something about this whole orchid thing doesn't make sense."

As she spoke the fog lifted a little more and we saw the *Emilia* just doubling the southwestern end of Big Koniuji. Natasha hurriedly shipped her oar and grabbed the starter cord.

"This is crazy," I said. "Just what are you going to do?"

The engine started with a roar. "Aleut rules," she yelled. "You move fast or you don't play." She opened the throttle wide and headed for the fogbank where the *Emilia* had disappeared. I looked over my shoulder but thankfully the *Seal* was nowhere to be seen.

When we rounded the point Natasha slowed the skiff and turned into the first bay. The fog was again thick. Very slowly we felt our way around its rim but found nothing. Natasha stopped the engine and pulled out our dog-eared chart and studied it.

"Too many nooks and crannies," she said. "You could stay hidden out here forever. It'd be great country for smugglers, if only there was something to smuggle out. Or somebody to buy what you smuggle in."

"You sure have a lot of piratical instincts."

"Yeah, I'm going to be the world's first freebooting missionary. 'A wild ass used to the wilderness, that snuffeth up the wind at her pleasure.'"

"More Jeremiah, chapter two?"

"Yup."

I took the chart from her and studied it, thinking it was time she learned some other parts of the Bible. Big Koniuji looked like Nagai's smaller brother—the same deeply indented coastline and tucked-and-rolled topography. We followed the shore and entered a large bay where the fog still pooled deeply. As we motored slowly along the western side we passed jagged reefs covered with rockweed that wavered and turned in the gentle surge. Near the bottom of the bay we finally came upon the *Emilia* drifting like a phantom, her white sides pearly in the fog light. "Ahah," Natasha said and laid the skiff gently alongside. Li Po appeared on deck and threw us a line.

"John Nelson and Natasha," he said as he helped Natasha aboard. "How nice to see you." I found this a bit bizarre under the circumstances but oddly enough I was pleased to see him.

There was a groove plowed in the cap rail. Natasha ran her finger along the splintered edges. "Max's calling card?" she asked.

"Fitzgerald, actually."

"Fitzgerald?" I said.

"We ran into them out by Chernabura but gave them the slip." Li Po said. "Shoal waters and poor light, the smuggler's friend."

Chernabura, I thought as we descended to the galley. *Where Bering and Steller had first encountered Aleuts.* The galley smelled as usual of musty wood and fuel oil. Jason Davis stood by the stove. "Coffee?" he asked, gesturing at the pot.

That was a bit much. "Coffee?" I sputtered. "Coffee? You maroon us and steal our stuff and now it's like some kind of tea party?"

"The amenities, young John, always the amenities." A sudden, terrible cough wracked Davis. His lips were deeply cracked and there was dried blood in the corner of his mouth. He looked as though he had been wrestling with shadows so long that he was about to become one. When he handed a cup of coffee to Natasha she held his hand for an instant but I felt no sympathy whatsoever.

"Where have you two been?" I asked.

"The outer islands, hunting sea otter. How's the flower hunt going?"

"That's none of your business."

Natasha had found her carpetbag. She knelt to rummage through it and unfolded a length of blue muslin. She ran her hand across the cloth lightly.

"We were going to leave that in Unga if we didn't find you," Davis said to her.

"Find us? You're the ones who lost us, remember?" I felt as if I was at the Mad Hatter's tea party. I saw my trunk in the fo'c'sle and dragged it out and opened the lid.

"Where's my vasculum?"

"The bottom of Izembek Lagoon. I don't need a reminder of Walter Arbuthnot carrying the damn thing in China, like a bull flaunting his scrotum."

"And the Wardian case?"

"That's mine. I paid for it in blood and folly. Tell Audrey to come get it if she wants it."

"Dammit . . ." I started to say but a quiet shout of warning came from Li Po on deck. We all three went up the companionway. The fog had lifted oddly, as though a cloud hovered at ceiling height. The mountain slopes were still shrouded in gray but the entire bay and the strait beyond was illuminated like a ballroom. In the middle of the strait was the *Seal*, headed our way.

"Waited too long," Davis said. He took the wheel while Li Po started the engine. The *Emilia* headed toward the rock garden guarding the west shore of the bay.

"He's faster than us but if we can get back in the fog we still might give him the slip," Davis said.

"There's a passage inside the rocks," Natasha said, pointing. "I've been through it on a fish boat."

"Chart only shows half a fathom."

"Full moon last night. Big tides. You can make it but Max can't."

"Why don't you just drop us off," I said. "Then you two can play your little games."

Davis looked at me. "You're sure they're only after us?"

Li Po stood in the bow, leaning on the bulwarks. The water puckered and swirled around submerged rocks. Others showed like gray-backed sea lions. I looked back at the approaching *Seal*.

"I doubt Max has any charts of these waters," Davis said.

"Like an old fur seal bull," Natasha said. "More balls than brains." She looked at me and put her hand over her mouth. "Oops," she said and then the *Seal* struck a reef, climbing partway out of the water and canting over with both booms swinging wildly. Two of the figures on deck tumbled into the scuppers. Only the man at the wheel kept his balance.

All three of us were watching the confusion when Li Po gave a sudden shout and the *Emilia* also struck ground with a series of shuddering thumps. "My fault, goddamnit," Davis yelled.

Quick as a cat Natasha pulled 67 alongside, jumped in her and started the engine. No one had said a word to her but Davis ran to the stern and passed her a line which she secured to the stern cleat of the skiff. She began to tow at full throttle, standing at the tiller, facing aft. The skiff yawed back and forth as Davis ran the *Emilia's* engine hard in reverse.

"Just past high water," he shouted to me. "If we don't come off we'll be stuck for a whole tide."

I looked across at the *Seal* which lay on her side about two hundred yards away. They had launched a small skiff but it could not possibly tow the schooner free.

"Goddamn, goddamn, GODDAMN," Davis said as the *Emilia's* stern slewed to one side and then she came free with a grinding bump. Natasha quickly cut the skiff's engine, cast loose her line and came alongside and climbed back aboard.

Still watching the *Seal* I saw a figure in a checked suit bracing himself against the rigging. Light glinted on a rifle barrel. "Look out," I yelled.

Jason Davis took a quick step and shoved Natasha down in the scuppers. The rifle cracked simultaneously. "Sweet Jesus," Davis said and sat down on the deck. Natasha crawled over and put one arm around him, cradling him. Li Po ran to the wheelhouse and put the *Emilia* in forward and cranked the wheel hard over, steering for open water. The rifle cracked again and I saw a faint splash astern. Natasha pulled her hand away from Davis's side. It was marked with blood.

I was still standing, my mouth agape. Li Po shouted at me to go forward and watch for rocks. Davis pushed Natasha aside and climbed shakily to his feet as I ran forward. He leaned against the rail, arms across his belly. Natasha took the wheel while Li Po pulled the hatch cover and jumped down in the hold. I scanned the surface for rocks but by now we were a ways offshore. I drew a deep breath.

Li Po reappeared and beckoned to me. "We're making water. I can't get at the leak, you'll have to pump."

The pump was located just forward of the wheelhouse. I fitted the long handle and began to work it back and forth till a jet of water began to spew over the side. Meanwhile Li Po swung the mainmast and foremast booms far out to starboard, causing the *Emilia* to list. He looked over the side. "Not enough," he said. "Help me move some barrels."

Together we grabbed a whiskey barrel and maneuvered it to the starboard rail. Jason Davis came forward to help despite Li Po's gestures for him to go back. Davis's shirt was bloody but he was moving almost normally. We wrestled two fuel barrels to the rail as well and lashed them there. There was a pronounced list now but we attempted to move one last barrel only to have it slip on the slanting deck. It knocked Davis into the scuppers and he lay face down for a moment clenching and unclenching his fists but then he struggled to his knees. Natasha watched with frightened eyes, unable to leave the wheel.

"Too old, Li Po," Davis said with a grin, his face totally devoid of color. "We're getting too old for this game."

We half-carried Davis back and leaned him against the wheelhouse. Li Po looked over the side and then once more went down to the hold while I returned to the pump. When Li Po came back he said, "That must have been a saw-toothed rock. We're only making a little water now but we're going to have to put her on the beach and patch her."

"Larsen Bay," Davis said. "It's got a nice gradual sand beach. We can careen her there."

"What about Gottschalk?" I asked. I looked back but we had rounded the point and the *Seal* was lost to view.

"He's going to be there a good while. He won't be off till the afternoon tide at the earliest. He can't know how badly we're holed. With luck he'll think we're headed back to Unga."

The fog had finally lifted. Our course was a direct line between the small islands Bendel and Turner toward Larsen Bay. Li Po took the wheel. I pumped till she was nearly dry then went below. Davis sat at the galley table with his shirt off. Natasha had cleaned away the blood but there was a discolored puncture and vivid blue bruises. His ribs were stark as whalebone.

"It's not so bad," Natasha said to me. "The bullet deflected off a rib and went around to his back. I'm going to cut it out."

"That damn Fitzgerald," Davis said. "We were almost out of range, but fools are always dangerous."

Natasha had put a knife in a pan of boiling water. She made Davis lean over the table, took the knife, hesitated, and then made an incision. I looked away as the blood welled. Davis made no sound but he put his head down and gripped the mast where it came through the table. Natasha was nearly as pale as Davis as she worked the bullet free and dropped it on the table. She gave me a stricken look.

"Judgment and retribution," Davis said. Sweat stood on his forehead. "That's part of your theology, isn't it, John?"

"More or less." I watched Natasha take a clean, white blouse from her bag and rip it into strips. She improvised a bandage and wound adhesive tape around Davis's chest. "But I don't get it. Gunfire and all. What's this got to do with botany?"

"Nothing, really. Thing is, nobody believes you're after plants. It was the same in China. All the peasants thought we were British spies. Caused no end of trouble."

"But these are white men," I said. Natasha rolled her eyes and pulled the tape so tight that Davis let out a yelp.

"You've got at least one cracked rib," she said. "You should see a doctor."

"Where, Kodiak? I've been stove in before. It'll mend." With trembling hands he rolled a cigarette, spilling much of the tobacco. He lit it and inhaled then coughed violently. He pulled a handkerchief from his pocket and coughed again. Bright spots of blood flecked the linen.

"In Siberia," he said, "I watched a fox cross a frozen lake. A brilliant splash of red against the snow. But a pack of wolves caught him there in the open. They tore him to shreds."

Natasha took the cigarette from his hand, snuffed it, and said, "Maybe they envied his color."

PART V

Nagai

Although we had carried with us for some days several dead soldiers and the dead trumpeter to bury them ashore, they were now flung without ceremony head over heels into the sea since some superstitious persons, at the start of the terror, considered the dead as the cause of the rising seas.

One asked, "Is the water very salty?" as if death were sweeter in sweet water.

> —Steller's account of the wreck of the *St. Peter*
> November the sixth, 1741

CHAPTER 23

The pump finally sucked air. I sat on the rail till my breathing returned to normal. We were making slow progress, running at half throttle and bucking the ebb. Ahead of us the high ridge of Nagai was a patchwork of light and dark—rock that shone almost yellow in the sun and green grass that stood out from the shadows, much as it must have looked for Steller coming in from the sea two centuries before.

We reached Larsen Bay about the second hour of the flood. While the *Emilia* drifted in the bay Natasha and I went ashore and pitched our tent and built a fire. Then we brought Jason Davis ashore in the skiff. An hour before high water Li Po and I ran the schooner inshore till she touched ground. Li Po rigged a double block to a buried drift log as a deadman then ran a line from its hook to the crosstree on the main mast. He took the lifting line from the double block back to the deck winch and as the tide receded we hove the *Emilia* gently on her starboard side. Lastly we unrove the line to the block and moored her to the same log.

Li Po and I climbed on the keel to inspect the damage. We found a broken plank just below the turn of the bilge. Li Po used a tool with a small, hooked head to pull some of the shattered wood free. I picked up a piece and broke it, exposing signs of rot.

"I'll let it dry overnight, before replacing the broken part of the plank," Li Po said. "If I put a sheet of copper over it, bedded in pine tar, it should hold but the old girl is showing her age. I might sister the cracked rib, but I don't know how much time we have."

"Are we really in any danger?" I was thinking more of Max than of rotten wood.

"Depends on what you fear."

"They took a shot at us."

"Fitzgerald did. For Max, I doubt the stakes are high enough."

"I just don't get the violence."

"These men are seal hunters, John. Blood is what they know."

"But that makes it all sound so random." I shook my head. I was still puzzled by Fitzgerald's role. Unless the shooting was a way to up the ante, to make Max believe the pot was worth the trouble.

"From what I've seen of chance and design and character, they all braid together like the strands of a rope."

"Don't get all inscrutable on me, Li Po. There has to be a reason. I mean, is this about the orchid or black ivory or what?"

"Davis told you about the black ivory?" Li Po laughed.

"Sort of. But isn't there also something about that woman Lena?"

"Something? I guess you could say that. Davis met her in Petropavlovsk, singing in a saloon. Max was there as well and Lena played them both, she was desperate to get to America. She gave Davis a gold rouble for passage but the day before we planned to leave he disappeared. I found him days later and miles away, passed out drunk in a Koryak village."

"And Lena?"

"She ran off with Max."

"But it all seems so long ago." Or could the genesis be even further away, back in Yunnan before the war with Audrey and Arbuthnot? Or further yet, with Steller and Brigitta Helena and Messerschmidt in St. Petersburg? Too many overlapping triangles, linked through the years as if by the stilted walk of a compass divider.

We lowered my steamer trunk to the sand and dragged it a little distance up the beach toward the campsite. Natasha had fashioned a sort of pallet from driftwood and Davis reclined against it while she prepared a stew of sea otter meat.

"Do you think you can float her on the morning tide?" she asked Li Po.

He shook his head. "Too much to do. Maybe by evening. We can't outsail Max so maybe it's best to lie low. The *Emilia*'s not very visible lying on her side and there's a lot of islands to search."

"Did you ever tell Fitzgerald specifically about Nagai and Larsen Bay?" Natasha asked me.

I had to think for a moment; the days on the *Victoria* seemed impossibly distant. "I don't think so," I said slowly. "I just mentioned the Shumagins, nothing more than that."

Natasha looked out to sea. There was a bit of a headland shielding us from the strait but we were not well hidden.

"The toad beneath the harrow knows / exactly where each tooth-point goes," Li Po said.

Natasha shook her head, unconvinced by the poetry. Waiting did not suit her temperament. She served us bowls of stew, virtually the first food we had eaten that day. Jason Davis refused a bowl and she tried unsuccessfully to spoon-feed him. Watching her nurse him my bitterness returned. I had almost forgotten that Davis had marooned and robbed us. Trying to hold my temper I walked down to my trunk and brought back my copy of Asa Gray. I opened the book at random. The pages felt good in my hand; the drawings and the text were from a world I knew.

"*Orchidaceae*?" Davis asked.

"*Gramineae.*" I looked down at the page.

"But you still believe in Steller." His face was a mask of shadows in the firelight.

"Why not?"

"Bering ignored him. His wife abandoned him."

"What's that got to do with his work?"

"He died of drink, John. His grave was robbed. Stray dogs devoured his bones."

"But his name is in the literature."

"Attached to an extinct sea cow? Even his grave is gone now. The river took it." Davis coughed, leaned over and spat in the fire. A trail of blood and spittle marked his chin. I put down the Asa Gray and helped myself to more stew.

"Did you ever consider that Arbuthnot might have been duped?" Davis asked.

"No, it doesn't make sense." But then nothing did.

"Perhaps there's as much to be learned from a hoax as from reality."

"Nothing I want to know." My spoon scraped the bottom of the bowl.

"I can't quite envision you as a plant hunter, John Nelson. Botanists move like inchworms, gathering endless data, but with plant hunters it's more a leap of faith. A plant hunter will risk everything on a single roll of the dice. I don't see that headlong passion in you."

"I came up here, didn't I?" I said, stung by the suggestion of timidity. "Only difference is I'm not gonna end up out here, wandering around like some forlorn pilgrim."

"I didn't mean it as a criticism, John. Which was Steller? Botanist or plant hunter?"

I hesitated. "Both, I guess."

"I suppose that's right." Davis stared into the flames. "And perhaps I was neither."

"Davis." I blurted out. "What really happened in China?"

Natasha grabbed my arm to silence me but Davis wanted to talk. "At a river crossing our crew was split," he said. "Audrey and Arbuthnot were on the far side. They'd swum the horses and mules across. Li Po and I were still on the near side loading the packs in a dugout canoe. That's when the bandits struck. They came running down the path, stopping to draw their bows. Women, mostly, or so it looked, in their long skirts."

"Enough," Natasha said to him. "You need rest."

"Two of our porters fell." Davis ignored her. "The others scattered. Li Po and I and the boatman dragged the canoe into the river but halfway across an arrow struck the boatman and we capsized. Li Po clung to the boat and was swept over the falls. I thought he was lost. I floundered ashore in a shower of arrows but Audrey and Arbuthnot were already gone. I could see their horses crossing the next ridge. Audrey never even looked back. I ran into the woods and just kept going."

"Why didn't you follow them?"

"Why didn't they wait?" Davis pulled the lucky rouble from his pocket and tried to walk it across his knuckles but dropped it. "Two days before, I'd found her in his arms on the kang in a mountain inn. And that wasn't the first time." He picked up the rouble, looked at both sides then flipped it, spinning, into the heart of the fire.

Not the first time. Did he mean not the first time with Arbuthnot or not the first time overall? Too many questions with answers that I did not want to know.

"You're sure Audrey's not coming?" Davis asked me as the coin blackened. "Hard to believe she could resist a new orchid. In the old days nothing would have stopped her."

"She wanted to come," I said with a little more sympathy. "Maybe next year." I remembered Audrey posing elegantly against a backdrop of hothouse flowers. In truth I could not begin to picture her on these barren shores. The jungle, maybe.

"She must have thought I was killed." Davis said, to himself not to me. He looked up at the moon whose eastern horizon held the first shadow of waning. Moonlight carved a path across the water, faint as asphodel.

CHAPTER 24

A pot of pitch softened above a fire Li Po had built next to the *Emilia*. He stood on the keel scraping the broken plank clean of paint. A piece of sheet copper and a little bucket of copper nails sat beside him.

"Will you be needing any help, Li Po?" I asked.

"Maybe later, John." Li Po looked at the still-receding water. "The tide should be high late afternoon."

"I kind of wanted to spend the day botanizing. Then maybe if I help you launch we can go our separate ways." I looked back toward the campsite. Jason Davis sat huddled by the fire, a wisp of smoke curling from his cigarette. Natasha sat close beside him and I felt the sharp sting of jealousy, an adder's bite.

"Li Po," I said, "you were at the river ford?"

He stopped scraping the hull and looked at me. "I almost drowned. I can't swim so I held on to the dugout till it drifted ashore way downriver. By the time I got back upstream everyone was gone, even the bandits. When Davis and I crossed paths in Siberia years later it was like he'd found a ghost." He smiled at the memory. "But I sometimes think my reappearance resurrected other memories. Ones that should have stayed buried."

"I just don't get Audrey running off with Arbuthnot. They're so different. It's not much of a marriage." But then I could not imagine Audrey with Jason Davis either.

"Go to the circus and sooner or later you'll see an ox yoked to a panther."

"Maybe." I headed to the tent to fetch my rucksack. This whole show was a circus but what did Li Po mean? Perhaps the two were drawn together because they were so different that neither could get the upper hand. Then the fall that broke his back set the bond in stone. And still neither would give up the contest of wills.

As I passed the fire Natasha looked up and said, "Where are you going?"

"Plant hunting. What I came here for."

"Wait, I'll go with you." She jumped to her feet and wrapped her black shawl around her shoulders. Her hair hung full and loose and she gathered it in one hand and freed it from the shawl as we began to walk south.

The day was clear and cold but a bit of wind thinned the mist that rose from the water as though the sea were breathing. We crossed a low, sandy ridge and began to follow a small creek toward the sea. Crisscrossed drift logs jammed its lower stretches. Two oystercatchers flew at our approach—black birds with long, red beaks. We found a single chick, almost fully fledged, crouched in the grass beside a log.

"Oh, the dear thing, let's not scare it," Natasha said and took my arm to draw me away.

"You sure have a lot of sympathy for anything sick or weak," I said irascibly.

"He's dying, John Lars."

"Of broken ribs?" I knew she did not mean the chick.

"Of something. I listened to my mother cough all that last winter. The tone changes, like when you drive a nail and the sound gets darker as the nail goes deeper."

We reached a beach with white sand as fine as flour. Shells of butter and razor clams paved the creek bed where it crossed the sand to lose itself in the sea. The shells crackled like autumn leaves beneath our feet. Offshore a thick kelp bed moved in the swell.

We turned and followed the windrow of kelp that marked the storm tide line. The carcass of a long-dead sea lion lay ribboned with dried popweed. The endless wind had abraded and desiccated the hide that stretched like a worn tent across the bowed ribs. A mouse or vole had gnawed an entrance between two ribs, the record of its comings and goings as faint as stitch marks in the sand.

"Remind me when we voted to cast our lot with those guys," I said.

"We didn't. Things just happened."

"Because Davis saved your life?"

"He didn't save my life, he just got himself shot."

I knew by now how impossible it would be for Natasha ever to admit she needed help.

"So now you're friends," I said.

"He's an outcast. I know what that's like."

"You can't decide things just based on loyalty."

"Why not?"

"You just can't."

"But if you can't tell who . . . Look, do you have even the faintest idea why you came here?"

"I'm doing a plant survey." I looked down. The first flower above the reach of the tide was a beach cinquefoil with small yellow blossoms and slender runners that reached in all directions as if seeking something unknown.

"No, you're not. You're just looking for that make-believe orchid."

"The orchid has to be real. I didn't come all the way to this godforsaken country for nothing."

"Godforsaken," she said slowly and looked back the way we had come. Wind and tide had already begun to obliterate the signs of our passing. The light had a blurred quality like incipient mist. "You and Davis, you can't see what's right in front of you."

"At least I can still tell right from wrong."

She studied me for a long moment. The sea lion's shadow just touched the yellow blossoms of the cinquefoil. "This is the North, John Lars," she said. "Light and dark are different up here."

She began to walk back north. I wanted to scream after her that I loved her. I was crazy in love with her but she was too much for me, the whole situation was too much for me. This country was too big and she was too quick, too strong, too smart.

I should have chased her down and thrown my arms around her but I turned and headed south, raging at myself. Within an hour I came to a large lake that nearly spanned the island. Presumably it was the lake advocated by Steller as a watering place. I skirted it, crossed a steep ridge and came to what must have been the small pond where Bering had instead chosen to draw water. I tasted the water and it was indeed brackish.

I looked around, trying to imagine where Nikita Shumagin lay buried. A lonely place for a grave; had his long sleep been untroubled? A hawk cried behind the wind.

Beyond the pond was a multi-peaked ridge that I climbed in a series of long traverses. Once on top I looked around. The eastern passes were empty but to the west near Sea Lion Rocks I saw a schooner inbound for Unga. I thought it might be the *Seal*.

I sat on a rocky ledge and took Palmer's scarf from my rucksack and wound it around my neck against the chill. I thought about Li Po saying that violence was commonplace in a seal hunter's life. Crack of the rifle, bright blade of the knife, hot spurt of blood—all so strange to me. When Professor Arbuthnot told stories about China I was hungry for a similar adventure but now I wanted out of what I had found. I preferred flowers to blood. I drew my scarf tighter and closed my eyes and concocted a fantasy in which I rescued Natasha from the *Seal*.

A shrill whistle awakened me. A marmot sat on a nearby rock, twitching its tail. I checked my watch: not quite two o'clock, I could go a little further before turning back. I followed the ridgeline southwest but there was nothing but bare rock and sparse vegetation on top. I dropped a hundred feet or so down the south slope and tried to follow the contour of the hill, thinking that the southern exposure might provide marginally better habitat for orchids.

The hill was steep and the footing tricky. I stopped to rest, feeling a bit discouraged. As I scanned the hillside below me I thought I caught a flash of scarlet unlike anything I had seen so far. It flashed, then was gone, then flashed again, faint but definite. I headed downhill, slipping and clutching at tufts of grass, till I reached a rocky promontory that overlooked the pocket meadow where I had seen the flash of color. It was gone. The meadow was drab green but then the scarlet flashed again.

There was no easy way down to the meadow but I found a cleft almost like a chimney and started down it gingerly, bracing myself against the sides. At first it went well and I was nearly there when I slipped, clutched at a rock, missed, and slid the last ten feet to end up face down on the grass. I lay there for a minute. My hands were scraped and I had wrenched my left knee rather badly. I sat up and then crawled over to where I had seen the flash of color.

A length of red ribbon was caught on a stalk of arrow grass. I sat back in disbelief. An eddy of wind waved the ribbon like a banner. How had it come here? The wind, of course, unless a bird had dropped it, like one of the ravens that fed Elijah. I freed the ribbon and wound it around my fingers. It was soiled and frayed, the bright crimson dulled but still more gaudy than the grass. I had the irrational thought that it had been there since Bering.

I stuck the ribbon in my pocket and pulled out my watch. The hands still pointed to two o'clock. In all the confusion I must have forgotten to rewind it. Suddenly the shadows looked a lot longer. I limped back to the cleft and took a tentative step upward but realized there was no way I could negotiate the bottom twenty feet.

The cliff face beetled out above me. Looking down toward the sea I thought I saw a possible route, a long slanting decline to the water's edge. Cautiously I set out, following the dwindling meadow, then scrambling awkwardly on the steep hillside. My left knee was on the downslope side, bearing most of my weight, and I had to stop frequently. I thought of the three waiting by the campsite but there was no way I could hurry. After what seemed hours I reached the water's edge on trembling legs. The tide was ebbing and the shadows were long.

I turned and limped back north. When I reached the salt pond I stopped briefly in the gathering dusk but thoughts of Shumagin's ghost drove me on. Too tired now to climb I tried to follow the shoreline and stumbled through a tussocky bog till I came to the edge of the large lake. Its surface bled the last light from the sky as though it were a mirror where both light and shadow went to die. I stood, bone-weary and penitent, and stared into the waters but saw nothing.

Another hour passed before I topped the last hill and saw our fire. The flames were windblown scarlet petals. The *Emilia* still lay on her side, a pale specter in the moonlight.

"Where have you been?" Natasha asked in a low voice when I collapsed beside her.

"I got lost." My fingers trembled as I unlaced my wet boots.

"We tried to launch the *Emilia* but Davis insisted on helping. He started hemorrhaging really badly and we had to stop."

There was a cooking pot next to the fire and I helped myself. I was expecting more sea otter stew but the meat was white and strangely seasoned.

"What's this?" I asked quietly.

"Peregrine. Li Po went to watch for the *Seal* and he took the shotgun."

"Curried falcon," Li Po said. He was mending a torn pair of canvas pants. "Captain Harold Snow's favorite dish. Very healthy with rice."

"I saw the *Seal* over by Unga, I think," I said when I had finished my bowl.

"Let's hope he's headed for Siberia," Natasha said.

"The Kolyma," Davis said suddenly. "The jumble of tusks and the stench of rotten blood in the hold. Dark as the grave."

Pale and haggard though Davis had been, now he was worse. He turned to me. "Did I tell you of Père Soulie? Jean-André Soulié? He was a French missionary and a very able botanist. Tibetan monks attacked his mission and hacked his people to death with their great two-handed swords. A few escaped and the Tibetans sent women scouts armed with poisonous arrows to hunt them down. Harpies. Soulie was tortured to death, his collection scattered. But why am I telling you this?"

He mumbled to himself, as if sorting through the storehouse of memory, trying to touch everything one last time. "The longbows were made of bamboo, the bowstrings woven from nettles. Aconitum poisoned the arrows. Listen for the bowstring, John. You can tell the difference."

The difference from what? The one that hits you and the one that misses? The shadow of waning had moved a little further across the eastern rim of the moon. A log broke in the fire and there was a hiss and then a ticking sound like a deathwatch beetle. I was so tired I could barely think and my knee throbbed like the slow ringing of a bell. I needed to lie down. I put down my plate and rose very carefully to go to the tent but Davis heard me and opened his eyes again.

"Did you find it?" he asked.

"No."

"Keep looking."

CHAPTER 25

"He died just before first light," Natasha said. She had stretched an old, gray sail on the ground and was cutting it with a pair of heavy shears. Her blue muslin covered Jason Davis. A heavy mist cloaked the ground though the sky above was blue. Sleep had not cleared my head but my knee felt almost normal.

Li Po and I lifted Jason Davis onto the sail. I was not prepared for the stiff, clumsy weight of rigor mortis. Natasha began to sew up the shroud, pushing a sailmaker's needle through the heavy canvas. Her lips moved softly. She was singing "From Greenland's Icy Mountains," but slowly, like a dirge.

This was all too eerie for me and I went down to the water's edge and pulled 67 ashore and took Hjalmar's pick and shovel from beneath the load. Natasha lifted her head from her work and I realized I could hear the faraway chug of a boat's engine. The engine noise grew steadily louder. For a moment we could see the topmasts of a ship headed south in Nagai Strait, a little ways offshore.

"The *Seal*," Li Po said as the noise faded. Natasha shook her head and bent to her stitching.

Li Po and I dug a shallow grave on the rocky hillside then laid the body in the grave. Natasha threw a small bouquet of windflowers into the grave and then turned and walked away. I expected Li Po to say something but without a word he picked up the shovel. When the first shovel full of dirt drummed on the canvas shroud I felt a jolt of nausea. I thought about the previous night. When I lay dying what mix of memories and dreams and regrets would braid together in my last moments?

An inquisitive fox watched us. When the mound was finished it yawned mightily and walked away. I carried the tools down and found Natasha by the water's edge, staring into the mist.

"You should have kept vigil with us," she said. "He asked for you near the end, something more he wanted to tell you."

"I was tired," I said lamely.

"Tired?"

"Look, I didn't think I was entitled to watch him die, all right?"

She wrinkled her nose. "What's that supposed to mean?"

Then we heard the motor again, approaching from the south now, still very faint. Natasha's eyes widened in alarm.

"I'll go look," I said and ran with a limp toward the headland at the southern end of Larsen Bay. I had no plan in mind; I just wanted to escape from Natasha's questions and from the sour aftertaste of death. I scrambled up the ridge and lay in the damp heather where the cliff fell away to the sea. Fog still blanketed the water and gulls circled the cliff front incessantly. Beneath their lonely voices I could hear the engine growing louder.

The masts and hull of a schooner gradually emerged from the mist, working northward. I could make out the figure of a man standing at the wheel on the afterdeck. Someone swathed in black sat on the rail near him. There was a lookout in the bow, leaning on the forestay. The fog was thinner now in Larsen Bay and I was afraid the *Emilia* would be visible when they passed.

A sharp nudge on my shoulder nearly sent me over the cliff. I turned and saw Francis X. Fitzgerald leaning on a walking stick and leering at me.

"Top of the mornin' to ye, young Nelson," he said. He was still wearing the checked suit, now torn and filthy. His derby hat was beaded with dew and as he leaned jauntily on his stick I could see a pistol shoved in the waistband of his trousers. My first, incongruous thought was, how had he managed to sneak up on me wearing such conspicuous clothing?

"What are you doing here?" I stammered.

"Captain Gottschalk was kind enough to put me ashore for me mornin' constitutional and I thought as how I'd drop by and say hello, you and me bein' old shipmates and all."

He spoke mockingly with an exaggerated brogue. I climbed to my feet and looked down at the *Seal*, which was just altering course to enter Larsen Bay.

"Max is a little bashful at heart and he thought it might be wise for me to go ahead and make introductions kind-of-like. It's been a slow season and him and me has taken a considerable interest in just what ye's might be doin' out here."

"I told you before I was doing a plant survey."

"Are ye now?" Fitzgerald took an iron grip on my arm. "All the years I've known Jason Davis, never've I seen him take an interest in such learned matters. Him and his Chinaman both. If they're in it there'll be the scent of money somewheres."

Still holding my arm he began to steer me back toward the campfire. "We seen ya on the ridge top yesterday," he said conversationally. "That blue-and-white scarf of yours sticks out a mile. We'd thought you'd gone to Sand Point."

When we passed the gravesite Fitzgerald asked, "Just what might this be?"

"Davis died last night. We buried him this morning."

"Is that a fact, now? How convenient for him."

In the bay the *Seal* rounded to and I saw the faint splash of the anchor being lowered. Natasha and Li Po sat by the fire. Natasha had the shotgun across her knees and was polishing the barrel with a rag, which was odd because the bluing had long since disappeared.

"Now I don't call this a very friendly greeting for another old shipmate," Fitzgerald said as we walked up. "Such an ugly gun for such a pretty lady. Why don't ye set it aside so's we can have a bit of a jaw about old times."

Natasha looked at him coldly and made no move. Fitzgerald tightened his grip on my arm and twisted until I could not help but wince. Seeing this Natasha laid the shotgun very carefully against a log but still within easy reach.

Fitzgerald let go of my arm and seated himself by the fire. "That's better. Now let's sit nice and sociable-like and wait for Max." Turning to Li Po he said, "Sorry to hear about the recent demise of your partner, Ching Ching. Or is it Captain Ching Ching, now?"

Li Po gave him a look of polite incomprehensibility.

"Now don't pull that dumb Chinaman shit. I know you speak English better than I do." Fitzgerald pulled a knife from his pocket and began to whittle a piece of firewood. "Jason Davis," he said speculatively. "I always took him for a sickly soul. Not long for this troubled world."

"Being shot didn't help matters," Natasha said tartly.

Fitzgerald tested the edge of his knife with his thumb. "But there wouldn't be any need to mention that in town now would there, missy?"

A keel crunched on the gravel as the *Seal*'s dinghy was beached next to 67. The Cossack had been rowing and he climbed out and pulled the bow ashore. Max and Lena followed. As they approached the fire I saw that Max was shorter than I had thought, shorter even than Lena. He wore a pistol and a heavy cartridge belt and carried a rifle in his right hand.

"Davis is dead." Fitzgerald jerked his chin in the direction of the grave.

A tremor crossed Lena's face, cloud shadow over still water. Her gaze flicked across the hillside and paused briefly on the newly made grave.

Max stood looking down at us. He was smoking a hand-rolled cigarette and his long teeth were discolored by tobacco. "So just what were you and Davis doing out here?" he asked Li Po.

"The *Emilia* was chartered by this young man from Yale College to do a survey. Flowers, that's what we were looking for." Li Po spoke calmly but with a hint of mockery that surprised me.

Max tossed the stub of his cigarette in the fire, grabbed Li Po by his queue and struck him full in the face. My stomach jolted and I tasted bile in the back of my throat. Natasha glanced quickly at the shotgun.

"Max," Lena said sharply but Gottschalk ignored her. He took a tin of tobacco from his shirt pocket and began to roll another cigarette.

"Just how did you plan to turn a profit off flowers?" he asked.

A little blood marked Li Po's lip but he appeared completely unruffled. "People will pay great amounts of money for certain flowers, I'm told. But we were just making money off the charter. It's better than salting gray cod."

Max grunted and lit his cigarette with a coal from the fire. "Nikita," he said to the Cossack and jerked his thumb at the *Emilia*. Together they walked down to the schooner and boarded her.

Nikita, I thought. His first name would be the same as Shumagin's. He gave off the sour odor of a bear and was about as communicative.

"He's mute," Fitzgerald said, following my gaze. "Got his tongue cut out by the Bolsheviks for some reason." Fitzgerald looked toward the *Emilia*. "Max is a little bent out of shape about Davis being dead. There's bad blood between 'em and Max hates to not get even. I half expect him to dig Davis up just to spit in his face." Fitzgerald laughed a little nervously and ran his tongue across his lips.

A clanging noise came from the *Emilia* and I looked up to see the samovar fly over the rail, soon followed by other goods. Lena looked up the hillside at the grave and her lips moved slightly but whether she was praying or arguing with her memory of Davis I could not tell. Fitzgerald sang an Irish ballad softly and whetted his thin-bladed knife on his shoe leather. His gaze lingered on Natasha, who sat with her head on her knees, nearly asleep.

Eventually Max climbed out of the hold and jumped down onto the pile of ship's stores. He gave the samovar a kick and walked over to my steamer trunk, opened it, and began tossing my belongings on the sand. I jumped up and ran down to them. "You can't do that," I said. "That's mine. Some of it belongs to Yale College."

Max ignored me. Nikita's face split into a demonic grin and he tossed some of my collection into the air. Sheets of pressed flowers scattered in the wind.

"Wait a minute," I said but Nikita put his foot on one sheet and ground it into the sand. It was the pseudoarnica I had found near Hooper Bay, two or three lifetimes ago.

"I can pay you to leave us alone," I said but Max slit the lining of the trunk with his sheath knife. He found my hidden cache of money and stuck it in his pocket.

"Look, my father's a rich man," I said, starting to babble. "He has powerful friends. The governor comes to dinner." Max grunted angrily and Nikita put a hand on my chest and with no apparent effort pushed me so sharply that I took two steps backward and sat down heavily. I could hear Fitzgerald's mocking laughter. I stood up and dusted my pants off and walked back to the fire with what dignity I could muster.

Max slammed the trunks shut and walked back to the *Emilia*. When he returned he had a pint bottle of whiskey sticking out of each pocket. Not the trade whiskey but some that Davis had stored in the cabin.

"Pretty slim pickins," Max said. "Where'd you get them sea otter, Li Po?"

Li Po gestured to the east. "The outer islands."

"You got a market for 'em?"

"Shanghai. Market for everything there."

Max pulled a sheaf of bills from his pocket, wetted his thumb and began to count them. "This all you got from trading?" It looked as though he had found neither the remaining opium nor the proceeds from its sale.

"Nobody much wants Russian tobacco and tea," Li Po said. "Not even the Eskimos."

"Jesus, is it any wonder? I got so tired of that crap when I was in the mines. I might burn the *Emilia* just to see the last of that stuff."

Max took a long swig from one of the bottles. Nikita came up from the boat carrying one of the tins of trade whiskey. He took a sheath knife from his belt and punched two holes in the top, then lifted the whole can and took a drink. Some of the whiskey poured down his beard as he drank greedily. When he set it down Fitzgerald poured himself a cup and nodded to the company. "Here's to the governor's dinner party." He winked at me and tossed back the whiskey. "You should water it down more, Li Po," he said banteringly and poured another cup. "You're cheating yourself."

"That sonofabitch Lucas," Max said. "That was my whiskey." He scowled at Fitzgerald. Obviously chasing the *Emilia* had been Fitzgerald's idea and if Max decided it was a wild goose chase life might not be a bed of roses for Francis X. Max took another long drink and said to Li Po, "So you two really was lookin' for flowers?"

"Flowers. And whatever else came along."

"Jesus, the things a man has to do to make a living in this country." Max nursed his bottle and stared into the fire. "Wait a minute," he said. He rose and walked down to the *Emilia Galotti* and returned with the Wardian case. "Just what the hell is this supposed to be?"

"It's for transporting live plants," I said diffidently. Max looked at me uncomprehendingly and I tried to explain. "You see, the water given off during transpiration can't evaporate because it's a sealed environment. So the idea is . . ."

I stopped as a slow flush began to spread across Max's face. Out of the corner of my eye I saw Natasha grin slightly for the first time that day. I half expected Max to smash me in the mouth. Instead he rubbed the back of his hand across his chin stubble.

"What the hell," he said and tossed the box aside. He shook the whiskey bottle to see how much was in it and then drained it with one long swallow and threw it toward the cove. He walked up the hillside to the gravesite, a little unsteady on his feet now. He unbuttoned his pants and urinated on the mound.

Lena grimaced and looked away. "Come help me," she said to Natasha. "A hot meal will do some good."

Li Po fetched some salted sea otter meat and the women began to fry it with onions. *Allium*, I thought—the genus name for onions. More useful than the *Orchidaceae*.

Gottschalk came down the hill, buttoning his pants. "Well, your friend's gone now," he said to Lena. "No more fancy manners and highfalutin' talk." He scratched his belly and looked me up and down. "Davis was helping you with the plants and shit?"

"Not really."

"I thought he knew all about that stuff."

"Not enough to matter," I said, thinking about Jason Davis's unfortunate life. Natasha pursed her lips in annoyance as she turned the frying meat.

Max walked to our tent and pulled back the flap. "What's that portmanteau thing with the leather straps?"

"It's a plant press. Here, I'll show you." I pulled a few sheets of paper from the press. Max scratched his bullet-shaped head and then touched a bog violet very gently with a blunt forefinger.

"They pay people to do this?" he asked in a puzzled tone. "Doesn't seem right somehow. What's the good in it?"

"Knowledge, I guess."

Max shook his head and opened another bottle. I spent a little time changing the papers in the press. There was an air of normalcy in the camp but it was thin and brittle. Max in person was more of a buffoon than I expected and oddly enough I kind of liked him. But I did not doubt his capacity for violence. I felt we were sitting on a powder keg and the randomness of everyone's behavior was not reassuring. I could not even tell if the people here were friends or deadly enemies. They were all locked in a dance where the steps followed no pattern I knew.

Fitzgerald and Nikita were still working on the tin of trade whiskey. While we ate, Max and Fitzgerald began to exchange stories of pelagic sealing. Li Po even added a few remarks. Max told an involved story about stealing pelts from a Russian-controlled rookery by disguising the *Seal* as a Russian gunboat. Nikita laughed uproariously, showing a mouth without front teeth but with long, lupine canines and the stub of a tongue.

By now the light was fading and the cold drawing closer. Li Po heaped wood on the fire. The moon was just rising over Big Koniuji Island. Natasha sat absently working her hair into two braids. Max eyed her and drew a speculative thumb across his lips. Catching his gaze, Natasha gave him a contemptuous look and moved closer to me. I felt that I offered poor security at best.

"Hey, kid," Fitzgerald said mockingly, "that the trophy you gonna take home? I thought you was huntin' flowers."

"She's just working for me. For the summer, that's all." I thought it would be safer for Natasha not to be linked with me.

"Look what I found in the islands. May I keep her, mother dear?" Fitzgerald laughed and looked at Natasha with small red boar's eyes. "The nut-brown maid."

Natasha stared into the fire wordlessly. Without actually moving she seemed to draw away from me.

"I want to go back to the *Seal*, Max," Lena said suddenly. It was an order, not a request.

Max locked eyes with her for a moment but then wavered. He shook his head as if trying to clear it of whiskey and said to Fitzgerald, "You two stay ashore and keep an eye on these birds. Y'oughta be able to do that much. I still can't figure out what's going on here." He stood and peered around as if trying to locate something.

"Natasha, you can come with us if you'd like," Lena said.

Natasha shook her head. "I think I'll stay here."

"Better you should come."

Natasha lowered her head, gathered a handful of sand and let it sift through her fingers without replying. Lena hesitated as if wishing to argue the point further. She gave Fitzgerald a cold glance and then looked at Nikita and spoke to him sharply in Russian. Nikita touched his forehead submissively.

Nikita accompanied them to their dinghy and helped launch it. Max nearly fell as he clambered over the gunwale. He collapsed in the stern and Lena took the oars to row across the moonlit cove.

"Well," said Fitzgerald, "ain't we the cozy little company." He shook the now-empty whiskey can and then strolled down to the *Emilia*. He returned carrying several of Jason Davis's brown bottles.

"Now," he said to Nikita, "I scarcely calls it fair that Max drinks the good stuff and leaves us the swill."

He gestured expansively and almost as if by sleight of hand drew his pistol and clubbed Li Po across the temple with its barrel. Li Po crumpled to the sand and Nikita leaped on him and pinioned his arms. Fitzgerald tossed Nikita a length of rope and the Cossack bound Li Po hand and foot.

With the pistol Fitzgerald gestured for me to sit on the sand and Nikita put a length of rope around my arms and pulled it tight. I could smell the whiskey on his breath and the sour reek of his unwashed clothing. He then tied my feet. Lastly Fitzgerald took a bandanna and tied it around my mouth as a gag.

"Hate to do this to an old shipmate, but I learned at my mother's knee you can never be too careful." He looked at Natasha. "Don't worry, sweetheart. Nobody'll get hurt unless you chooses."

He handed Nikita a bottle and sat back by the fire. Nikita drank long and deep then belched and stared stupidly into the flames. Fitzgerald threw more wood on the fire. In doing so he stumbled over the Wardian case. He looked at it and then threw it on the fire. The glass broke on impact.

"Jason Davis won't be needin' it anymore and that's a fact," Fitzgerald said. "Or was it yours? I kinda forget."

I lay on my side, my arms already numb from the bonds. I watched the flames play across the polished wood and pictured Jason Davis giving the case to his young bride.

Nikita drank again and then again until he had finished the bottle. He threw it away with a grunt then stood and looked around, rolling his head. Suddenly he went down on his back like a felled ox. He struggled to his knees and crawled toward the tent. Halfway through the door he collapsed and lay as if dead.

"Pity the man can't hold his drink," Fitzgerald said. "Comes from bein' Russian. To us Irish it's like mother's milk."

He sang a few phrases in a lilting voice then said, "You know, I rather fancied a career as a tenor. I believe I could have rivaled the great McCormack but luck was against me. Took a dark turnin'."

Looking at Natasha he said, "Now why do you suppose so many of the great old ballads are named for young girls?—'Kathleen Mavourneen,' 'Molly Branigan,' 'My Dark Rosaleen.'"

He began to sing, "Kathleen Mavourneen, the gray dawn is breaking, / The horn of the hunter is heard on the hill; / The lark from her light wing the gray dawn is shaking. Kathleen Mavourneen, What slumb'ring still?"

As he sang he walked over to where Natasha sat with her head bowed. He put a hand on her shoulder and caressed one of her braids. As he sang the last line of the stanza she looked up and spat in his face. He jerked her to her feet by pulling on the braid. She made no cry but tried to knee him in the groin. He blocked her knee and grabbed her shirt with his free hand. She twisted free, tearing her shirt open, then ran to the opposite side of the fire and stood with her fists clenched, staring him down.

"I love it when they play hard to get," Fitzgerald said. "It's so romantic in the moonlight."

Natasha picked up the coffee pot sitting in the ashes and hurled it at Fitzgerald. He warded it off with a raised forearm but the top came off and the hot coffee and grounds splattered him. He cursed just once and then pulled out his handkerchief and mopped his face, smiling malevolently all the while. He began to whistle "Kathleen Mavourneen" slowly as he replaced the handkerchief. He leaned down and picked up the shotgun.

Natasha picked a burning brand from the fire. She was breathing rapidly but still made no sound. I strained at my ropes, almost choking on the gag. I looked across at Li Po. A trickle of blood marked where the pistol's front sight had raked his scalp but he lay perfectly still, watching. I felt a surge of anger at his calm.

Fitzgerald edged around the fire. Natasha circled opposite him holding the brand in both hands. Fitzgerald came to where I lay and casually placed the muzzle of the shotgun against the back of my neck and leaned on it slightly. I put my face down in the sand and closed my eyes and began to pray. I felt the cold, round shape of the muzzle and heard the click of one hammer being cocked and my bowels turned to water.

"All right," I heard Natasha say and the pressure of the gun barrel eased. I opened my eyes and watched Natasha drop the brand in the fire.

"What was that, my dark Rosaleen?" Fitzgerald said mockingly.

Natasha said nothing but fumbled with the last untorn buttons of her shirt and then with a swift motion pulled off both shirt and undershirt. She stood bare-breasted with the shirt clutched to her stomach, her head bowed. Then she straightened and looked at Fitzgerald almost brazenly, her eyes flashing. She looked at the tent where Nikita lay.

"Not here," she said and turned and walked toward the *Emilia Galotti*, throwing the shirt across one shoulder like a matador's cape.

"Wait a minute," Fitzgerald said but she paid him no mind, almost sauntering now, her back pale as a moth, growing less distinct as she left the circle of firelight.

Fitzgerald broke open the shotgun and threw the shells in the grass, then pulled his knife and held the blade against my cheek.

"I do believe your young friend has taken a fancy to old Francis X. She's a bit country-bred for my taste but when you can't get chicken ya have to settle for seagull."

He pricked my cheek lightly with the point of the knife, straightened, and began to stroll toward the *Emilia Galotti* singing, "*It may be for years and it may be forever? Oh! why art thou silent, Kathleen Mavourneen?*"

Fitzgerald reached the schooner and climbed the ladder. The moment he disappeared Li Po jackknifed his body toward the fire. With his bound feet he kicked a red-hot chunk of wood from the coals and then squirmed around and held his wrists to it. I could smell the burning of the hemp rope and his cotton jacket. Sweat burst from his face and his jaws clenched as he strained at the bonds. Strand by strand they gave way. Without stopping even to look at his burned wrists he crawled toward the tent. He hesitated momentarily above the sleeping Nikita and then carefully drew the sheath knife from the Russian's belt. He cut the rope securing his ankles and then limped over to me.

"She is too reckless," he said. "We must hurry." He cut the ropes holding my arms and dropped the knife in my lap. While I sawed at the ropes around my feet he picked up the shotgun and began to search for the shells Fitzgerald had tossed in the grass.

From the *Emilia* came a string of laughing profanities and then a clamor as if someone had tripped and fallen in the cabin. There was silence for a few heartbeats and then a desperate shout that ended on an odd, gurgling note. A figure appeared from the companionway and darted across the sloping deck only to slip and fall in the scuppers. As I freed myself another figure appeared, one that stumbled and grabbed the rigging for support then extended an arm. I made a running start only to trip and fall headlong, my feet made clumsy from being bound.

"Natasha," I screamed as I tried to stand up.

There was a muzzle flash and the report of a pistol from the deck. Li Po had been running awkwardly, loading the shotgun as he ran. He dropped to one knee and fired. The explosion sounded twice as loud as the pistol. The figure by the wheelhouse jerked backward, turned and toppled overboard.

A savage blow from behind knocked me face down in the sand. A knee landed in the small of my back and a rough hand seized my collar. I could smell Nikita's whiskey breath but then a rabbit punch to the back of my neck split my world into shards of lightning, leaving me unable even to shout a warning.

Through blurred eyes I watched Nikita run toward Li Po who swung around to meet him. Li Po struck Nikita in the stomach with the shotgun but did not pull the trigger. Nikita straightened with a grunt and Li Po chopped at his knees with the gun barrel but Nikita used his superior weight to force Li Po to the ground. He wrested the gun free and threw it aside and grabbed Li Po by the throat.

My mind and body were still disconnected from the rabbit punch but I scrambled forward on all fours and tried to tackle Nikita around the knees. Without letting go of Li Po he kicked me hard in the stomach. I doubled up and rolled aside, gasping. I could see Li Po twist around, his eyes bulging as he struggled to break Nikita's stranglehold.

Then Natasha sprinted out of the darkness. In one move she scooped up the knife that lay glinting in the firelight and leaped on Nikita's back. She sank her hand in his hair, pulled his head back and slashed him across the throat.

Nikita gave a strange, voiceless bellow like a stricken bull. He turned and seized Natasha who struck at him again with the knife. Blood was squirting from his face and neck. He grabbed her knife hand and she sank her teeth in his wrist while he hit her in the body with his free hand. Li Po had squirmed free and he took the shotgun and brought the stock down hard on Nikita's head, driving him to the sand. Li Po raised the shotgun and hit the seal hunter again and then again as if driving the final spike in the railroad to hell.

I had managed to reach my knees. Natasha was no more than ten feet from me. She, too, sat on her knees with her head down. Blood marked her arms and shirt. She made a low, moaning sound, almost a keening. The crack of a rifle came from out in the bay and a fountain of sparks flew up from the fire. Natasha leaped to her feet and ran off into the darkness.

Li Po stood over Nikita as if catching his breath. He bent down and touched the man's throat then looked out to where the *Seal* lay floating in the moonlight. The rifle cracked again and more sparks flew. Still carrying the shotgun, Li Po hobbled off into the night.

I wanted to follow them but when I gained my feet a wave of pain and nausea made me drop back to my knees and I retched in the cold sand. A seagull that had perched for the night on the *Emilia's* canted foremast took wing and circled the boat and flew off, crying like a lost soul. From somewhere out in the bay I could hear the splash of oars but whoever was rowing was headed away, north along the shore. The sound grew fainter till at last I could hear nothing but my heart thudding within my chest.

I stood up gingerly. Odd flashes of colored light interrupted my sight. I walked carefully down to the *Emilia* and found the body of Francis X. Fitzgerald lying on the pile of jettisoned goods. Buckshot had torn his right shoulder, but there was also a jagged wound in his throat that exposed the trachea. Blood from this made an irregular blotch like a complex crimson flower on his shirt. *The Queen's Gambit*, I thought.

I fetched a piece of canvas from the nearly empty sail locker and spread it across the body. I looked at the fire and momentarily saw two distinct sets of flame but then my vision cleared. I walked back, warily skirting Nikita before realizing that he, too, was dead. I found the sail from which Natasha had cut Jason Davis's shroud and covered Nikita with it. I winced as I did so and looking down saw that two fingers of my left hand were bent grotesquely to one side, broken somehow in the melee. I had not even felt it till this time.

I sat down by the fire to keep vigil for I knew not what. Amidst the coals I could still make out the intricate dovetails of the Wardian case, barely discernible and rapidly turning to ash.

CHAPTER 26

The sun rose before the moon set. By first light I saw Natasha walking slowly along the beach, wading ankle-deep in the water. She had discarded her shirt and trousers and wore only her long, white undershirt. The morning was cool and mist rose from the water, yet she walked slowly and delicately as a deer.

When she reached the fire I greeted her by name but she did not answer. She started to walk to the tent but when she saw the imprint of Nikita's body in the blankets she turned away, then knelt by the fire and held her hands out to the flames. Her left eye was blackened and a torn piece of cloth was wrapped around the knuckles of her right hand. Blood discolored this bandage. I tried to put my coat around her shoulders but she shrugged it off.

I had stuck Nikita's knife in a log. Natasha reached for it, tried the edge, then hacked off both her braids and threw them in the fire. They burst into flames and began to shrivel. She watched them without a flicker of expression. There was a burn mark on her right palm and I remembered her throwing the coffee pot at Fitzgerald. A thousand years ago now.

Hearing the squeak of oarlocks I looked up and saw the *Seal's* dinghy approaching. Lena was alone at the oars. I went down to help her beach the dinghy. "Fitzgerald and Nikita are dead," I told her, "and Li Po ran off. Where's Max?"

"On the hills, watching. In the dark we could not tell what was happening. I put him ashore and he told me to go back and stay aboard but I had to know." She looked at the two shrouded bodies. "It's my fault. I never should have left her. I should have known."

She gathered her skirts and walked to the fire. Natasha looked up and Lena placed her fingers under Natasha's chin and very gently turned her head and studied the blackened eye.

Natasha twisted away. "I couldn't . . . It was so dark in the cabin. I couldn't even find a kitchen knife. I had to let him touch me."

She began to cry and Lena sat beside her, put an arm around her and began to stroke her butchered hair. Natasha buried her head against Lena's shoulder and I could hear her muffled voice saying. "The other one, the one like a bear. I found a bear's den one winter. I could see the steam from its breath and smell the stink even through the snow."

Lena continued to stroke her hair and rock her gently. When the sobbing eased, Lena said, "Not so very long ago I had to flee my father's home. When the Red Army came. I traveled with a maiden aunt but she died in the Urals. Raped and murdered by Cossacks while I cowered in the woods. I crossed Siberia alone. I ended up singing for tips in a waterfront saloon." She stopped and smiled wanly. "I'm telling you this because . . . " She hesitated again. "If someone like Fitzgerald had come to my father's estate I would have shrunk from him in terror. But after crossing Siberia I would have cut his throat without regret. And sat on his chest to rifle his wallet. You see, only God knows our fate and our strength."

Natasha kept her head buried and both arms around Lena's waist. Lena began to sing very softly, something about the soul's great sadness. I felt like an unwanted intruder and turned and walked down to the *Emilia Galotti*.

Two seagulls perched on the sail that covered Fitzgerald. I shooed them away and climbed on board. A trail of blood led down the companionway. The cabin was a shambles. Fitzgerald's knife lay in a corner. I picked it up but it almost burned my hand and I tossed it up the companionway and over the side. By the settee I found the arrow with the bone point that had struck the mast back in the Yukon delta.

So long ago now. Blood streaked the shaft, obscuring the decorative carving. So this was what Natasha had found in the dark.

I took the arrow to the sea and scoured it clean then stowed it in my trunk. I gathered the clothing and papers strewn on the sand and repacked them. Natasha lay by the fire on a bed improvised from coats. I looked up the hill toward Jason Davis's grave. I felt a flash of anger that he was not here to help us but maybe that was his particular fate—like a character written out of the play before the final act.

Max Gottschalk came walking down the hill, still wearing the holstered pistol and carrying a rifle. "What the hell happened to her?" he said when he reached the fire. Natasha lay with her knees drawn up to her body and her right arm with its bloody bandage shielding her face.

Lena shook her head in warning but Max had already turned away. He walked down to the *Emilia* and picked up a corner of the sail that covered Fitzgerald, then let it drop disgustedly. On his way back he gave Nikita's sail-covered body an irritable kick.

"Give 'em a simple job," he muttered. "Where's Li Po?"

"In the hills somewhere," I said.

"Goddamn. He's the only one with any sense around here." He cupped his hands like a trumpet and shouted, "Li Po," and again, "Li Po-o-o."

A moment after the echoes died I saw Li Po picking his way across the rock-strewn hillside. Max walked again to the *Emilia* and returned carrying four sea otter pelts still tacked to drying boards. When Li Po reached the campsite he stopped on the opposite side of the fire and nodded at us all calmly. I felt tremendously relieved to see him. When I had first met him in Nome I had thought he looked sinister and piratical but now I found his lined features as reassuring as the faded pages of an old book.

The stock of the shotgun showed newly splintered wood. Li Po cradled it casually, as though he were an English gentleman grouse hunting on the moors, but he kept his right thumb on one of the hammers and his eyes never left Max's face. Max held his own rifle over his shoulder. He swung it down and Li Po brought the shotgun to half cock. Hearing the click of the hammer, my stomach clenched but Max pointed his own rifle at the ground and made a deprecatory gesture with his left hand.

"I'm takin' half your pelts," he said, gesturing at the sea otter. "Jason Davis don't need 'em and anyway you two owe me."

Li Po held out his hand palm upward as if conceding a bargaining point.

"I know about your opium business," Max said. "If ya wanna go partners I got a little money to invest. A man's gotta try somethin' and this little adventure has sure been a bust."

"Perhaps something could be arranged," Li Po said, his first words since the melee of the night before.

Jason Davis dead and buried. Fitzgerald and Nikita dead. Li Po and Natasha beaten or worse. And the two talked as if it had been an inconvenient business transaction.

"Well, ya know how to find me." Turning to Lena, Max said, "Time to catch the tide down the straits. Write this place off."

"Shouldn't we bury those two?" I blurted out.

"Up to you, kid. You got enough flowers for a funeral." Max showed his wolfish grin. "Me, I'd let the crabs feed on 'em. Be the most useful thing they ever did."

Lena knelt and gave Natasha a long, wordless hug, looking over Natasha's shoulder toward the gravesite as she did so. Without a word she kissed Natasha on the forehead then together with Max walked down to their dinghy and launched it. When they reached the *Seal* Lena disappeared below without a backward glance. Very quickly the *Seal*'s anchor came aboard and she headed out to sea, Max alone at the wheel.

"Would you really go partners with Gottschalk?" I asked Li Po.

He touched his split and swollen lip. "Like Max says, a man has to try something." He broke the shotgun and leaned it against a log. I could see that the chambers were empty. He must have found only the one shell in the grass, which meant his play with Max had only been a bluff.

He and I skidded the bodies down to our skiff. They were both large men and it was heavy work. Li Po took a length of rope, looped it around a thwart, ran it across the gunwales and tied one body on each side by the wrists. Fitzgerald's head hung limply, his scalp dead white beneath his bald spot. Li Po emptied both men's pockets and kept a watch and a few dollars from Fitzgerald's.

"Something for my troubles," he said, catching my eye. He brought two lengths of chain and wired one to each body. As he worked I saw that his wrists were red and blistered. "Can't have them washing ashore too soon," Li Po said.

We launched the skiff and headed out the bay traveling slowly with our grotesque cargo bumping the sides. When we were a little way out in East Nagai Strait Li Po cut the motor and with one slash of my jackknife the two were gone forever. The only valediction that came to mind was the ballad "Kathleen Mavourneen."

High water was just before noon. We had beached the *Emilia* at the top of the tides and the moon was now three days past full. At high tide the water reached partway up the schooner. She wavered but did not quite float. Li Po bent several lengths of line together and then walked over to where Natasha sat silently by the fire. "We're going to have to kedge her off. We'll need your help," he said to her.

Together we manhandled the schooner's anchor into 67. We took the skiff a little ways out in the bay and Li Po and I dropped the anchor overboard while Natasha sat impassively at the tiller, the wind riffling her chopped hair.

Back on shore Li Po said, "We can't start the engine with her canted over. We'll have to work the windlass ourselves." He fitted three wooden bars to the capstan and as the tide rose we strained mightily on the slanting deck to move the *Emilia* inch by grudging inch. Pulling with all my strength I found myself leaning against Natasha's leg, the muscles of which were taut and trembling. She flinched away like a frightened deer.

With each click of the windlass we shifted the *Emilia* deeper in the water till at last she floated. Li Po started the engine and anchored offshore then went below. Natasha stared down the dark companionway and raised a hand as if to flip her braids out of the way but they were gone.

"You had to let him touch you?" I blurted out. I swear I meant it as a question, a sympathetic one, but anger and bewilderment flared in her eyes as though a furnace door had opened to show the fire within. But then the door clanged shut.

"I didn't let him do anything," she said and climbed over the rail into the skiff.

"But what did I do wrong?" I called after her. "What was I supposed to do?"

She turned her head away. "I don't know. Nothing, I guess," she said almost inaudibly.

We ferried ashore in silence. Natasha walked up to the fire but I lingered by my big steamer trunk that sat tilted on a bed of dried popweed. The decals for Shanghai, Rangoon, and Calcutta looked tawdry in the daylight. The newest label said "Not Wanted On Voyage."

Li Po came ashore around nightfall and we made a simple meal. When he had eaten, Li Po cleared his throat and said, "There is the matter of the charter."

I thought it a bit odd to pay someone for being marooned but without a word I opened my money belt and gave him the entire contents.

"Thank you," he said

"When do you plan to leave?"

"Sometime tomorrow. The fall storms are coming. Time to think about a winter haven."

"I want to go home," Natasha said without looking at me.

"Sure . . . ," I said slowly. "But give me one more day. Just one. I have to go all the way to the end of the island. Just so I can say I did it all."

"If that's what you want." She stared into the fire.

"Look, I have to try. I have to finish what I started. It's what you showed me. And I owe something to somebody, only I don't know what." I looked up at the stars. Clouds were massing and the moon had not yet risen. I tried again to picture the orchid but I could not even conjure its shadow.

"I don't know if I believe in the orchid anymore. Maybe it was like the sea ape—some strange illusion. Or maybe the letters were frauds. I don't know, but I have to see."

Li Po coughed discreetly and said, "When I was a boy the British in Shanghai had a fox hunt. But there were no foxes so they had two men on horseback lay a trail of bits of paper for the hunt to follow. A paper chase."

"So . . . ?"

"Two winters ago in Shanghai Jason Davis spent much time in a shop in the Russian Quarter. The Jew who ran the shop made passports and other documents."

"What was Davis doing there?"

"He would not tell me but I think now he was having those letters made. This man Glickman was very clever."

"But why?"

"As bait," Natasha said unexpectedly. "He wanted to lure that woman out here. Or at least talk to her through the letters."

"Only the wrong fish took the bait?" I shook my head as I chased the permutations, trying to reconcile them with what had come to pass. "That doesn't make sense. Why did you give me a ride from Nome, then?"

"We needed your money." Li Po laughed. "So first we said no and then we said yes. Davis was a little taken aback when you first arrived. You were like a mirror in which he could see himself as a young man and he didn't know what to do with you."

"I blindsided him, I guess, showing up in Nome. But why did he maroon us?"

"I don't know. Something changed. That morning in Izembek it was like his bones could no longer stand the touch of his flesh."

"You should have stopped him."

"I did stop him. He wanted to leave you alone, take Natasha with us. But I said you would die without her."

"And yet he came to Nagai."

"He said he wanted to look for sea otter. But I think he still hoped that woman would appear. He believed the wheel had to come full circle. Only it never does. Not in that way."

"At least he loved her," Natasha said. "That counts for something."

"Not much," I said. Natasha shook her head in annoyance and rose to fetch more wood. I had been thinking not of Davis but of Audrey and her manipulations. Had Audrey ever really loved anyone? I was sure that Davis marooned us when he figured out that Audrey and I were lovers. I could not admit that in front of Natasha even though she may have figured it out.

Li Po looked into the flames as if considering the many aspects of fire. "And maybe Davis came back because he feared you might actually find the orchid."

"But how can that be if he only imagined it?"

Li Po did not answer. Natasha tossed a log on the fire. A bit of cedar by the scent, one that had been caught in the gyres of the North Pacific only to be cast ashore on Nagai. A whirlwind of sparks ascended to the heavens. Each speck of light seemed to hesitate before fading to obscurity.

CHAPTER 27

Quietly I laced my boots and picked up my rucksack. At first I made slow progress in the landscape of shadows and vague outlines but then the sun cleared the eastern horizon and showed the flint-hard ridge beneath a gunmetal sky.

By mid-morning I had reached the causeway known as Saddlers Mistake, a thin spit of land with drift piles on both sides and grassy turf down the middle like a skunk's stripe. Beyond lay the mountainous ridge that formed the southernmost part of Nagai Island. I crossed the spit, asking myself: who was Saddler and what his mistake?

My knee had begun to twinge with every step and I had to scramble uphill on all fours. My stomach was still sore from Nikita's kick and my broken fingers trailed uselessly as I dug my hands in the scrubby brush. I stopped to rest and saw the *Emilia* outbound in the channel, sails set. Li Po was alone at the wheel. I waved but he did not see me.

I climbed in a zigzag fashion, casting about like a hound for any flash of crimson. I chased this chimera through the long afternoon till finally I reached the cliffs that overlooked Mountain Point, the outermost part of the island. There I found nothing but grass and barren rock and the immense vista of the North Pacific, and heard nothing other than the keening of gulls and the sandy whisper of grass stems scraping against one another.

I walked to the cliff's edge and pulled from my pocket the red ribbon that I had found three days before. How had it come to this island? I held it up to the wind and it twisted and wound around itself like a snake. Then I let go and watched it tumble out of sight, still dancing with the wind. I could not tell if it reached the sea.

At my feet was a tuft of wheatgrass with a long, slender culm and a spikelet of miniscule flowers so dense they bowed the stem. The lines of the grass were as sweet and succinct as anything God had ever made and I knew that this would have to be enough. I pulled the grass and stuck it in my rucksack and started down the hill, wondering if all knowledge was purchased with such pain and confusion. Who had spun the web that caught and brought me here? Or had it all been random? A chessboard where the players were arranged arbitrarily and even the black and white squares alternated without pattern.

For the last time I climbed the island's central ridge. My knee was so sore that I descended haltingly, one slow step at a time like a pilgrim at the close of his journey. I reached camp long after nightfall. The *Emilia* was gone and Natasha was nowhere to be seen. I built up the fire and by its wavering light read the last of the Steller letters, the one supposedly written from Bering Island where they lay shipwrecked:

Dec. 8, The Captain-Commander died today, two hours before dawn. He suffered terribly but was calm at the end. We are now like a ship without a rudder and I cannot believe we shall ever leave this island. You may never read this letter but all my writings are now like torn scraps of paper scattered by a merciless wind. Still, I think of you constantly, trying to recall the rapture of our first days together. I remember how intoxicated I was by the soft caress of your eyes while poor Messerschmidt still lived, by the light touch of your hand, the sweet promise of your voice. But then I recall the same look bestowed on so many others after our marriage. Will no one understand the torment of my heart? As the Captain-Commander lay dying he was consumed by vermin. He lay half buried in the sand and foxes circled incessantly, drawn by the scent of death. Just so does jealousy consume my heart. From the wreckage I saved the orchid I shall name for you, but in truth I scarcely know your name, except that it is the same as my own . . .

The letter broke off abruptly. The last communication, but who was speaking to whom about what? I crumpled the paper and threw it in the fire where it flared briefly and went out.

In the morning Natasha sat by the fire, back from wherever she had wandered. Together we launched 67 for the last time. A tumult of seabirds surrounded the skiff as we rounded Mountain Point and set course for Unga. I did not sit in the stern with Natasha but forward with my trunk, facing aft towards the hills of Nagai. Before we had left the campsite Natasha had dug through the firepit till she found Davis's blackened rouble. She scoured it briefly in the sand then stuck it in her pocket.

When we reached the village Natasha took her carpetbag and started up the hill to where Misses Devlin and Dennison stood waiting. That night at Hjalmar Mork's kitchen table I told him the story while he cleaned and re-bandaged my fingers.

"These are pretty ugly," Hjalmar said. "You best see a doctor."

"What I really need is a US Marshall."

He stopped wrapping the bandage. "What for?" he asked warily.

"Why, to report what happened. Three men are dead."

"People disappear all the time out here. Leave it be."

"But it's the law."

"Think you can keep Natasha out of it?"

"None of it was her fault." I stared at the single kerosene lamp that illuminated the table. A streak of soot marked one side of the glass chimney.

"By your own story she had a hand in the killing."

"In self-defense."

"You sure you can convince a judge of that? A half breed girl with a background of trouble?"

"I'll get her a lawyer. The best."

"Maybe so, but what school board would hire her after all this comes out?" He paused. "Unless you can lay it all on that Chinaman."

"Li Po? He's a friend, too."

"Then let it lie. Nobody's gonna be askin' after them three."

I looked out his window at Delarof Harbor, its surface like hammered silver. I did not care about Fitzgerald or Nikita but I thought something should mark the passing of Jason Davis. Then I thought of what my involvement in a murder trial might do to my father's political ambitions and I almost laughed aloud at the irrelevance, at the hollow vanity. I almost wanted a scandal, just to ruffle his feathers. But Hjalmar was right: what was buried had to stay buried.

"The mail steamer's due in Sand Point tomorrow," Hjalmar said. "The *Starr*. She'll be leaving for Seward in the evening."

"I don't know if I can be ready."

"She won't be back for a month. Best be on her." Hjalmar got up from the table and washed his hands in the kitchen basin.

The next morning I packed my belongings, cleaned the skiff and arranged a ride to Sand Point. One of the few things left to me was a letter of credit from the college bursar. I bullied the storekeeper into giving me three hundred dollars against this scrip. I gave Clyde two hundred and told him to split it with Gus Masek when he came to fetch 67. Fifty dollars was the price of a steerage berth all the way to Seattle. Which left fifty more.

That afternoon I went to the schoolteachers' house and was told, rather frostily, that Natasha was in the schoolhouse. I hesitated at its door; a plover flying low above the graveyard made a plaintive cry. I knocked and entered.

Small desks were arranged in rows. An American flag stood in one corner and a world map adorned the west wall. Natasha had been unpacking boxes of books and shelving them. She said hello and then picked up a book and studied its spine. She was wearing a long dress, dark green with a floral print. Her black eye had faded and someone had taken scissors to her butchered hair; now it was quite short and lay neatly like a skullcap.

"I'm leaving this afternoon," I said. "There's a steamer at Sand Point."

"Yes, I'd heard."

"I wanted to say goodbye. And give you this." I tried to hand her my last fifty-dollar bill.

She put down the book and faced me with her arms folded in front of her. With her hair shorn her face looked more Asiatic than before. The sharp planes and almond-shaped eyes reminded me of the carved ivory talisman Jason Davis had given me. Her blue-gray eyes were startling in that face.

"It's not much . . ." I stopped, tongue-tied. "I just . . . I just wanted to thank you for all your help."

She looked out the window and then back at me. "I'm sorry you didn't find what you were looking for, John Lars."

"I don't even know if it exists." I reached out to her but she moved just enough to leave my hand dangling.

"I'll write to you," I said and she nodded politely. I stood uncertainly, then put the money on the table and left. I doubt she ever picked it up. Outside the plover was still crying in the graveyard.

Half an hour later I was in a battered fishing skiff with an old Aleut man at the helm. I sat on a thwart that was speckled with fish scales. Before we turned the point and lost sight of the village I saw a figure in a long, green dress standing on the grassy knoll watching us. The wind was caught in her skirts. I raised my hand in farewell.

Alyson

"So the orchid was fake after all?"

"I still can't be sure. The letters were probably forged, but it's possible that Jason Davis found a new orchid during his wanderings. Maybe not as spectacular as the one in the letters but still new to science. So it could still be out there. Remember, the last thing Davis said to me was 'keep searching.'"

"That could mean a lot of things."

"Yeah, you're right. And most probably the whole thing was a hoax."

"Pretty elaborate hoax. How could he even be sure that dame got the letters?"

"It wasn't as improbable as you might think. Not like a message in a bottle; more like fishing. Davis would have known that Audrey collected orchid prints. Being a crook himself, he could have easily found a forger in Shanghai. And a shady art dealer. Then all he had to do was concoct a lure, cast it to the right spot, and wait for a strike."

"But why do it at all? He was better off without her."

"Davis knew he was dying. What happened in China still haunted him, and he wanted to lay those ghosts to rest. Bring Audrey out to his home grounds and somehow settle accounts. Audrey was hard to let go of. I knew her for only a few months and she still visits my dreams."

"That sounds awful."

"Actually, you might have liked Audrey. She was tough and intelligent. Devious for sure, and manipulative, but this was 1924, and she had to fight for anything she wanted. And cheat to get it."

"But what about Natasha? She was the real fighter. Did you ever get in touch with her? You should have."

"I wrote her more than once, and Hjalmar too. But no reply. So I just got on with my life. There was this feeling I hadn't acted well. Hadn't measured up in some way. Plus, I needed to shut the door on what happened on Nagai. It's not like the movies. Seeing people die violently is soul-shattering. I mean, Jesus! Two men lying there with their throats cut and a girl you loved did it? And knowing you should have had the guts to do it yourself?"

Alyson studied me for a long minute. "That cruise you went on last summer. That was about Natasha, wasn't it? And that picture in your bedroom?"

I didn't answer. In the faint light from the streetlamps, the flowers in the garden showed muted colors. What would be blooming now on Nagai? Lupine? Monkshood? I shivered at the memory of those unforgiving shores.

"It's late, kid. Maybe we better hang it up," I said.

"You can't wimp out on me now, Uncle John. You have to finish the story. That's what Natasha taught you, right?"

"She taught me a lot more than that." I took a swig of scotch, shook the bottle, and handed it to Alyson.

"There's still a bit left," I said.

CHAPTER 28

The *Starr* was less grand than the *Victoria*. Before becoming a mail boat she had worked in the halibut dory fishery and the steerage berths were sixteen bunks in the old fo'c'sle. I lay in my bunk swaddled in gloom. In Seward I boarded the SS *Alaska*. She was far more spacious, almost as big as the *Victoria*, and I found a corner where I could work on sorting my sad jumble of flowers.

My notes were torn and tattered, the pages pocked by campfire sparks, the ink blurred by rain. Yet I had more than two hundred specimens. As I worked I stopped and turned certain flowers in my hand, trying to understand what they meant to me. Tundra rose. Spring beauty. Mistmaiden. Now forever linked with a time and place. And a person.

I wrote a letter to Professor Arbuthnot outlining what I had, and had not, accomplished. I planned to mail it as soon as we touched shore so that it would precede me to New Haven and I would not have to break the news of failure in person. I also wrote a long letter to Natasha but the day before we reached Seattle I posted it overboard.

The ship docked the last day of August. I had to catch the train east immediately for fall classes but my mother insisted I see a doctor about my hand. The bones had knit but the fingers were stiff and bent, the knuckles oddly swollen. The doctor wanted to re-break the fingers and straighten them but I declined. While I was in Seattle my father was in the other Washington—D.C.—and I did not have to describe my summer adventures to him. In fact I never did. After what happened on Nagai his ambitions for himself and for me appeared foolish.

When I reached New Haven, I found that my fears about explaining my work were unfounded. Professor Arbuthnot had secured an appointment as assistant curator at Kew Gardens and had departed in August. He had left the Marsh Garden in disarray and the temporary curator was completely nonplussed by my appearance with specimens to be cataloged. In the end he simply hired me to do the work and thus I alone sat in judgment upon the great Steller's Orchid Expedition.

Audrey Arbuthnot was still in New Haven overseeing the sale of their house. I sent her a note and she invited me for tea. She met me at the door and led me to the now-empty conservatory. Autumn light slanted across the marble floor. The orchids were gone.

"I'm afraid I don't have any good news to report," I said.

"I gathered from your letter that the summer was rather a trial for you."

"I did manage to cover the whole of Nagai but more sketchily than I would have liked. It took all my energy just reaching the island and battling the weather."

She laughed. "The plant hunter's fate. But at least now you have stories of your own to tell."

"I guess so." I remembered Jason Davis dying and the shadows that had darkened his face and the bright flower of blood on Fitzgerald's shirt. Jason Davis had loved this woman. Should I tell her of his death? How deep was the pool of connected memories and what was owed to whom? I was not sure, but as I sat in the sunlit, empty room I found myself unable to speak of those windswept shores.

Audrey touched my knee. "In truth Walter was so pleased by the Kew appointment that nothing could have darkened his mood. And I almost hate to tell you but a month or so after you left we got a letter from our Shanghai dealer trying to extort more money. Something about the letter made Walter suspect that it was a bunco scheme from the beginning but there was no way to let you know."

Bunco? That was not the word I would have chosen. "I lost your Wardian case," I said.

"Lost?"

"Well, it was destroyed, in an accident."

"Not important; it was just a bit of baggage from the past." Audrey leaned back in the couch and considered me. "The summer was good for you. You've changed, grown. Walter is organizing an expedition to Burma; perhaps there's a place for you."

"I'm afraid I'm not that much of an orchid fancier."

Audrey locked eyes with me while she coiled a lock of hair around one finger, a move that back in the spring had meant checkmate. But now, I stood to take my leave. A brief frown knit her brows, then she accompanied me to the door. In the bright sunlight I could see a hint of parchment in her skin. I looked for a trace of the girl who had so captivated Jason Davis. Had that girl really existed? Or had the image Davis carried in his heart been born in the cold and empty North?

Audrey gave me her hand, the touch as light and soft as the wing of a butterfly. And as brief. I turned and walked away.

The gray cloak of winter wrapped around New Haven. I cloistered myself in the lab and library. More than once I fell asleep at my desk only to jolt awake, imagining that I heard the cries of sea birds and that the stone walls of the library were the cliffs of Nagai.

My plant collection produced nothing very earthshaking but I did find one new subspecies. Somehow Natasha's Bible had come south with me and in it I found two stalks of the blue-eyed grass she had found in Northeast Bight. This flower had not been described before and I named it *Sisyrinchium littorale christiansenii*.

In the spring I finally mustered the courage to write Natasha. I told her about the blue-eyed grass but never received a reply. I left New Haven in June, not even waiting for the commencement exercises. I returned to Seattle but not to my father's house. I had accepted a place as a graduate assistant at the University of Washington. The botany department became my home. I wrote again to Natasha but again no reply.

Throughout my career I focused on the *Gramineae* of the Pacific Northwest. I studied the tall grasses in the river bottoms and the short prairie grasses on the hills of the Palouse. I did a series of papers on the succession of grass after fire. But always I returned to the edge of the sea, to the salt chucks where the eelgrass wavered with the tides. I tried to understand how any grass could be tough enough to withstand the salt and the constantly changing current.

My father's political ambitions came to nothing. He was devastated by the '29 stock market crash and died soon after. My mother lived until the last days of World War II. In 1937 I married one of my graduate students, a girl with long brown hair and a quick laugh, but something was lacking and after two years we parted almost amicably.

In 1971 I saw an obituary in the *New York Times* for Audrey Gould Arbuthnot, who had died "at her home in London." The article said that she had been predeceased by her husband Walter.

I went then to the university library and spent half a day searching the botanical literature but I did not find an orchid that bore Audrey's name. However, in an old florilegium of Southeast Asia I found a color plate of "Audrey's asphodel," a greenish flower much quieter than any orchid.

Palmer and I kept in touch through the years and he persuaded me to return to New Haven for our fiftieth reunion. Palmer was now a widower. He had liver-spotted hands and overly bright dentures but he remained merry as a cricket. He tried to drag me to every possible social function but I resisted, preferring to walk the streets of New Haven alone. Dutch elm disease had decimated the campus and Hillhouse Avenue was now devoid of trees. I mourned the loss of the elms, some of which I had known better than I had known my classmates. The Arbuthnots' home appeared unchanged. I stood at the gate and remembered the first time I had knocked at that door and met Audrey. Odd how young she now seemed in my memory.

When I returned to Seattle I found myself thinking more and more of that summer on the edge of the world. Of Jason Davis, Li Po, Max Gottschalk, and Lena. They would all be gone now. Natasha alone would still be alive. I sat down and wrote her a letter that was pages long. I addressed it in care of the Unga postmaster. Two weeks later it came back marked "Undeliverable as Addressed." There was a Sand Point postmark on the back.

The seed of memory had come to bloom, however, and that winter I found a brochure describing a natural history cruise to the Pribilofs and the Shumagins and I booked passage. In July I boarded a small cruise ship along with a gaggle of elderly adventurers.

The Pribilofs were wild and beautiful but I could not shake the artificiality of the packaged tour. When they showed us the killing grounds I wandered away from the group and tried to imagine which of the tumbledown houses had been Natasha's childhood home.

Less than a week later we were in Sand Point, which was now a busy fishing port with prefabricated metal buildings and dust and noise and constant bustle. To my amazement, tied up to the cannery dock unloading fish was the *King & Winge*, Olaf Swenson's old boat. She had been rigged as a longliner, with a metal bait shed covering the afterdeck and rows of plastic buoys bright as salmon eggs tied along her bulwarks. She needed paint and attention but she was working still and I took this as a good omen.

I had persuaded the tour operators to offer a daytrip to Unga for those interested. A dozen or more of us passengers set out very early in two inflatable Zodiacs powered by large outboard motors. I chose the one captained by a pretty blonde girl who was tightly wound and tended to treat elders with the forced cheerfulness of a kindergarten teacher. As I took a seat I felt in my pocket for the ivory amulet that I had carried as a lucky piece for more than fifty years.

Unga proved to be a ghost town. At the landing in Delarof Harbor there were no boats, not even a rotting hulk. Two horses with shaggy coats worked the tide line, pulling at the kelp. While the other passengers milled about I walked up the hill into town. The grass was high, the buildings dilapidated. The church had partly collapsed and now served as a stable for the horses, judging from the depth of manure. The old school had been replaced by a utilitarian concrete structure that looked more decrepit than the frame buildings.

There was smoke coming from the chimney of Hjalmar's old house, the only sign of a human presence. I knocked at the door with an eerie feeling that Hjalmar himself might answer but an elderly man appeared and invited me in for coffee. The house was clean but contained a hodgepodge of furniture gathered, no doubt, from the abandoned houses. The walls were covered with framed pictures.

The man introduced himself as Jacob Alexey and said that he was the sole remaining resident. I told him that I had visited Unga fifty years before and asked him if he had known Hjalmar Mork.

"He moved to Kodiak many years ago. When I was a boy. I heard he died there," Jacob said.

I took a sip of the instant coffee and looked at the crowded kitchen shelves—boxes of cornmeal, cans of Campbell's soup, a giant can of Crisco. I looked again at the living room walls and saw that one of the pictures was the drawing of Natasha I had made on Unga Spit. It had been framed but behind the glass the paper had yellowed. The glass reflected the table where we sat.

"Do you know Natasha Christiansen?" I asked Jacob.

He considered for a moment then shook his head.

"That was her maiden name. I don't know if she ever married. A pretty girl? Half Aleut, half Norwegian? She had long, dark hair and gray eyes. She worked in the school here."

A faint light appeared in Jacob's eyes. "Ah, she was my teacher," he said. "But she died, long time ago. Drowned."

Suddenly I felt very old. I had always felt that if Natasha died I would sense it in some way. I stared at my drawing of her, its graceful lines now faded. I had been a better artist than I remembered. Where had it all gone? And why are we all fated to become so much less than we might have been?

Jacob rose and beckoned me to follow him. He was wearing blue jeans and a flannel shirt that was buttoned at the collar and curious homemade sandals, fashioned by cutting open the tops of a pair of red rubber boots. He was short and so bowlegged that he walked with a rolling gait like a sailor.

I followed him to the cemetery. The grass was high and unkempt but the two gnarled trees were apparently unchanged. In the corner by her father's grave Jacob showed me a tombstone on which was carved:

In Memoriam
Natasha Christiansen
Lost At Sea
1904–1926

I could not believe it. All the years I had carried her in my mind, pictured her, talked to her, and yet she had been dead so long that the words carved on her gravestone were already blurred and weathered. I looked out at the ocean, past my fellow tourists wandering in their bright coats. I watched the gulls circling.

"She was my teacher," Jacob said again. "She was coming back from the outer islands alone." He gestured at the distant strait. "Out there. Her skiff washed up."

I returned with Jacob to his house and asked him if I could purchase my drawing of Natasha. He agreed but would not accept money. Instead he wanted the bright orange floatation jacket I wore. It bore the cruise ship's name and was not mine to give but I handed it to Jacob and he took down the picture, leaving a less faded patch of wallpaper between two outdated calendars.

Jacob accompanied me to the landing wearing the jacket which reached to his knees. The blonde guide looked with disapproval at Jacob in the coat of one color and began to take off her own to offer it to me but I ignored her and climbed into the bow clutching the framed picture to my chest. I felt a tremor in my heart.

Max Gottschalk had been strong. Li Po had been stronger yet, but Natasha had been strongest of all. I thought of her quicksilver, indomitable nature and could not picture it coming to an end in an open boat. What storm could have beaten her?

The wind was rising. The girl in the stern opened the throttle and I huddled lower against the weather. I could see the bright orange dot that was Jacob making his way back to Hjalmar's house and I wondered how much of the past I had imagined, how much had been a dream. I searched the headland for the figure of the girl in the green dress but not even the ghost was there. The wind picked spray off the troubled water and across the strait I could see the dark hills of Nagai.

Biographical Note

Tom McGuire came to Alaska with two college friends. Fifty years later he still hasn't found reason to leave. He has worked as a salmon fisherman, carpenter, and North Slope oilfield worker. He and his wife have raised four children in a house they built on the banks of the Chilkoot River. Grizzly bears are frequent visitors. Tom has also paddled thousands of miles down (and up) northern rivers. He has published a book, *99 Days on the Yukon*, that describes a summerlong trip with legendary canoeist Charlie Wolf.